REBECCA REID is a writer, commentator and former digital editor of *Grazia*. As a journalist she writes a column for the *i* and contributes regularly to the *Sunday Times*, *Glamour*, *Cosmo* and *Stylist*. As a commentator she regularly contributes to *Woman's Hour*, Jeremy Vine and *Good Morning Britain*. Her first play is due to open in London in 2026. Rebecca has previously written five books (four thrillers, one non-fiction) but after almost a decade of journalism about sex and relationships – not to mention the demise of her own marriage – she finally felt ready to pen a love story. The first of these was *Seven Rules for a Perfect Marriage*.

For Eliza & The Board

STELLA IS STARTING OVER

REBECCA REID

BLOOMSBURY PUBLISHING
LONDON • OXFORD • NEW YORK • NEW DELHI • SYDNEY

BLOOMSBURY PUBLISHING
Bloomsbury Publishing Plc
50 Bedford Square, London, WC1B 3DP, UK
Bloomsbury Publishing Ireland Limited,
29 Earlsfort Terrace, Dublin 2, D02 AY28, Ireland

First published in Great Britain 2026

A catalogue record for this book is available from the British Library

ISBN: PB: 978-1-5266-8231-4; EBOOK: 978-1-5266-8234-5

2 4 6 8 10 9 7 5 3 1

Typeset by Six Red Marbles India
Printed and bound in Great Britain by Clays Ltd, Elcograf S.p.A

FSC www.fsc.org MIX Paper | Supporting responsible forestry FSC® C018072

Stella

The most surprising thing about my husband leaving was how embarrassing I found it.

And listen, I know how that sounds. I'm not saying it was the *only* hard thing about it – just the one that I was totally, completely unprepared for. I had genuinely never suspected that we might split up, but I had a sort of abstract idea that if we did it would be some grand, dramatic fight, like something out of a film. I'd have one tear running down my face, he'd have an old-fashioned suitcase and a sense of dignified resignation. That sort of thing. So when I came home earlier than expected from the 'Under Six Plus Boppers and Groovers Mummy and Me Shake It Together!' class that I thought I'd booked for Wednesday morning but had in fact booked for the previous Monday, and found my husband crouching on the floor going through our travel toiletries, it wasn't quite the sexy French cinema bombshell I'd imagined. I asked him what he was doing, he said nothing. I asked why his suitcase was half packed and he said 'no reason' and then I went to feed our daughter for what felt like the fifteenth time that morning. He came downstairs carrying the suitcase he'd packed 'for no reason' and told me that there was, actually, a reason, and that the reason was 'I'm leaving you'.

Not the easiest statement to respond to, especially while the baby, who was desperately hungry but refusing to consume any milk, was arching her back like a cat who didn't want to get in the carrier to the vet. I think I probably laughed. The idea of Gavin leaving me, Gavin who was devoted to me and adored me and continually told me how much more fun I was than any of his friends' wives – felt implausible. But then he stood there for a while, in our bedroom, and I realised he was serious. And I laughed again. And then, before I could say anything devastating, he was gone. Nothing else had changed. The temperature of the room was the same, the baby was still screaming, my phone was still on the same battery percentage and every world leader was unchanged, but everything about me, and my world, and my life, and the life that I was expecting to build, the family I had been talked into creating, was different. Mostly destroyed. And even though someone else destroyed it, it's me who had to do all the rebuilding. Which started with telling people.

I told Louella, my sister, first. She heard the first four seconds of my breathing at the end of the phone and knew what was up – down to the last detail – without needing to be told. Sort of impressive, but then we have seen each other almost every day since she was born so also maybe just a symptom of overexposure. She told me she was leaving work, which was kind but less dramatic when you understand that she works for some kind of internet company where she sends five emails a day and they pay her six figures.

'He's an evil cunt,' she said as she used her key to open my front door. 'How? Why? What did he say? How did he explain it?'

'Why?' is a very good question and not one I thought to ask. The sum total of the questions I had asked by this point was, 'What are you doing with all of the mini L'Occitane shower gels?' and, 'Why do you have a suitcase packed?'

Since then (twenty-three weeks ago, not that I'm counting), everyone has been really nice about it. People sent flowers, came over with wine; my university friends got me a massage voucher that I can't use because I can't leave the baby for long enough and various other child-free friends who are frightened of small babies offered to babysit in a generous and completely unrealistic gesture of love. I'm desperate to leave Rose, gagging for freedom.

Sometimes I imagine closing the front door of my house and walking down a street without a pram or a nappy bag, and it seems more exciting than any fantasy I've ever had. But when the prospect of leaving her becomes real, it's gut-wrenching. She's the only company I have, the constant companion to my life. Her wants and needs rule my life, and it's exhausting and draining and overwhelming, and yet, if I actually stopped for a moment, I might have to think about the reality of my situation and I have absolutely no desire to find out what that might feel like.

There's also something hard to swallow about all the sympathy. All the COOK ready meals and offers of help were their ticket price to the show. The lasagnas and bunches of flowers came with messages, and the messages always said the same thing, in slightly different phrasing: 'What happened?' They wanted the details, the specifics, the ins and the outs of our horrible life, because there's nothing more reassuring or validating than someone else's marriage falling apart. If you're a couple, it's delicious because you've outlasted them. If you're single then it's a refreshing reminder that being conventionally alone is much better than being someone who had a baby and a big white wedding, and then ended up alone anyway.

In fairness to these people, I asked for it. I was the smuggest smug married since Bridget Jones's dinner party mates. I married Gavin – handsome, slightly older, successful – aged twenty-five. A child bride, I joked at drinks with my friends, acting embarrassed to be getting married at an age more commonly seen in a tradwife mommy blogger than a London-based creative who worked as a writer for an interiors magazine. The first of my friends by about half a decade, being engaged became my entire personality. And as my friends passed my ring around, putting it on their right hand rather than their left for fear of jinxing themselves, I felt like I'd done the only really important thing I'd ever do. I liked my job and my gym, and nights out with my girlfriends, but there was a small part of me that had always privately, a bit ashamedly, been waiting for the 'real' part to start – the part where I could have a house and babies. Before we were engaged, I had the good grace to hide those feelings but the second I got a diamond on my hand, my restraint just disappeared.

Because Gavin was five years older than me, and because we were getting married young, we did everything else young too. I was the first to buy a house, the first to get a big, grown-up car, and eventually, when I turned thirty and decided that I was finally ready, just as my friends were moving in with their partners, I was one of the first to get pregnant – the first who had intentionally got pregnant. Once again, I floated through life being un-fucking-bearable, telling people we couldn't believe how easily I'd got pregnant, that we thought we'd have months of trying like all the blogs I read said but, mysteriously, it just happened on our first go. When Rose was born, almost eight months ago, via an easy and uncomplicated birth, I looked down at her and across at Gavin and thought, *I wish everyone could be this lucky*. And then two months later, when Rose was literally eight weeks old, he left and in a matter of minutes I became a single mum to a tiny baby.

When you see it all written down like that, you can't help thinking that maybe I had it coming to me. I really wouldn't blame anyone who thought I'd had more good luck than anyone deserved, and I'd invite that person to take a look at my life today. There are six drying racks of baby clothes in my house because, in a brief spurt of trying to get my life together, I decided that not having enough drying racks was the organisational issue with my laundry system. I was wrong. The prospect of putting everything away is too overwhelming and I've decided that I'm just going to use things straight off the racks and cut out the middle man of putting them back in Rose's bedroom. I've told myself it's basically like having a hanging rail, which is a perfectly respectful and accepted way to store clothes.

The health visitor, the woman who comes to see us intermittently to check that Rose is growing and not being given Red Bull in her bottles, told me that it's 'extremely unusual' for a dad to leave that early. She said it with total neutrality and I had absolutely no idea what I was supposed to do with that information. 'They usually wait a while,' she told me. 'Until the kids are older.' I just nodded and then sat in silence while she weighed Rose and then repeated the same facts about breastfeeding I'd been told seven times that month and confirmed that I was on maternity leave and would be going back to work when Rose was one year old.

Anyway. Last night I accidentally went to sleep with damp hair so it's now a surprising look that's sort of frizzy on one side and completely lank on the other, which is especially unfair because Rose woke up nine times, so I slept for about ninety minutes total. I'm also wearing dirty leggings from my 'back when I had money' wardrobe that are too small, so there's a band of fat hanging over the top, and if I were to bend over, which I'm going to avoid, you'd be able to see my underwear, which is thigh to belly button and made of a sort of industrial cotton. Rose is clean, her toys are clean, the house is sanitary and other than that, everything is a fucking disaster.

And, as if that wasn't bad enough, I'm about to see my ex-husband (technically, legally, still my husband, in real terms my ex) for the first time in six months.

Gavin has seen Rose during that time, just to be totally fair to him. One Saturday a month, his mother, Sue, formerly (though again, still legally) my mother-in-law, arrived – tight-faced and apologetic, also clearly very embarrassed about the situation – and took Rose out in the pram to see Gavin, who apparently met them in the park. I spent that ninety-minute window pacing up and down in the house, thinking about all the things I could be doing with my free time, achieving nothing because I felt queasy about being away from Rose, and happily the whole thing was over quickly. It wasn't a good system, not compared to the system where Gavin and I spend Saturday mornings walking in a sun-drenched park, sipping on oat flat whites and taking adorable candids of each other with the baby, which is how I'd envisioned our life playing out. But it was a tolerable system. Just about. Better, by a fucking mile, than this new system where Gavin comes to my house – *our* house – and I have to talk to him while wishing he would wrap his arms around me and tell me that everything from the last six months was his evil twin and that he is back and so is our life together.

The door goes and I'm standing literally behind it. He can see the outline of my body, so the entrance I'd planned (I leave him waiting a couple of minutes then come down, pretty and flushed, in jeans and a white blouse, holding Rose) isn't possible. I open it and I'm knocked sideways by the bizarreness of seeing a face that I've studied in every possible light, moment, attitude, a face that I saw basically every day for a decade and then suddenly didn't see at all for six months.

'Hi,' he says. 'Can I come in?'

He still has keys to the house, I assume. He didn't give them back. I'm glad he hasn't attempted to use them.

'Sure.'

He takes his shoes off, toeing them off, then pauses for a moment. Instead of leaving them in the middle of the floor like he would historically have done (to my annoyance), he puts them in a neat pair, to the left of the door. He's wearing socks that I bought him. Well, a pair from a five-pack of striped socks from Waitrose that I bought on a Sunday morning on the basis that we might as well just share socks seeing as we shared everything else.

Rose squawks.

'Hello, my love!' he says, reaching for her. I want to grab her and smack his hand away. I offer her out to him. He takes her, supporting her wrongly – or if not wrongly, awkwardly. To my absolute delight, she cries.

I take her back. 'She's a bit clingy at the moment,' I say, trying to pretend that I'm not pleased. 'She really only wants to be on me.'

'Sure,' says Gavin, looking distraught. Now I feel guilty, and sad for him, and still completely delighted that she patently prefers me.

'Do you want a coffee?' I ask.

'Yeah,' he replies. 'That'd be great.'

We got the coffee machine for our first wedding anniversary, our present to each other so that we could make lazy brunches at home. Balancing Rose on my hip, I scrabble one-handed in the door of the fridge, among jars of baby food, trying to find the packet of grounds. It's still got a clip on it to keep it fresh. A yellow one. Gavin put it on there, the Sunday before he left. Did he know that he was leaving me by then? Did he open the new packet of coffee grounds on that Sunday knowing that he'd make one coffee from it, put it in the fridge and then disappear from my life?

I try to open the clip while holding Rose and wobble. She slips slightly on my hip.

'I'll do it,' Gavin says eventually, after watching me struggle. I don't argue. I sit on the sofa at the far end of the kitchen, Rose on my lap, playing with my necklace, and watch as Gavin brings the coffee machine back to life.

'The tank's totally empty,' he says, after a few moments of silence.

'Yeah,' I say.

'You're supposed to refill it fresh every time you make a coffee.'

I haven't touched the coffee machine since he left. I couldn't.

'Yeah,' I say. 'I know.'

He makes the coffees. I put Rose down for her first morning nap and we sit holding our coffee cups like props at the opposite ends of the sofa, as if we haven't seen each other's arseholes.

'I wanted to talk to you,' Gavin says eventually, looking into his latte. 'About Rose.'

'What about Rose?'

'About visitation.'

I think I probably knew this was going to be about that. It didn't seem likely that Sue was going to play baby steward every weekend until Rose was old enough to take an Uber over to wherever Gavin ends up living. But also, quite a big part of me had been hoping we might be able to just keep things this way forever.

'Right,' I say. I panic-Googled this morning about how to talk to your ex-husband and it said to try and say as little as possible, to get him to do the majority of the talking, and to communicate exclusively about the child. 'What were you thinking?' I ask. *How many times a month are you going to take my daughter away from me after abandoning us both?*

'I'd like to have her every other weekend.'

The oat milk burns in my throat and I think I'm going to throw up all over the green velvet sofa that I told him

I didn't want us to buy because it was such a millennial cliché. Every other weekend? He's seen her for twenty hours in the past six months and now he wants her every other weekend? She's only just become aware that my body isn't a part of her body, she can't spend every second weekend miles away from me.

The article I read said that you have to be calm, measured and restrained in how you speak to your ex, that you must not say an outright 'no' to anything. 'No,' I say, trying not to cry.

'No?'

'No. You can't take her every other weekend – she's too little. She's only just stopped breastfeeding. She's not even one yet. She's a baby. And you don't know how to do it, you don't know which spoon she likes or which *That's Not My* book she likes—'

'I'm not going to learn those things unless I spend more time with her,' he interjects.

'She's not a project for you to learn on, she's a person, and these are, like, the most formative years. She's a baby, she needs her mum.'

'She needs her dad too, Stella.'

I mean, I was inclined to agree until he left. I always thought that having two parents was better than having one. But is it actually an asset to have a relationship with a man who, with absolutely no warning or explanation, just decided to disappear from your life? Does Rose really need to spend regular time with a man who abandoned her? Because I'm not finding it a particularly enriching experience myself. 'Then why did you leave?' I snap. 'If she needs her dad, maybe you should have stuck around?'

He takes a deep breath. 'You know why I left.'

I don't, actually. I've got some badly written WhatsApps where he attempts to spell it out and I've got the working theories of my various friends. But I don't know why, and, honestly, I'm really not sure what could have been so completely horrific about our situation that it would have induced him to leave. I can say with absolute certainty that I'd have changed anything he asked me to change, fixed anything he asked me to fix, done basically anything imaginable to convince him to give it another go. But I wasn't given the chance to do any of that because his decision was made without consultation.

'Look,' I say, trying to sound calm. 'I know she needs both of us, I want her to have both of us, but she's too young for weekends right now and you don't have the experience you need, you've got to build up—'

'Okay, let's build up.'

I have a horrible feeling that he might have used some LinkedIn negotiation shit on me because I can see exactly where this is going and I don't know how to stop it. 'Yeah, we can build up, but slowly—'

'Okay. Look. Why don't I take her one evening a week?' he says gently. 'I'm staying at the cabin in Mum's garden. It's a two-bed, it's nicely done, it's all childproof. So Mum can be around the first couple of times to make sure I know what I'm doing and then we'll be in a routine. I'll pick her up in the afternoon, take her home, do her bedtime routine, get her up, give her breakfast and then drop her back with you. How does that sound?'

It sounds worse than sticking a cotton bud all the way into my eardrum until it hits my brain.

'I don't think you're ready,' I say, weakly.

'We weren't ready when we had her,' he argues. 'It's a learning curve.'

'If you wanted more time with her then why didn't you just...' I trail off. This isn't dignified. I'm about to make the same point I've already made and it's not going to change anything.

Gavin looks out of the window, clearly unable to meet my eye as he says, 'I'd really hoped you'd be able to do this with me, without us needing to involve anything legal. But she's my daughter too. And if I have to, I will.'

'Okay,' I say, eventually.

I want to say, 'How is it fair that you left me, you took away my husband, my security, my stability, and now you get to take my baby away from me once a week?' But of course, I don't. I say again, 'Okay.' I sigh, because I need him to leave before I lose the ability to hold back my tears. 'We can try it.'

Stella

The second most surprising thing about your husband leaving you, at least if you have a baby, is that you just sort of… carry on. It would be nice to crawl into bed and cry but most days there isn't time, and on the occasions that I've had half an hour spare I've genuinely attempted a bit of scheduled crying and found that – probably unsurprisingly – feelings don't work like that and the tears won't come.

I didn't have many break-ups before Gavin because I married the first proper boyfriend I ever had (possibly my first mistake). But when a situationship did end, or a boy I was obsessed with stopped messaging me back, I went full wallow. I loved a break-up in the same way that I loved a hangover. It's not technically a nice feeling but it is sort of satisfying to lean into the discomfort. Comfortable clothes, comforting TV, comfort food, the whole nine yards. Fun, because the heartbreak was a graze rather than a stab wound, and eventually sufficiently boring that I'd jack it in and go back to living again. This, unfortunately, was different. This was a bit like a bereavement and a limb loss tied into one. My routine, my home, my confidant, my financial security, my sense of who I was as a person, all gone up in smoke. Poof. Every shared memory, in-joke, every story about holidays together, all the gossip and the lore lost because I'll never be able to explain them to anyone else and probably wouldn't want to even if I could.

Surprisingly, the most helpful tool I had to get me through the unrelenting misery of post-Gavin life was Rose. Rose didn't just want things, she needed them, and there was literally no option other than to get up, change her, feed her, get her dressed, take a lightning-fast shower if I'd got too grotty to tolerate, and then take her out in the pram, telling myself that the cold March air was good for both of us.

But it's Thursday. So Rose is about to go on a sleep-over with the person I'm angriest with on the face of the earth, and I'm going to magically transform from having 24/7 sole responsibility for my child to being totally alone. Since the moment she was conceived, I've been away from her for a handful of hours. She lived inside me and then always in the same room as me. The longest I've ever been without her was when she saw Gavin for those park visits, metres from our home, and I spent those pacing the house, chewing the skin off from around my fingernails.

Gavin arrives promptly at 4.30 p.m. I had been praying he'd be late enough that I could refuse to open the door. But he isn't.

'That's a lot of stuff,' he says faintly, looking at the bags by the front door.

I've packed her clothes, dummies, bottles, premixed formula, nappies, wipes, more nappies, more wipes, snot sucker, baby Calpol and various different books. There's also the travel pram, the travel cot and the car seat.

'Yeah,' I say. 'Babies come with a lot of stuff.'

'Maybe I can get some duplicates. For my place. Then you won't have to pack all of this up next time.'

'It wasn't any trouble,' I lie. It took me two hours because Rose screamed if I left the room to get something.

I buckle her into the car seat and then burst into tears as I watch his car, rented from one of those pay-per-hour services, pull away from the kerb. It's like a physical pain in my chest. I go back into the house, sit down on the sofa and stare at the wall for a while. Then I clean. Once I've cleaned, I reorganise. Then it's dinnertime.

I open the fridge and stare into it until it starts beeping. This fridge was the most exciting, and most expensive, thing I've ever bought. Double doors with an ice maker, like the cool girls at my school always used to have in the noughties. Gav and I jokingly called it my first child when it was delivered because I took so many pictures of it. It was briefly the background on my phone. It's enormous, designed to see us through at least two children. It currently contains six pots of weaning-friendly baby food, a satay chicken ready meal that went off two days ago and half a bottle of wine from when Louella came over. I pick it up and look at the label. It's something complicated and biodynamic because Lou is too cool to drink an M&S sauvignon.

I pour a glass and drink it quickly, then pour another one, feeling massively pissed because I barely drink these days. It's a nice, fuzzy, numbing kind of insulation. Then I feel worse about feeling slightly better, in case it means that I'm actually an alcoholic. So I do three quizzes on my phone all titled 'Are You an Alcoholic' and conclude that no, I am not. Then I cook the ready meal and eat it, worrying that it's going to poison me but figuring that having food poisoning is one of those things that is much easier child-free, and at least I'd be thinner as a result. Next, I put on the television and scroll through the options until I'm so bored and angry at not picking anything that I turn it off.

Do you want to finish watching White Lotus*?* the TV screen asks.

No, I don't. I started it with Gavin. He's probably finished it. Arsehole.

What about Game of Thrones*?*

Again, no. We rewatched it when Rose was born until I started worrying that the noises and violence were going to traumatise Rose (at that point, three days old).

At 10 p.m. I've officially run out of things to pretend to be distracted by and I allow myself to go to bed.

I wake up at 6.30 a.m. yet don't move, needing to wee but so tired I can't make my legs work, counting down the minutes until Rose will be home. I open my phone again and go to my conversation with Gav, just in case he has magically messaged me, admitting that he can't manage Rose on his own and saying that I can come and collect her. He hasn't. I swipe back on our conversation. We speak so rarely now that within a couple of minutes I'm six months back and there are endless pictures of Rose, messages from me asking him to bring me things from other rooms because I'm nap-trapped under a sleeping baby. I scan his replies, looking for signs that he was plotting his escape. Then I scroll further back, back to when I was pregnant. Pictures of me grinning into the mirror, showing off a swollen side profile. His replies about how beautiful I am, about how proud he is of me, how he can't wait to spend the rest of his life raising a mini Stella. How did any of this happen? Where did any of that go?

A week later I recount the story of my first evening of freedom to Louella. She's in my headphones as I push Rose in her pram, on the way back from 'Jump & Jiggle With Mummy, Six Months Plus'. Louella, by contrast, is on her way home from reformer Pilates, which looks really easy but apparently actually isn't.

'Hang on, I'm switching to my AirPods,' she says as I tell her the part about rereading my messages with Gav. 'Sorry, did you say that you had your first night of freedom and you ate an expired ready meal, did a bit of emotional masturbation over your ex-husband and then went to bed?'

'Yeah,' I say.

'Did you get food poisoning?'

'No. Ironclad immune system, me,' I say mournfully.

'So you ate loads of microplastics and you didn't even get skinny out of it.'

'We're not supposed to say stuff like that any more,' I retort, pulling the pram shade down to block the sun from Rose's eyes, as if I hadn't had the exact same thought process when I ate the meal. 'We're supposed to pretend we don't care about being thin.'

'You actually did look skinny last time I saw you,' Louella goes on. 'Can I do a matcha with almond, please?' she addresses what I assume is a trendy barista.

'Yeah, divorce will do that to you,' I say.

'My boss got divorced and she got really fat,' Louella counters. 'So I actually would check your privilege on that one. Anyway, your night sounds fucking tragic and it's not happening again, so we're doing something today.

What time does Gav pick her up?' Louella makes the name 'Gav' sound like 'skin infection'.

'Four-thirty,' I say, feeling sick.

'Okay, great,' Louella says, sounding brighter. 'I'll find something fun for us to do and message you the address. Meet me there, okay? Wear the Sézane jeans I got you with a navy jumper and ballet pumps, not white trainers.'

She hangs up without saying goodbye. I roll my eyes and then, after I've once again packed up Rose's entire life, I get ready. Rose is napping, so I've got an hour, and instead of doing anything productive for the house I blow-dry my hair and curl my eyelashes. By the end of the process, wearing the outfit Louella dictated, I look in the mirror and to my surprise, recognise the person looking back at me as the girl I used to be, rather than the mumsy-looking woman I've been catching glimpses of in shop windows.

'You look great,' Gav says with a tone of surprise.

'Thanks. This is her stuff, and this is a cool bag of purées I've made for her – you can use a normal teaspoon to feed her, just obviously watch her at all times while she's eating.'

'I thought you said she just has whatever the adults are eating?'

This is technically true, because we are mostly doing baby-led weaning. But last week her clothes came back with a stain that looked and smelled very much like an adult lasagna, which is full of salt, which babies aren't allowed, and I really cannot bring myself to ask him to read an entire book about weaning. 'We're just doing purées for now,' I say. It's a lie, but only little one.

'Oh. Right. Okay.'

Rose screams when I hand her over and I want to claw her back from Gavin and move to a country with no extradition treaties to the UK. But before I know it I'm walking to the Tube. On my own. With a tiny handbag. I've checked seven times if I've got everything I need, because carrying a handbag with no nappies, wipes, bottles or change of clothes genuinely feels like I've lost an extremity. I listen to music on the Tube. I get off at Tottenham Court Road and don't even look to see if they've got step-free access. For a moment I forget to feel sad about Rose being gone and then I'm smacked with a wave of sadness tinged with extra guilt.

When I get to the pin Louella dropped for me, she's standing outside, wearing a floor-length cashmere coat, hair slicked back into the kind of bun that makes her look like an off-duty model and makes me look like Miss Trunchbull from *Matilda*.

'You look fit,' she says, hugging me.

'You look really rich,' I reply.

'Thank you! The coat's rented and it came with someone else's fake eyelashes in the pockets.'

'New or used?' I ask.

'Oh, very used. Previous owner's eyeshadow all over them. We're going in here.'

'Conjunctivitis-y. Fun,' I say as she steers me into a massive, glossy co-working space. 'Where are we going?' I ask.

There are signs everywhere reading *HER MAGAZINE*. I have a horrible feeling I know where this is going.

'Oh my god,' I say, looking around at the dozens of other middle-class women carrying tote bags. 'Is this some kind of panel discussion?'

Louella nods. 'Kind of.'

'If this is a self-help event I'm going to push you in front of the Tube on the way home,' I say, teeth bared.

'I'm on the Overground so that's not happening,' she snipes back.

'You said this was going to be fun. Self-help is not fun.'

Louella looks guilty. 'I know, and I lied, but there's a Mexican-Iranian pop-up we can go to afterwards, and I'll pay, and this won't be fun but it will actually be useful. I promise.'

We take our seats in the main space where there are rows and rows of chairs filled with rows and rows of different versions of the same woman. Louella and I are one hundred per cent on brand. At the front there are four chairs and a big screen that reads, *Navigating Modern Love*. Underneath, it explains that we are going to understand how to be better at dating because of these three experts: Jessica Rhodes, co-author of *Seven Rules for a Perfect Marriage*, William Green, author of *The No-Method Method*, and Lexie Leung, author of *The Mantourage*.

'I cannot tell you how much I hate this,' I whisper to Louella. 'I already tried not having a method, I already had what looked like a perfect marriage and I don't know what a "mantourage" is, but I do not want one.'

'If you complain one more time, we're not getting margaritas at dinner,' Louella says, taking pictures of the stage for her socials.

Eventually the room is full and the panel sit down. Jessica Rhodes is a pregnant redhead, William Green is a tiny, dark-haired guy with little round glasses and Lexie Leung is Asian, and has a full fringe and the kind of triceps I can only dream of. Everyone claps, the host introduces the panel and then they start talking. At which point, I think I can forgo a margarita because I'm going to complain to

Louella non-stop after this. The redhead woman is saying some sensible stuff about relationships but I'm not in a relationship and I don't think most of the other women here are, because who's paying money to go to a romance lecture when they've already got a partner? And the guy keeps saying that not trying and not doing anything is the best way to find happiness and, like, yeah, okay, William, how did you get an entire book out of that?

Just as I'm wondering whether I could pretend to faint so I can leave, the host backtracks. 'Wait, Lexie,' she says, her bright pink manicure wrapped around the microphone. 'There might be some people here who haven't read your book or followed you on socials – can you explain what the mantourage is?'

Lexie smiles and lifts her own microphone to her mouth. 'Sure,' she says, taking a long pause. 'So, I grew up in a family where marriage was expected, ideally in your mid-twenties, certainly before your late twenties. And alongside that expectation was my own desire – I wanted to get married and have a family. But I'd been at medical school and doing my doctorate, so I'd barely dated. And I realised that if I wanted to find the right man, I needed more experience, but I didn't have a lot of experience. So I took inspiration from the medical school where I'd studied. When you're training to be a doctor you do rotations, so you spend time in lots of different types of medicine – sometimes you're in dermatology, oncology, paediatrics, and, at the end of it, you've got more experience of being a doctor and you understand what you're best at. So I put together a kind of rotation of men, who were all different archetypes, who offered different benefits and of course each had their own flaws. And I dated them simultaneously for six months – they were all aware of this, obviously. I'm not like a man – I wouldn't do this dishonestly!'

Everyone else laughs, but I'm rapt. 'So then by the time I'd finished this rotation system I understood what worked for me, what didn't, what I had to offer, what I wasn't able to compromise on. It's essentially an accelerated study programme for dating. And if you're someone who hasn't had a lot of experience but wants to be ready for a marriage, I feel like this is a great way of hacking the system.'

Dozens of hands go up with questions for Lexie. Louella pokes her pointy, red fingernail into my leg. 'You should do that,' she mouths at me.

The Mexican-Iranian place has a queue around the corner when we arrive, but Louella knows someone and, apparently, we magically have a reservation at a place that doesn't do reservations. Inside it's just loud enough to be buzzy but not so loud you can't hear each other talk. The windows are steamy and the tables are made of dark wood, and everyone looks deeply attractive because of the warm, yellow lighting. We order a load of small plates; I get the margarita I've been dreaming of, and then she inevitably returns to the subject of the mantourage.

'I'm sorry,' she says, which means she's absolutely not sorry. 'But I feel like that was fate. We were literally supposed to be at that talk – that was meant for you.'

'It's not fate,' I counter, secretly thinking she might have a point. 'It's generic advice that is demographically appropriate for us.'

'Potato pot-ah-to,' Louella replies, scraping the last of the Baharat guacamole out of the bowl. 'You know that

Gavin will be porking someone else within weeks. If he isn't already.'

Over dinner, I put up a massive resistance to the idea of trying Lexie's method. I claim that I don't want a relationship ever again, which we both know isn't true because I'm painfully co-dependent and I'm desperate to have more babies before my uterus shrivels up. I claim I don't know how to date, that I don't want to date, that I'm scared of dating, that I'm not ready.

But a bit of research isn't going to kill me, is it? At home the next day, I dig through the bright pink goodie bag we were handed on the way out of the event (allegedly worth £299, mostly full of tiny samples of beauty products I don't want) and pull out the copy of *The Mantourage*.

At the back of the book it has a sort of section of worksheets, as if I'm nine, and I find the idea of filling it in deeply humiliating. It's phrased the same way that my *Teen Dream Diary* was, when I was eleven. In fact, if this book were pink and fluffy with an extremely breakable padlock on it, then they'd basically be the same thing. But Rose is napping, and I said I was going to do this properly, so I'm filling it out. In a swirly, patronising font, Lexie Leung has invited me to assign archetypes to the men that I'm seeing.

There's no need to fill every archetype, Lexie says, helpfully, as if I could date twenty men at the same time. *But try to pick one from each category and keep at least three people in play at any one time. Three is a magic number for a reason – it's the perfect way to keep your rotation fresh, but allows time to forge a connection with any worthwhile potential partner.*

Okay. Fine.

Category One:
THE PROVIDER
THE FATHER FIGURE
THE LEADER
THE TEACHER

Half of these sound like they should be on a register. In what world do I want to date someone who could be my dad or my teacher? Like, there are literal laws in place to prevent those things from happening. I mean, obviously back in the day I wanted to snog my history teacher but I'm an adult now and I know what statutory rape means.

Category Two is basically impossible, because there's no one I know who is meaningful or likely to turn into anything meaningful. The options are: *THE WORKMATE*, *THE FOUNDER*, *THE ARCHITECT* and *THE CHEERLEADER*. I read the descriptions, all of which focus on the idea of building, creating and supporting each other. Once upon a time, I would have put Gavin down for this. He's the one who was so sure we could make this house beautiful, that it might finally be the career transition I've been talking about for years, the way to jump from writing about other people's houses to designing them, that maybe I could use it as a shop front for making and selling things. Only it turns out that the tool he's best with is a fucking sledgehammer and his pet project is smacking it into our lives.

I feel cross with the book. How are you supposed to know this many people well enough to be able to fill each category?

If Category Two was hard, Category Three is even harder:

THE POET
THE THINKER
THE ARTIST
THE DREAMER

Arguably all synonyms for much the same thing but at this point I'm picking holes in the book because I'm cross with myself, not Lexie Leung.

I look up from the book, up at the house around me. Entirely empty, walls still unpainted, drying racks loaded with even more tiny clothes. The silence is enormous and I keep replaying all the things Lou said, things I already know. I take my make-up off, put my pyjamas on, get into bed and then, for the first time in my life, I download a dating app.

Dominic

I'm trying to work out how many hours of my life I've spent on stag dos. So far I've got to 324 – nine stags in total, using thirty-six hours as a standard measurement to account for some of them being shorter than a full weekend. Actually, I realise, clearing the calculator on my phone because I can't do mental maths, I've forgotten one. It's 360 hours, not 324.

This one was a good one, in fairness. When you hear 'stag do', you picture a group of rowdy men dressed in fishnets and gimp masks, harassing the locals and snorting something questionable in the loos of a filthy club. That is very much not us. A smiling Dutch girl one of the guys got talking to in the Rijksmuseum called us 'the least threatening stag' she had ever seen, which I felt was quite a significant compliment. She wasn't wrong, either. Far from sinking a six-pack each on the train home to drain the last of the juice from the weekend, we're scattered across the economy carriage of the 10.13 a.m. from Amsterdam to London (one change at Brussels, annoying but significantly cheaper), all very keen to get home despite having had a perfectly nice time.

Tim, the groom, is sleeping, head pressed against the window, and Theo is doing the same, only he's using Tim as his pillow. Charlie and Graham are playing snap because they bought a pack of cards in the Eurostar departure lounge, with big ideas about poker, and then realised they don't know how to play anything other than snap. Two of the stag's mates from work, whose names I didn't fully get at the start of the trip and therefore have avoided calling anything all weekend, are sharing headphones to watch a film on an iPad. Tim's younger brother, Ed, has gone to see if they've got any of the 'really cool Dutch crisps' in the bar car.

I try to get my phone to connect to the very not working Wi-Fi so I can see if Orla has messaged me.

'How're you feeling?' Ed is back, holding three packets of said crisps. I look up.

'Not bad,' I say. 'I was pretty restrained, went harder on the first night. Always the trick.'

'Lucky you,' he replies. The train lurches and he looks even more nauseous. 'I had seven beers last night.'

He reads in my face that I clearly think these are amateur numbers, and says, 'I haven't been drinking this year, solidarity with Jules and all that.'

'I didn't know you were having another one,' I reply, my enthusiasm entirely genuine. Ed and his wife had a nightmare getting pregnant with their first kid. I remember Tim glumly telling me at the pub that he was worried they might ask him to be a sperm donor. I reassured him that given he was eleven before he could tell the time, they probably wouldn't want his DNA. 'That's great news,' I add.

'Yeah.' He looks bashful. 'Nice to have a weekend away before the madness starts again. And I reckon it's the last stag I'll go on, now Tim's finally locked someone down. Getting a bit old for it all these days.' As he finishes the sentence he seems to realise that he's said something potentially offensive because his face falls. 'I only mean…' he says, with no idea what he's going to follow it up with. I laugh, to put him out of his misery.

'I know,' I say. 'Fewer and fewer of us singles left.'

My laugh has done too good a job of reassuring him because he beams and then doubles down. 'Not even fewer – none. You're literally the only one left.'

'No,' I start, looking around the carriage. 'I'm not the only…' I trail off. Because of all the men in our group here, I actually— yeah. I actually am. 'Fuck me,' I say. 'You're right.'

He looks worried. 'But you like it that way, right?'

The train crackles with an announcement, first in Dutch and then in English, telling us that we're about to arrive into London.

'I'd better sit down,' Ed says. It's not a flight, he absolutely doesn't need to take his seat for landing, but I sense he thinks he's put his foot in it and wants to escape.

His guilt is entirely misplaced. I was surprised to realise that all of our gang are married, but certainly not upset. Like he said, I like it.

We're out in the station before my phone finally decides to start working. Orla has indeed messaged me. Her flight has landed – good old Ryanair, not going to risk paying compensation by being a minute late. She's navigating customs and then she'll be in a cab, which gives me two and a half hours to be ready for her.

It's a cold, clear day. Sunday lunchtime. We all say our goodbyes, exchanging hugs and excitement about the wedding, and then they're all on the Tube, or trains to the countryside, where their wives and kids are awaiting their return. I, on the other hand, decide to walk from Kings Cross to my flat, a pleasing twenty-ish minute stroll over to Barnsbury.

I stop at M&S to get supplies: steak, because if I try to cook anything else it'll ruin the illusion that I'm a competent adult; rocket salad, because someone I dated in my twenties insisted that plates needed salad and I've realised she's right; and a packet of chocolate mini rolls because Orla told me last time I saw her that her mother didn't let her have sugar as a kid, so she's never enjoyed any chemical-riddled party foods. Then I stop at the florist by the Tube to get something to make the flat smell nice, and the wine shop for the velvety red she was so taken by on her last visit. Seduction shop completed, I let myself in through the front door and then the door to my flat, and note with relief that I did not leave a load of laundry in the washing machine as I'd been intermittently telling myself I probably had.

I take a long, hot shower to get the train off me, then I pull on a pair of cords and a wool jumper she'd liked last time. I change the sheets, put on some music and then start half reading, half pretending to read. I splay the book cover down when the intercom goes, hoping she'll notice that I'm halfway through something that won a lot of very highbrow literary prizes.

'Hello?' I answer.

'Did you want to buy some drugs?' she says, voice loud.

'Absolutely not, I'm waiting in for the Mormons,' I respond, buzzing her in.

She manages to look sexy even while pulling a wheelie suitcase, which is quite an achievement. 'Trying to get me in trouble with the neighbours?' I ask, kissing her.

'Always.'

Orla finds my relationship with the people downstairs extremely amusing. They're a stern-looking couple in their early twenties who put a *TRADITIONAL VALUES* sticker in their window. Orla is fully aware that I have a decent number of female visitors come through the flat, and takes great joy in both being one of them, and being provocative about being one of them.

'You look gorgeous,' I say, entirely truthfully. She's just got off a plane but she's the kind of very thin, very pale woman who looks neat even when she should really look rumpled. Her dark hair is pulled back severely, her skin a blinding contrast against her black T-shirt when she takes her coat off.

'Can I have a shower?' she asks. 'I—' She stops herself. I imagine she was probably going to say something about being worried that she smells, and then realised that we're not quite familiar enough for that.

'Of course,' I say. 'There's a robe on the back of the door and a hairdryer—'

'I know.'

The first time she stayed she laughed at me for the Aesop products in the bathroom, the hairdryer and the make-up wipes. Actually, first she accused me of having a girlfriend. Then, after I absolutely insisted I didn't and offered to let her go through the wardrobes to check for clothes, she laughed at me. 'You really have enough girls through here to justify this?'

At the time I was surprised she'd said girl rather than woman, given that she's an academic, and a feminist. But then this was three, four years ago? So she would have been in her mid-, maybe late twenties. More of a girl than a woman, arguably. I answered her honestly, at the time. Told her that yes, I absolutely do have enough women come here to justify it. She asked me how many and I said one, maybe two a month. Plus a handful of friends who returned time and time again for what was hopefully a low-pressure, high-enjoyment rematch. And after she'd asked me a laundry list of questions about how any of this could work, I took her to bed. And the next time she was in town, she messaged me, *Fancy a rematch?* And then I blinked and time passed, and we've done this for three nights every three months for three years. Thirty-six rematches. All from that one fateful right-swipe on an app when she was in London for a few days.

'I have bad news,' Orla says, when she comes out of the shower. Her cheeks are pink and she's wearing the towelling robe. Smiling up at me through her thick, dark lashes.

'Has the shower shelf come off the wall? Because the guy who installed it was incredibly dodgy and I told him that—'

'I'm in love with you,' she says.

Right.

Shit.

She's still smiling, which gives me the horrible feeling that she might think I'm going to say it back. I can't say it back because I'm thinking that I'd much rather she'd told me that the shower shelf had come off the wall.

'Is that… okay?' she asks, her smile fading.

'Of course it's okay,' I tell her, pouring her a glass of wine. She accepts the glass, holding it between both hands.

'Do you—' She pauses. 'I mean, if I have to ask…' She swallows. 'I take it you… don't?'

I'd love to lie to her. I really would. I'd love to tell her I love her, then take her to bed and see what she's like to fuck when she's just been told that she's loved, and then tomorrow do the same thing, and then block her the second she gets on the plane back to Dublin and pretend none of this ever happened. But for all the obvious reasons pertaining to my inconvenient moral code, I can't do that.

'You being here is incredible,' I say, slowly. 'Genuinely. I spent the entire weekend in Amsterdam thinking about counting the freckles on your shoulder blades, and asking what you thought of the last Rooney novel.' I force myself to look her in the face, because she came here to tell me something that I mistakenly allowed her to think I was going to not only celebrate but return, and honestly the more this experience pains me the better I'll feel about it afterwards. 'But, no. I don't. Not because I couldn't – if I let myself then I would, absolutely. But I'm not like that. I don't want all the stuff those feelings entail. Life-wise. So I've sort of… guarded against it.'

She takes a long drink from her glass and then nods. 'I get it,' she says.

We stare at each other for a while. I think quite a long while. 'D'you fancy a fuck anyway?' she says, half laughing, with a twist of a sob in the middle of it.

After we shag, we sleep next to each other, my arms wrapped around her narrow torso, and then in the morning she leaves and I pretend to be asleep.

Stella

Everyone I know has been painfully anti-dating apps. All I've ever heard is horror stories. The men are grim, the chat is dry, the profiles are agonising. But in the week I've been on Tangl, I've come to realise that my single friends are spoiled. If they think this is bad, they should try asking the same person what they want for dinner and hearing 'I don't really mind' in response for an entire decade. I don't know where all the negativity is coming from because I can tell you, right here, right now, dating apps are fun.

After I got home from dinner with Lou, I did a deep dive on Instagram, TikTok and various women's magazines into the best dating app and concluded that Tangl was where it's at. It's described as 'open-minded' dating, and it has options for you to look for couples to date. On day one, I admit, I was a little bit like one of those Amish teenagers who goes to New York and sees electricity for the first time. Everyone's profile had loads of complicated acronyms, and everyone seemed to talk in a complicated language. NSA, GGG, FWB all left me very confused initially, but now I'm a dab hand (no strings attached, good giving game, friends with benefits). I've uploaded three pictures, because since Rose was born, I've only had three decent ones taken of me, and before that I'm obviously pregnant, which might attract some quite weird people, and before that it's so long ago that I look dramatically better and my literal worst fear apart from getting murdered by one of these men is that I get accused of catfishing.

This Thursday, some of my girlfriends are coming to dinner to 'cheer me up', which is very sweet of them, and when they put the date in the diary two months ago (this is how long it takes to get four women in their early thirties in the same room), it was much needed. But right now, the idea of wasting a night talking about their actual careers, houses and lives, when I could be making small talk with boys on the internet, is less than appealing.

I've literally never done this before. I was too much of a baby to try the apps when I was at uni, and then I met Gav, so there wasn't any need to. But oh my god, the dopamine hit you get when you open the app and there are all these men just waiting there, it's insane! I've never even been bought a drink in a bar by a guy who isn't Gavin and now I've got like seven of them just sending me messages. And sure, if I met them, half of them would turn out to be losers, probably more than half. But that doesn't matter. At the moment they're not real. They're deliciously, delightfully fictional and the only thing that matters is that they're interested. In me.

It also transpires that it's pretty distracting. I've tried to keep it to evenings and naptimes because I keep reading studies about how babies with phone-addicted parents don't develop empathy, and I need Rose to grow up empathetic so she likes me more than Gavin. But my self-control is limited, and it's turning into an issue with my girlfriends.

Kate, Olive, Steph and Louella all arrive on time, which means they've been for a drink together after work. I'm hurt by this, even though I shouldn't be. I told them to come around seven; they're here around seven. The fact that they stopped for an Aperol outside the pub on the way home doesn't mean that they weren't excited to see me. And it doesn't mean that they like Louella more than they like me, an ongoing concern of mine. Louella and I are only eleven months apart because our mother thought that breastfeeding was a contraceptive device. I was born in September, Louella in August, so we're in the same school year and therefore both, conveniently and very inconveniently, share a friendship group. Obviously it's nice and I shouldn't complain about it, but having Louella – who is stunningly beautiful and effortlessly cool – as a sister is not totally without its challenges and I do sometimes wonder if I might have turned out a bit emotionally healthier if I'd at least had a couple of my own friends.

Anyway, they all file into the house, looking around, I think probably searching for signs of progress. When Gavin and I moved in it was deeply, painfully unloved. The previous owner had locked it up and moved abroad, and it had sort of rotted from the inside. We bought it for a bargain and then spent all of our time doing it up. I learned to wallpaper, learned to tile, learned to cut the most impressive straight edge around a power socket with a paint brush. We were seventy per cent done when Gavin left, so thankfully the open-plan kitchen-living room is decent, as is the TV room; our bedroom and Rose's bedroom are done, and we've got a working bathroom. The rest of the house, all the hallways and the downstairs bathroom, are still untouched from the 1970s. Not a decade famed for its decorative elegance.

'It looks stun,' Kate says, putting the wine down and throwing her coat on the sofa. It does not look stun. We're at a full seven drying racks, all covered with Rose's clothes – mine are festering in the laundry basket upstairs – and there is a carpet of plastic blocks across the entire floor. All of the post is in piles on the kitchen table and the vegetables I've been chopping are cluttering most of the counter space.

'And you look stun,' Olive adds. I really hope this is less of a lie than Kate's comment about the house.

We gather around the table, fill our glasses and start the download. Kate has given her boyfriend an ultimatum: propose or split. Olive is thinking about leaving her job because she found out that a guy a level below her is getting paid more and when she asked why, her boss explained it was because he'd just become a dad. Louella has had mastic Botox in her jaw to stop her from clenching all the time and none of us believe that's why she did it, and Steph is stressed because her sister is doing a terrible job planning a very expensive destination hen do for her when what she really wanted was a lunch followed by karaoke in London. I listen to all of this, genuinely interested. But every time my phone buzzes, my hand reaches for it and flips it over and I literally cannot stop myself.

I'd put it on silent but if Gavin called because there was something wrong with Rose and I missed the call, I'd never get over it. Every time I check the phone I tell myself off and resolve that I'm not going to look at it again. And then it buzzes and I look at it again. Chris, a 37-year-old software designer originally from New York, now living in Shoreditch, is asking me to recommend somewhere for a newbie. I consider telling him that 'Elephant Rhyme Time' at the Wandsworth library is pretty exclusive and worth putting your name down for, but think better of it.

'Stella, what the fuck?' Olive says eventually.

I jerk my head up and look at them. They're sitting around my table, which I'd hastily covered with a pretty blue-and-white tablecloth minutes before they arrived, all staring at me.

'What?' I ask.

'I just asked you three questions and you were staring at your phone the whole time. Is it Rose?'

I want to lie, but I'm afraid that would tempt fate. So I tell the truth. 'No,' I say. 'It's not Rose.'

'Then what are you so obsessed with?' asks Kate.

Louella looks smug. 'Go on,' she says. 'Tell them.'

I don't want to tell them, but obviously no one has ever escaped a 'go on, tell them' without telling. 'I joined a dating app,' I say. 'I'm doing the *Mantourage* method.'

They all explode. Mostly laughing at me for calling it 'a dating app' like I'm someone's grandmother.

'What's the *Mantourage* method?' asks Kate.

I explain about Lexie Leung. 'God, I'm so glad I'm not single,' Kate says. 'This sounds so tiring, I don't know how you're doing it!'

'Which app?' asks Olive.

'Are you sure you're ready?' demands Steph. 'Don't you need to be alone for a while?'

They continue asking questions without giving me a window to answer them and I let it wash over me, then eventually I refill my glass of wine and look at Louella. 'It's her fault,' I say.

'I just pointed out that she's had basically no dating experience.'

'That's true,' agrees Olive, archly.

'I feel like before she's ready to date to find an actual partner, she needs to put some points on the board,' Louella says languidly. They listen to her, because everyone always does. In fact, everyone who was asking me if I was entirely sane before now murmurs their agreement. 'She's literally only had sex with two people,' Louella adds.

She's probably got a point. You can't just jump back into having another husband with that kind of body count.

'Lou!' I retort. 'It's three – I've had sex with three people.'

'Liar, you gave William C a blow job. It didn't go all the way in and you know it; you're rewriting history.'

'That wasn't my fault. I should get to count it as three because we got to the point of penetration,' I retort, louder than intended. The others are used to this, so it doesn't rankle, but Kate, who is always the sensible one, takes a deep breath. 'Look, I don't want to sound like a downer, but is this healthy? Are you ready to be dating? You literally just had a baby. Is it even safe? Ryan and I didn't start having sex again until nearly a year after Rufus was born.'

I did not literally just have a baby, I had a baby eight months ago, and Kate would know that if she'd done anything other than arrive wearing a lot of perfume when Rose was a newborn, bringing an insanely expensive cashmere Babygro, and then continually tell me that we should go for 'day wine' on a weekday when she's got a free afternoon, but never actually respond to my suggestions for actual dates.

'Yeah,' I say, looking into my glass. 'Yeah, I get that.'

My face is burning red, which is probably partially the wine but also the abject mortification of thinking that they were going to want to hear about my Carrie Bradshaw antics and instead getting told off.

'She's not trying to be mean,' Olive offers, typically the peacemaker. 'We're just worried about you. Gavin's been gone for, what, four months?'

'Six.'

'Six months, and the baby is still really small. There's so much time for dating. Shouldn't you just be focusing on being a mum?'

Everyone nods earnestly.

Even in the moment I'm aware that tonight, when they've gone home, I'm going to think of ten brilliant things I could say to this. I'd really like to be able to explain that most weeks I can go forty-eight hours without saying more than one line of dialogue to another adult, that this massive unfinished house is so quiet at night that it gives me psychosomatic tinnitus, that sometimes I get on the bus at rush hour when I don't need to because I want to feel the weight of other people's bodies next to mine because I'm so achingly, bone-crushingly, physically lonely, and that these app guys have magically turned into a virtual support system for distraction and amusement. But right now, I've got nothing.

'Yeah,' I agree. 'I guess that's probably true.'

'How *is* Gav?' Kate asks, her head tilted to one side. 'How's it going?'

'It' is Gavin's newly realised (or newly admitted) big dream, and the reason that he left me. Despite having worked in finance for the better part of two decades, six months into my pregnancy with Rose, he came home from work and told me that he wanted to quit his job in order to become a stand-up comic. This surprised me for two reasons, firstly that we had never actually been to see any comedy together, and secondly because I was six months pregnant with what was set to be a pretty expensive baby. I admit, I didn't handle it that well.

Firstly, I laughed. Which actually isn't the worst thing given that he apparently wanted to make people laugh for a living. But then I looked down at my bump and looked around at the house we'd bought, which was literally falling apart, and said, 'Gav, I don't think we can afford for you to quit your job right now.'

And he nodded, and we went to bed, and we never talked about any of it again. Until he left, and then explained via a drunken stream of WhatsApps that he had left me because I 'didn't support his dreams'.

'He's fine,' I tell Kate. 'I think.'

'I saw on Instagram that he'd had a gig,' Steph ventures.

Steph should have done the decent thing and known that when I said, 'Please stay friends with him, we're keeping things amicable,' I meant *block him on everything or you're a disloyal snake.*

'Yeah,' I say, trying to sound cheerful. 'He mentioned that his comedy course had an end-of-term event.'

'Maybe he'll turn out to be decent at it and you guys will be able to make things work?' Kate offers.

This is the stupidest thing I've ever heard anyone suggest because even if Gavin became the next Lenny

Bruce there is nothing on this earth that could compel me to get back together with a man who walked out on me and our daughter. Anyway, they all talk for a little while about how great it would be if we could get back together and I don't have the energy to point out that if you miss six months of your child's life before they're a year old because you want to tell knock-knock jokes then you deserve to rot in hell.

Louella meets my eye, and I can tell she's gearing up to tell them that they're handmaidens for the patriarchy. I shake my head a tiny, almost invisible amount and she nods back, backing off.

'Okay, Steph, we need to hear about this hen and about wedding prep,' Kate says, changing the subject. 'Do we like the new sister-in-law or do we hate her?'

I'm not going on the hen because my mum and Louella are the only people who can have Rose for two nights, and Louella's going on the hen, while Mum is (perpetually) busy. Well, actually, presumably Gavin could, but when I was added to the WhatsApp group with its flurry of emojis and deposit requests, that wasn't the case, and anyway, two nights away at some luxury cabin feels like the kind of trip that belongs to a different me. I listen, or at least pretend to listen, and eventually someone suggests splitting an Uber and they leave, to go home to their husbands, bringing stories of my horrible life for their edification. Louella hangs back.

'Don't listen to them about the dating thing,' she says. 'They're pricks.'

'Yeah, well, they're my only friends, so I kind of need them to not be pricks,' I snap. It's obviously not Lou's fault but the shame is making me bitchy.

'Why don't you make some new friends?' Luella moots.

This annoys me even more. 'Oh, genius idea,' I say. 'Yeah, I'll just make some new friends, famously really easy in your thirties.'

'People make baby friends, right?' Louella says, taking a drag on her vape. 'You did those baby classes? I thought you liked some of them?'

'Can you do that outside, please?' I chide, because getting shitty with her about the vape is easier than explaining that I've barely spoken to any of our antenatal friends because I can't bear to tell them that unlike all their lovely, loving husbands, mine has fucked off.

She puts the vape down. 'Look, don't have a go at me. I'm just saying that lot were awful all evening and we should just prioritise other friends for a bit.'

'They're our best friends.'

'And they're pricks. They're probably jealous.'

I can't help laughing. 'Jealous? I developed six new moles on my body while I was pregnant, some of which are significantly more 3D than I'm comfortable with, and the haemorrhoids they said would disappear postpartum are still very much sitting on my arsehole, so I'm never going to be able to have anal with anyone, which by the way is something that young, single people seem to be literally obsessed with, and I'm getting divorced at thirty.'

'Stella, that is unbelievably chic.'

My face clearly tells her that I'm incredulous about this.

'I'm serious,' she goes on. 'I mean not about the moles or the haemorrhoids – you should really see someone about those. But being a young divorcée is so fucking chic. Plus, you've got a house and when it's finished it's going to be sick, and you've already got a kid so you don't have to worry about your fertility. And Gav is a cunt, but he's paying the mortgage, and your maternity package is decent and you've got savings, and Mum gives you money because she feels bad for you. So I'm going to say the thing you don't want to hear, that you need to hear, which is that it could honestly be a lot worse. Those bitches wish they could already have the house and the kid – they're like, so many steps behind you. Okay?'

I take a deep breath. She's wrong about them being jealous. But she is right about Rose. And about my finances. It could be worse, and thinking about myself as the hardest done by woman in London isn't helping anything or anyone.

'Thank you for being nice,' I say, giving her a hug. She squeezes me and the relief of being touched by another adult is extraordinary.

'Love you,' she says. 'Now you get back on the app and you find the hottest man in London to fuck, and then we're going to show that load of jealous bitches a load of photos. Ideally nudes.'

Five minutes after she leaves, Louella sends me a link to a Harley Street haemorrhoid removal clinic and a message: *Voucher for your Christmas present?*

Dominic

In the week after the Orla incident, I find myself feeling oddly miserable. Not just the kind of usual worried, depressed feeling I get when someone I went to school with wins an award or gets promoted, but something heavier, a proper mard. I think it might be guilt. I've messaged her a load of times asking if she's okay, if she wants to talk, all that stuff, and she's not replied. She doesn't owe me a reply, obviously, but I can't help feeling like an utter shit. Yeah, I was intensely clear about what I had to offer when we started talking but she's not exactly the first person to think that what someone says and what they feel might not match up.

Anyway, it's Saturday morning, almost a week after Orla's premature departure, and adding to my sense that the world is a bad place is the fact that I've got to go to the other side of London for my nephew's birthday party. River (not my name suggestion) is turning two, which means he doesn't know what a birthday party is or what a birthday is or what the passing of time is. But Georgie, my sister, has been making a balloon arch for an entire week and made it very clear that this event was not optional. I set an alarm for early because I'm not going to be the cliché child-free brother who arrives late and forgets to bring a present, and I'm in the car before I'd usually even be hitting snooze.

When I arrive at the party Georgie opens the front door and then goes back into the Victorian terrace without saying hello. 'Mini pittas are burning!' she shouts, disappearing. I follow her down the hall and into the open-plan kitchen and living room. She's got AstroTurf in the garden and bifold doors that everyone who has kids is obliged to have (as an architect, I'm well aware). It's a nice house, like it's the kind of house that people work really hard to have, but my god it makes me even more sure that I can't do any of this.

'Hello, love,' my mum says, putting her arms around my neck. She looks older than she did last time I saw her, a few months ago, which makes me feel deeply guilty. 'Did you bring a present?' she asks.

Obviously I brought a present. I point at the box of rainbow stacking cups I've placed by the door.

'Wow,' Mum says, like I've brought an actual unicorn with me. 'Who wrapped that?'

'I did!' I say, sounding like a whiny little boy. Why is it so surprising that I, a thirty-four-year-old man, might own a roll of wrapping paper and scissors? 'Where's Dad?'

She points to the garden where Dad and Georgie's husband, hilariously named George, are trying to put up a banner reading *This Is My Second Rodeo*. I look at it, bemused.

'No,' Mum says. 'Me neither.'

'Sorry,' Georgie says, looking harassed. She comes back into the kitchen with her behemoth toddler, my nephew, on her hip in a position that is presumably turning her spine into a sort of 'S' shape. 'There's just such a lot to get done.'

I take River and throw him up and down in the air for a bit, working out what kind of weight I'm lifting and whether I should start drinking creatine, or at least find out what creatine is, while Georgie arranges different chopped-up fruits into the shape of a rainbow and then dabs 'yogurt clouds' on the ends. Eventually her friends start arriving, complete with other much smaller toddlers, and we're all sent outside into their garden, which looks a lot like the *Big Brother* garden from the noughties because of the previously mentioned AstroTurf.

I realise after half an hour that driving here was a mistake because Georgie has stacked the garden with bottles of booze. I want to ask if this is normal for a kids' party taking place in the middle of the morning but that'd probably sound judgmental.

'Cheers!' shouts one of her friends, taking the cork out of a bottle.

'Prosecco o'clock!' says another extremely similar-looking woman.

One of their husbands sidles up to me, sitting next to me on the sun-drenched bench. 'I'm Ollie,' he says.

'Dom,' I reply.

'Which one's yours?'

I point at Georgie. He looks confused. 'That's my sister,' I explain.

'Oh!' The realisation dawns on him. 'No kids?'

'No kids.'

'And you're spending your Saturday doing this?'

'I mean, he is my nephew.'

'You must be absolutely hanging,' he says, weirdly excited by the idea. 'Big night last night?'

Last night I watched *The Red Shoes*, a 1948 film about a pair of haunted ballet shoes, and ate an entire bag of frozen gyoza.

'No,' I say, bemused. 'I'm fine.'

Over the course of the morning, about six other people discover that I'm the child-free brother and then make a comment about how hungover I must be. Eventually, once I've forgotten absolutely everyone's names, the kids start screaming and hurling food at each other, then George and Georgie give everyone a party bag and send them on their merry way. My mum and dad go home, Mum driving because Dad might fall asleep at the wheel (this has never happened and there's no suggestion that it would ever happen but Mum likes to worry about it anyway). I pick up *Paw Patrol* plates and napkins from the garden floor, and shove them into a bin bag. Georgie comes back from putting River down for what sounded like a very intensely resisted nap.

'Sorry,' she says, picking up what I think may be someone else's paper cup of Prosecco. 'I've barely talked to you.'

'It's fine,' I say. 'You had your public to deal with. It was a great party.'

'It was a second birthday party, Dom. It was boring as shit, you don't need to be sarcastic.'

'I wasn't being sarcastic!' I argue.

'Are you hungover?'

'Why does everyone keep asking me that?'

'You just look a bit… off.'

Someone's untouched piece of cake is sitting on a plate on the garden wall, so I decide to adopt it. I peel the white icing off the top, relishing how it tastes exactly the same as it did when we were kids.

'I'm fine,' I say, my teeth slightly sticking together. 'Just had a shit week.'

'Why?'

I shrug. 'Romantic stuff.'

She looks surprised, which is fair because I don't give much away to any of my family when it comes to dating. 'Like what?'

'I was seeing this girl and it was supposed to be casual. We got on really well. She lives in Dublin. We've had a kind of regular-casual thing going for a while. But then she got feelings for me, and I ended up really hurting her, and she won't return my calls and I feel like a piece of shit.'

Georgie rolls her eyes. 'Where did you meet her?'

'A dating app.'

'Which one?'

I don't think Georgie knows anything about dating apps, but I tell her anyway.

'Dom!' she says. 'You tit. That's for people who are *dating* dating. Like husband, marriage, babies dating.'

I give her a perplexed look because Georgie is married with a two-year-old; this isn't her world.

'I'm not dead,' she retorts. 'I read stuff, I have friends, I know stuff. If you're dating to find someone who actually doesn't want a commitment, you need to go on Tangl.'

It is fairly embarrassing that Georgie, married, knows more about this than I do, so I don't admit that I have no idea what she's talking about.

'Good idea,' I say, nodding along. 'Yeah. Okay, that's a plan.'

'Good,' she says. 'Now, I love you but please go home. I'm supposed to sleep when the baby sleeps.'

'He's two.'

Georgie points towards the gate. 'Out.'

Stella

Despite my oldest friends deeming me some kind of tragic nymphomaniac, my enthusiasm for Tangl doesn't seem to be slowing down. In fact, I've fallen into a routine where I do a swiping binge before the start of 'Jump & Jiggle With Mummy' and then spend the whole thing, while jumping up and jiggling and worrying about my pelvic floor, thinking about all the matches that could be rolling in like little rewards while I can't look at my phone. Then after the class, when Rose is exhausted from being thrown in the air and expected to hold maracas, I watch the other mums – who all seem to know each other – go off together, then I park up at a bench with a hot cup of coffee and a sleeping baby, and devour every single match. A treat.

This week, the same routine. We get up, get dressed, get fed, plod our way down the road and through the park to the class, revelling in the fact that the sun is out. I make it through the class without wetting myself and afterwards, instead of the coffee-and-a-flirt routine, I keep walking to the supermarket and do a food shop. I fill the basket under the pram with fruit because Rose basically only eats berries at the moment (must google a second mortgage later as a result) and I try to find something I can bring myself to eat. As is kind of standard at the moment, nothing looks tempting. I tell myself over and over again as I walk around the shop, thinking about the prospect of being elderly and living alone, that this is good for me. The app was a distraction. A crutch. I have to feel my feelings, not hide behind distractions. Lovely, distracting distractions.

I expect Rose to wake up in the shop but she doesn't, so now I've got a quandary on my hands. If I go home she'll inevitably wake up because she's got a sort of sixth sense about our house and the prospect of getting to go in her Jumperoo (brightly coloured plastic, makes loud noises, purchased by my mother who I still haven't forgiven). If I go back to the park and get a coffee, she'll probably sleep for another half an hour, and won't be overtired by the time her nap rolls around. So I sit on the bench, face in the sun, and try to think about how nice it is to be outside in nature. Think about the blue sky, and the green grass, and all the ducks on the pond. And feeding the ducks at the pond with Rose in a year or two. And how I'll be the only person at the pond feeding the ducks without a husband or a partner. And now Rose is never going to have any brothers or sisters because her father is a feckless arsehole who abandoned me for the most embarrassing, pointless reason imaginable. And before I know it, I'm unlocking my phone and the picture of Rose's round, pink face is replaced by the loading logo for Tangl. The letters each light up gold and shiver and then, bam, 148 new matches.

I am starting to get a slight twinge in my left thumb as I swipe through all the pictures from these men, indiscriminately saying yes to anyone who looks like they've had a shower recently. Opening the app has given me an almost worryingly lovely sense of relief, the closest thing I can compare it to was when I finally got the epidural I'd been claiming I didn't want during Rose's birth. All the loud thoughts about my future and Rose's future, and how I'm going to afford the mortgage, feel a little bit quieter as messages roll in.

Heyyyyyy

So you're a designer… (that's how I sell myself on my profile) *maybe you could help me sort out my new bedroom?*

I like that puppy in your second pic!

I'm smiling down at my phone, deciding who to reply to first when another one flashes up. It's from a man named Dom, who I don't even remember swiping on. He's tall and dark-haired with a stubbly beard and freckles. He sends me a waving emoji, which I initially ignore because I'm learning that men who just send emojis don't have great chat. But then there are three dots to indicate that he's typing, and Rose is still asleep, so for some reason, I wait.

Are you an electric or a manual staple gun fan?

I'm sure it's entirely accidental, but this is actually a fantastic question, because just before Rose was born, I caved and bought an electric staple gun so that I could upholster a chair for her bedroom, and it was possibly the most life-changing thing I've ever purchased. *Electric,* I reply. *Obviously, no contest.*

Okay, he replies. *But are we talking mains or battery-powered?*

Mains, I reply.

Oh, he says. *I'm hand-held only.*

That's a shame, I write, smiling down at the screen. *I'm not sure I can do a mixed-faith marriage.*

He doesn't start typing and for a moment I worry that the word 'marriage' might have spooked him, but then I rationalise that any man who is freaked out by an obvious joke about marriage is probably a bit unhinged, and then he's typing again.

No, come on, he says. *It's 2025, we can do this. There might be prejudice, but I believe in us.*

I laugh again. *Maybe*, I reply.

Let me buy you the dirtiest martini in London and then we'll see where we are, he replies.

I am not going on dates. This dating-app thing is a distraction. It's a Steri-Strip, a gauze, a way to keep the wound clean while it heals; it is not a plan or an intention and I am absolutely not going to go for a drink with a complete stranger.

But still. A resolution is a resolution. Chats, not dates.

Fine, I type, as Rose opens her eyes and reaches up for the pram canopy, batting at the plush whale I hung there to amuse her. *It had better be a filthy martini though.*

Stella

I am going on a date. A first date. My first 'first date' in ten years. Actually, if we're being totally realistic, my first 'first date' ever. Gavin and I met because I was a temp at the office where he worked. He spent the first two weeks of my working there gearing up to ask me out, and then failed to do so. We both went to 'team drinks' (ballsy from me who was very much not a member of the team) around the time they realised that I was absolutely unforgivably bad at spreadsheets and replaced me with someone competent. I hung on until everyone else left, then bought myself another large glass of wine, Gavin got himself a beer and we stood outside, me smoking and him trying to act like he wasn't cold. I told him how I wanted to be an interior designer but it turned out you have to have loads of rich friends who'll pay you to do their house to do that. He told me how he wanted to do basically anything other than be a forensic accountant, which was unfortunate because he'd spent a lot of years being a forensic accountant. And then we just sort of kept hanging out. No Italian restaurant with a candle in a bottle, no cinema where he yawned and put his arms around my shoulder, just a gentle slide into being Stella-and-Gav instead of Stella and Gav.

I was living off the charity of a friend with rich parents who had a spare room, and when that good luck ran out because her dad realised she wasn't charging me rent, Gav offered to let me move in. He owned his own flat because he'd chosen a sensible job in a sensible industry. So in I went. I sand-blasted his IKEA furniture on the balcony, reupholstered his hideous chairs, made cushion covers on my sewing machine and turned what looked like a brothel-inspired Airbnb into our home. So when other people talked about first dates, and the magic of falling for someone, and the delicious agony of not knowing if they'll message you back, I thought, *yeah, that sounds fun but this weekend we went to the farmers' market and I baked focaccia*, and that was honestly equally diverting.

The downside of having been an accidental tradwife in my twenties was that I have literally no idea how this date is supposed to work. Worst of all I don't know what to wear. The sensible option is to message Louella and have her tell me what to wear. But then she'll know that I'm going on a date, and she'll make me tell her where and when, and then she'll make me describe it all afterwards and, for some reason, despite having told Louella everything always, I don't want that. If it's a hideous, embarrassing, awkward mess then I want to be able to take that to my grave.

After pulling everything out of my wardrobe and even, in real desperation, looking at the clothes in the spare-room wardrobe that Gavin left behind (thankfully, even I realised that wearing one of his blazers for an androgynous look would be more likely to read as suburban head teacher), I come to the conclusion that I need to go shopping. And that's fine, because Gavin is coming to take

Rose at 4.30 p.m., and the shops are open until, like, 6.30 p.m. and I can go straight to the date from the shops.

Predictably, this doesn't work out.

At 4.30 p.m., Gavin messages me: *So sorry, stuck on the train, there asap.* This means that I can't start getting ready because he's known me for ten years – he'll notice that I'm dolled up, and he'll ask where I'm going, and I'll go bright red and he'll know I'm going on a date. So I don't get ready. I build a tower with Rose, do a puppet show for Rose, read Rose the same book seven times, make her dinner, and then eventually he arrives at 5.50 p.m. He can tell from my expression that I'm furious.

'I'm sorry,' he says, standing on the doorstep, not out of breath and not looking like he'd done any rushing from the Tube at all. 'I was working,' he explains, as if that makes this absolutely fine.

'Gavin, you literally don't have a job,' I say, giving in to the rage, sort of excited by how angry I feel. 'How can you be nearly two hours late because you were "working" when you don't have a job?'

'Okay, well, it's an hour and twenty minutes – which isn't two hours – and it was literally for a gig. I had to go up to Stevenage for a lunch slot at a club and—'

'Sorry, you were performing at lunchtime on a Thursday in Stevenage?'

He has the gall to look genuinely affronted. 'That's how people get their starts, Stella. It's not like, day one, *Live at the Apollo*.'

'Okay, but who's watching comedy at lunchtime on a Thursday?' I reply. Then I catch sight of the time on my phone. 'Whatever,' I say. 'I've packed up all her things – is there any progress on getting some baby stuff at your house?'

Gavin makes a sad face and I wish I could push him down a manhole.

'I'm keeping an eye on Marketplace and stuff, but baby gear is expensive and she's not going to need this stuff for much longer so it's a waste to buy loads,' he says, in a pseudo-gentle tone.

Rather than slamming the door on his fingers, I hold Rose for a long cuddle, smelling her hair and studying her face. There's a slight scratch on her cheek where she caught herself last night and I feel bad for not filing her nails better. Also probably best to make a mental note that she had the scratch when I handed her over so I don't accuse him of damaging her when she comes home, a bit like when you take pictures of any previous damage on a rental car. I tell Rose how much I love her and then buckle her into her car seat.

By the time she's gone and I've shed a few tears (fewer than last time, personal growth) it's 6.15 p.m. and I've got to be at this date in half an hour. I shove myself into a clean top that I had remembered as being really lovely and flattering and nice but now transpires, outside of the changing room where I tried it on, to show me for what I really am, a slightly tubby thirty-year-old woman who looks like shit and doesn't deserve to have a nice time. I run upstairs, throw open the wardrobe doors and yank things out, trying on different tops until my hair is static. Then I decide that maybe the trousers are the problem, so I take them off and put tights on.

I ladder the first pair of super-sheer ones that I ordered during a 3 a.m. scroll while feeding Rose because I'd read that super-sheer was what the cool girls were doing – as if I was either cool or a girl at this point. I'm on my second pair of tights and have now emotionally committed to wearing a skirt when I realise that I'm about to be really bloody late. I pull on a black skirt, knee boots, a white T-shirt and a jumper, and decide that while this isn't a great outfit, I don't look insane. I look like a human woman who is going out for a drink, and that's just going to have to do. I dash some more lipstick on because the original application is now all over the inside of the clothes I'd tried on, and call an Uber because I've left it too late to take the Tube.

Dom has told me to meet him at a wine-shop-cum-bar a ten-minute drive away. I googled it to make sure that it wasn't some kind of crack den or human trafficking location and it showed a very pretty French place calling itself a 'cave', on the corner of a tree-lined street. It must have opened while I was pregnant with Rose and therefore actively avoiding places serving the wine I really wanted to drink but couldn't. It apparently does French wines and small plates, and has delighted reviews from dozens of people. Only when I arrive, it looks like they're hosting a premiere because there are crowds and crowds of people standing outside. I pause, trying to work out what the hell is going on, when Dom comes up behind me.

'Jesus,' he says. 'What the fuck?'

'Hi,' I say, looking up at him through my eyelashes because I read once in a teen magazine that it's sexy. 'Nice to meet you.'

'Nice to meet you,' he says, clearly slightly distracted. 'Sorry – I just can't work out what's going on – why is every single person in London here? Can I get you a drink? You look great, by the way.' He kisses me on each cheek, still looking slightly dazed. We battle our way towards the door and he holds it open for me.

He catches the attention of the very pretty waitress with a septum piercing. 'Hi,' he says, leaning in so she can hear him. We have a table for 7 p.m.?'

The waitress looks guilty. 'I'm so sorry but we've gone viral so we've stopped doing reservations.'

We both look blankly at her. 'Someone made a TikTok about us,' she explains slowly, realising that we're out of the loop. 'So now we've got too many people trying to get in and we're doing first-come, first-served. You can take a drink outside if you want?'

Dom and I exchange glances. I'm very ready for a drink, and clearly so is he. Eventually the waitress gets us a bottle of Mâcon-Villages (we're not risking having to come back in here again) and we go outside. He holds the glasses between his legs while he rebalances all our stuff, and arranges it on the little table attached to the side of the building. 'Are you sure it's not too cold?' he asks.

'No, no, I'm fine,' I say.

'I can ask them to turn that heater on,' he offers. 'Though I'll probably be there for about three hours.'

'Don't,' I say. 'I like being outside. I stood outside with my husband on our first date and that was January.' Why the fuck have I said that? Why is, like, the fifth thing I've said to this man in our entire experience of each other the words 'my husband'. What is wrong with me? This is why I wasn't supposed to go on a real-life date.

Dom looks surprised. 'Husband?'

I'd given a lot of thought to how I was going to raise the concept of being a mother. Some terrifying article I read at four in the morning last week told me that predatory men will target single parents.

But while I'd spent all the time deciding how I would broach the topic of Rose, it had totally escaped me that I might need to mention that I'm still legally married and in the process of getting divorced.

'Yeah,' I say, focusing on the rim of my wine glass. 'I was married. I mean, technically, on paper, legally I'm still married. I'm getting divorced but it's this, like, insanely time-consuming process so it'll be literally ages until I'm technically single.'

'I'm not feeding you a line,' Dom responds. 'But you seem pretty young to be divorced.'

'Well, again, not divorced, getting divorced, and also thank you, and also, yeah. I got married at twenty-five.'

'Fuck me.' Dom whistles. 'Well, that'll do it.' He looks at me for a minute, like he's considering whether to say something or not. 'This is a nightmare. I was, too.'

'You were what?'

'Married.'

This is a genuine shock. I look down at his left hand which doesn't have a ring, or the indent of a ring. My finger is still narrower at the base than anywhere else, where my wedding and engagement ring trained it to be smaller. His isn't.

He sees where I'm looking. 'It wasn't very long. We got married really young, like you. We met at school, got married out of uni, everyone said we were mental and it turned out they were right because it was a disaster.'

'How old were you?' I ask.

'Twenty-three,' he replies.

'Oh, fuck you.' I laugh. 'I was twenty-five and people are usually like, so impressed with me being a child bride.'

'I won't lie,' he smiles, 'I do automatically dislike anyone who beats me on the getting-married-young front.'

'So what happened?' I ask. 'Apart from the fact that you were too young to rent a car, let alone get married?'

He looks up at the sky, then takes a deep breath. 'I cheated on her. And then she cheated back, which I guess she had every right to do, and then we cheated on each other, until eventually she'd shagged my best friend and I'd slept with a load of women I didn't even like, and we took a look at each other and realised we were ruining our lives.' He takes another sip of wine. 'Sorry, that's a lot. I don't usually tell people that. Actually, I never tell anyone that. Have you put something in my drink?'

I laugh. 'No. I'm sorry though, that sounds really hard.'

'Yeah. Largely my own making. But not an easy time. I kind of realised towards the end of it that I wasn't ready to be anyone's husband, so I've tried to avoid it since.'

'I get that. The idea of my clothes in the same washing machine as someone else's, or my books on the same shelf, makes me feel like I'm going to throw up.'

He laughs, and I sense that I've said the right thing.

'Yeah,' Dom says. 'I mean, don't get me wrong, I like the idea, for one day. I'd love to use my DIY skills to play house with someone but I just don't seem to be there yet, on any other front, apart from putting curtain rails up. Is this your first date since you became single?'

I decide that I'm in for a penny, in for a pound at this point. 'This is technically the first first date I've ever been on,' I reply.

'This? Me?' He looks genuinely aghast. 'It's your first ever first date and I've brought you to the outside of a TikTok-trendy wine bar? Shame on me. Absolutely dreadful.'

'Well, maybe if there's a second you can do something more impressive,' I suggest. There's a flash of something across his face, something like concern. 'Don't worry,' I add. 'I meant what I said before. I'm not looking for anything serious.'

'It's not that,' he replies, refilling both of our glasses. 'I was just internally panicking about what I could do to impress you on a second date.'

I smile. 'I'd be happy with something really simple, just like jaunt over to Paris, a quick browse around Harry Winston, a night at the Plaza Athénnée, that kind of thing.'

'Phew.' Dom smiles. 'I was worried you'd want to fly long haul.'

We both laugh at this only medium-funny exchange, I think at the relief of having diffused a moment of tension.

'The "not looking for anything serious" thing is also helpful,' he adds. 'Because I know how this sounds, but I just—' He breaks off. 'I know my own limitations, you know. I'm really over accidentally hurting people.'

'Ready to hurt people on purpose?' I quip.

'Yep, yeah, just really hoping to do some deliberate emotional damage going forward.' He smiles.

'It says that on your profile though, right? That you're not looking for anything serious or long term?' I say, frowning. Have I mixed him up with someone else?

'Sure,' he says. 'But sometimes people think that might change, or it's just a temporary thing, or—'

'I'm inclined to believe people when they say they're not in a position to get into a relationship,' I say. 'Possibly because I'm not in a position to offer anything meaningful. My life is an absolute shitshow.'

He laughs. 'At least you're self-aware.'

'Yeah, well, I think about myself almost non-stop,' I say. I'm surprised by how much I like him. In the last half-hour he's taken me to an overfilled bar where we don't have a reservation and then told me that he cheated on his wife, and that he doesn't ever want to commit to anyone, and yet somehow – maybe it's just how totally honest he's been – it's endearing.

He leans down, brushes my fringe away from my face and then very gently presses his lips to mine. I freeze for a moment, trying to remember how you do this. I kiss him back and he takes my enthusiasm as an invitation, meeting my tongue with his. I feel it as much between my legs as I do between my lips, and, for a second, I worry that my knees might actually unlock and leave me lying on the cold, grey pavement.

I pull back, grinning. 'First first kiss in a decade,' I say.

'You're welcome,' he replies.

Dominic

I cycle into the office on a Lime bike because it's warm outside and I'm fully committed to the spring vibes. Then, halfway through the cycle, I realise that I'm seeing Stella tonight and curse myself. Why would I cycle when I have a date? Specifically, why would I cycle when I have a date with Stella who is a) brilliant and b) has been very clear that we're going to have sex. I can't turn up at her house with bike crotch.

It might sound unromantic but I find her approach deliciously refreshing. We've been sending each other filthy messages since our date last week, and a couple of days ago she told me she had the house to herself on Thursday night and she wondered if I wanted to come over. And then, when I said that sounded nice, she launched into a long stream of conversation about how she'd like to have sex but it was totally fine if I didn't and there was no pressure or expectation, a stream of consciousness that only ended when I told her that I've thought of basically nothing else since we first met and that, yes, I would really like to fuck. So now I've got all the excitement at the prospect of going there, and none of the lingering dread I usually get that I've misread the situation and I'm set to massively embarrass myself.

At the office I make a cafetière of coffee for everyone – or rather, three cafetières, while regretting offering to make everyone coffee. We have a meeting about a building where the client wants to put bathrooms on every other floor to save money (illegal, as well as mean) and at lunchtime I nip into Boots to buy some condoms and a packet of baby wipes in case I've got a sweaty sack from cycling, and the nice wine shop down the road from Boots for a tasteful bottle of 'thanks for having me over' wine. The afternoon passes painfully slowly; I spend most of it looking out of the window at Clerkenwell Green and the bright late-winter sunshine casting shadows on the tombstones. But eventually it's six, and I can leave.

This is not my first rodeo, as Georgie would say. It's not even my hundredth rodeo, I don't think. But I'm nervous. I'm always nervous. I want this to go well, I want us both to enjoy it. I want us to have mutually gratifying sex (ideally far better than what she was having with her ex-husband because I'm nothing if not competitive) and then enjoy a peaceful night's sleep before agreeing that this was fun and we should do it again in a month or so. I get on the train at Farringdon, headed towards Dulwich, and then follow Google Maps from the station.

When I arrive at the address she's given me, I stop, stand and look at the building, trying to work out how I could have got the address wrong because there's no way this could be her house. It's an old Victorian house with an

SUV on the drive. I go to WhatsApp and check, but yes. This is it. This is the address she gave me. Then I look on Google Maps to be completely sure that there aren't two Murphy Streets in Dulwich, but there aren't. This is it. Maybe it's her parents' place and she's house-sitting? Or inherited it? I'm just psyching myself up to press her high-tech doorbell when the door opens.

'The neighbours will ring the police if you stand there long enough,' says Stella, smiling at me. She's wearing a white top, low cut and pretty, with jeans and bare feet. Her toenails are pale pink.

'I thought I had the wrong place,' I say. 'This is insanely… grown-up.'

'I'll tell you a secret,' she says, ushering me in. 'I am a grown-up.'

The hall gives way to an open-plan kitchen and living room. There's an island with stools, the same bifold doors that Georgie and George have, a green velvet sofa and some kind of floor mat. Also covered in toys. The fridge has a blotchy hand painting on it, and a leaflet for something called 'Jump & Jiggle With Mummy'. It smells like cooking and fresh flowers and laundry.

'Do you want a glass of wine?' she offers. Her face is slightly flushed, like she might have been drying her hair ten minutes before I got here.

'Yes,' I say, looking around, trying to make sure that my eyes are processing this place correctly and that there are a load of books with ducks on them in a pile on the coffee table. 'So your housemate's out tonight?'

She laughs, which is surprising because it wasn't a funny comment. 'Yes,' she says. 'With her dad.'

'Nice.'

I turn to look at Stella and behind her on the floor is a basket full of stuffed toy baby animals. 'Are you… house-sitting for someone?'

Stella looks bemused. 'No.'

'You live here?'

The expression on her face makes me think that I must have missed something. 'Yes?'

'But why is there so much kid stuff?'

She looks even more bemused. 'Because I have a kid?'

I sense she might now not be the only one with a bemused expression. 'What?' I say.

'I told you? On our date?'

Did she? I think back to standing outside my formerly favourite – now blacklisted for becoming a TikTok hotspot – bar, chatting away, her talking so fast and the people around us so loud that I occasionally missed something she said.

'I thought you said you could be a kid,' I say weakly. 'Like, you could act like a kid sometimes.'

'That would be quite a weird thing to say,' she responds. She looks worried.

'Are they… here?' I ask, dropping my voice in case I'm liable for waking up a baby. Stella laughs.

'Of course she's not here. Her dad takes her on Thursdays – just said that?'

'I thought you were talking about your actual housemate.'

'Why would my adult housemate be staying with her dad every Thursday?' She laughs again.

'I don't know!' I say. 'I just didn't realise – I didn't think…' I trail off, aware that I might be about to make this insurmountably weird. 'People are strange, I didn't want to press it!'

'Do you want a drink?' she says. 'Or are you so freaked out that you're going to fake a work emergency and leave?'

'There's not really such a thing as an architectural emergency,' I say. 'Usually just people wanting to put more balconies on things and that's not really urgent.'

'Good,' she says, going to the fridge and taking out a bottle of wine. 'It's really not a big deal, you know? Just think of her as my housemate. My little, tiny housemate.'

I laugh. 'Is she a good housemate?'

'She doesn't pay rent, which is a pain, but she also never drinks my wine or steals my clothes, so on balance, pretty decent.'

I laugh again. 'Sorry,' I say. 'I didn't mean to be weird about it, I just didn't realise.'

'It's really fine,' she says. 'I get that it's kind of weird to have your second date at a, like, family home.'

'I sort of assumed you'd be living in a house-share with, like, one uni friend and a lot of Oliver Bonas,' I admit.

'Not so much,' she says. 'Garden?'

It's not really warm enough to be outside, and going outside takes us further away from the bedroom, which is, I assume given Stella's very explicit communications, the goal. But it's still light at nearly 7 p.m. for the first time this year and we're too British to resist that. She opens the back doors and we go out into the garden, which has a wooden table and chairs. I wait for her to sit down and then sit next to her, rather than across the table. I lift a strand of her hair that has fallen forward, in front of her shoulder, and put it back into place. She smells like citrus and I can see a blush creeping along her neck. That's a good sign.

'This is great,' I say. 'A proper garden.'

'It really isn't. The people who had it before had treated it like total shit and I've been trying to make it look half decent, but I've only got like half an hour at a time to work on it. It'll get there, though. Eventually.'

'I could help,' I hear myself say.

She raises an eyebrow. 'Really?'

'Sure. Like I said the other day, I like playing house. I'm just not so good at doing "house" for real.'

There's a pause, which, if we weren't awkward semi-strangers, would be filled with us acknowledging that it might be weird for me to help sort her garden out when we're very much not looking for a relationship, but that she could use the help and that I've got two window boxes and nothing else to play with, and I really miss getting my hands dirty, so it could also be a perfect arrangement.

'How was work?' she asks.

'Fine,' I say, trying to think of something funny. 'No buildings I've worked on fell down so I call that a win. How was yours?' I ask, remembering that she works in interiors, so that should be safe ground for us, chat-wise. Not that we've actually had any issues on that front. Or that being able to ask her about cornicing would actually save any kind of conversational drought.

'I wasn't at work today,' she says, looking at the stem of her wine glass.

'Oh, right, day off?'

'I'm on maternity leave.'

I try to keep the surprise off my face and it clearly doesn't work because she laughs at my expression.

'But we talked about your job?' I say. 'Before?'

'I'd just done a keeping in touch day. And I am going back – it is still technically my job.'

'Wow,' I say, because I'm not sure what else to do. 'I mean, honestly, impressive work.'

She looks down, dropping her gaze, and I sense that I've said the wrong thing.

'I'm on mum mode most of the time,' she says. 'But my ex has our daughter once a week now and I just felt like I wanted something to do – something that wasn't, like, a yoga class or drinking alone.'

'Hey, I'm absolutely not judging you,' I say, probably too quickly, but genuinely horrified that I might have sounded like I think she's doing something wrong. 'It's just that the only person I know who has had a baby is my younger sister and she basically refused to do anything or go anywhere for, like, a year after my nephew was born because she kept saying she'd "done enough".'

To my relief, Stella laughs. 'Oh, god, is she one of those really amazing mums who breastfeeds for years and years and then makes all their own purées from organic vegetables?'

'I'm afraid so,' I say. 'That kid's going to end up in therapy for having nothing to complain about.'

'Not a problem Rose is getting.'

'Oh, no, she's got it made. Imagine how great it would be to know from, like, birth, what your big trauma you blame everything on is going to be?'

She laughs again, which is another relief because I've pushed it a bit here. 'You're right,' she says. 'Plus, built-in excuses for the rest of her life. Any time she behaves like a dick, she can just be like, it's not my fault, my dad left when I was a baby.'

'Exactly! George and Georgie's kid has got nothing.'

'George and Georgie?'

I forget that this isn't normal when you say it without context. 'My sister is called Georgie. Her husband is called George.'

'Oh, wow,' she says, clearly trying to be polite. 'What's your nephew called?'

'River.'

She puts on an expression of warm neutrality. 'Oh, that's lovely.'

'It's really not.'

She laughs. 'Okay, I mean, it's not what I'd have chosen.'

'My mum literally begged her to change it. I think she probably offered money; she's convinced that he's going to be bullied senseless at school.'

'Oh, they've all got mad names, though the ones getting bullied will probably be called Harry or Tom.'

'True, and the kid's built like a brick shithouse so at least he'll be able to hold his own.'

'Yep, and you can make sure to teach him the art of a devastating one-liner and then he's got it made.'

The garden is warm, warmer than it should be for this early in spring. It smells like trees and grass and optimism, and once again I am reminded that I should start taking a vitamin D supplement because everything in the world feels better on an evening like this. 'How long have you lived here?' I ask.

'Just over a year,' she replies. 'We bought it when I was pregnant, did a load of work, then had the baby and sort of stopped. So the downstairs is great, the upstairs is fairly hideous.'

'I'm sure it isn't.'

'Want to see?'

I'm taken aback. She's looking straight at me, with a half-smile across her lips. She's wearing a pink-brown lipstick which reminds me of the poster of Rachel Stevens from S Club 7 I had on my bedroom wall as a teenager, and I'm thinking about Rachel Stevens but I really shouldn't be because, yes, I do want to see. I want to see her bedroom very much. I'd assumed, perhaps slightly sexistly, that she'd be nervous.

'Yes,' I say, trying to stop the stream of nonsense inside my head. I would.

I follow her upstairs, internally repeating to myself that of course I'm going to be able to get it up, she's very attractive and I've only had one glass of wine. She closes the door opposite her bedroom, and as she does so I catch a glimpse of pink and floral. Clearly the baby's room. I avert my gaze because somehow it feels invasive to even look; the baby hasn't invited me in, after all. I follow Stella into a big bedroom, facing onto the garden. The floor-boards have been stripped and painted white, the walls are pale blue and her bed has a sort of four-poster structure, almost like a goalpost.

She stands next to the bed and bites her lip, looking like she's suddenly very unsure what to do. 'You all good?' I ask.

She nods. 'Yes.'

I run my hands through her hair – it's really spectacular hair – and down her body and then, for only the second time ever, I kiss her, full on the lips. Her tongue meets mine and I let my hands slide across her waist, gripping her firmly, waiting to see if I encounter anything less than marked enthusiasm. She keeps kissing me, which I take as a good sign, and I go to lift her up. She squeals and makes a pretence of being too heavy, which she absolutely isn't, and then wraps her legs around my waist while we snog furiously. Eventually I drop her gently onto the bed and pull off my shirt. She looks up at me, her eyes lock into mine and then, to my complete and utter shock, she starts crying.

Not just one little tear sliding down her cheek – I've known women who weep like that a little bit when they've just come – a proper, heart-hurting, wrenching sob. And she doesn't stop. For a second, I completely freeze. 'Did I hurt you?' I pat the bed to try work out if I've dropped her on something sharp or angular but there's nothing, and she's crying so intensely that I can't make out what she's saying.

'Are you okay?' I ask again, standing up and stepping back just in case I'm coming off intimidating or something. 'I'm so sorry – did I…? What did I…?' First Orla, now Stella. How do I *keep* making women cry?

'Sorry,' she says, through her sobs. She pulls herself up into a sitting position. There's mascara running down her face so I search for a tissue, but there's nothing. I hand her my shirt and she wipes her face with it, then realises it's my shirt. 'Sorry,' she says again, and the sobbing restarts. 'It's not you – genuinely – it's not you.'

'Do you want a hug?'

She shakes her head and I take another step back. 'Shall I wait for you downstairs?'

A nod confirms that this is the best course of action so I go downstairs, very aware of the effluvia on my shirt, and do the *New York Times* crossword on my phone, while replaying the last ninety minutes and trying to work out if there's something I've missed and if so, how to apologise for it. A while later, I'm not totally sure how long, Stella comes downstairs, wearing the same outfit with a jumper on the top.

'You're still here,' she says, surprised.

'You said I could wait downstairs?'

'Yeah, no, of course. I totally did, I just thought after that absolute freak show you'd probably have left.'

'I wanted to check that you were okay.'

She goes to the fridge and takes out the bottle of wine we'd made a dent in earlier. She fills her own glass and then looks at me. 'Do you want one?' Mistaking my hesitation for a lack of enthusiasm, she says, 'You really don't have to.'

'I'd like to, though.'

She fills both of our glasses and then takes a blue-and-white bowl of hummus out and puts it on the table, pulling a box of breadsticks – or rather, 'grissini' – from the cupboard and puts them in front of me. I'm starving and don't wait to be asked.

'Fuck me, that hummus is insane,' I say, as soon as I've swallowed. 'Is it the fancy one from M&S?'

'No,' she says, sitting down across the table. 'I made it. And yet my husband still left me.' She laughs.

'Crazy,' I reply. 'I'd stay married to someone really evil for hummus that good.'

'Right?'

There's a silence, and I can hear French pop playing on the speaker, I presume via Stella's phone. 'I'm really sorry,' she says. 'About what happened upstairs.'

'Me too.'

Another silence.

'It wasn't anything you did,' she says.

'Oh, thank god,' I reply. 'Hang on, are you sure? You don't have to say that, I'd really rather know, if I did do something—'

'Really. It wasn't you. It's just – that was my bedroom with Gav, it was like, our bedroom, and I've obviously never had anyone else in there, and no one else has, like, taken their clothes off, or touched me, and when we kissed the other day that was great so I thought I was really ready for this but turns out I'm actually not, and I'm just really sorry for dragging you into all of this and making you give up your evening to like, come and watch me cry because I'm clearly not over my ex-husband.'

'It's really fine,' I say, putting my hand on her forearm. 'Genuinely. It's not a big deal – we had a drink, we had a chat, you're great company, if you're okay then everything is okay.'

She smiles at me. 'You can call an Uber now.'

For some reason this really doesn't feel like a natural next step. But then she also might well be asking me to leave and the last thing I want is to hang around when she's desperate to get rid of me. 'What are you going to do?' I ask.

She half laughs, but her eyes fill with tears and I wince, really wanting her to stop crying. 'Probably make some pasta, drink some more wine and watch a reality show about Mormon wives.'

Okay, good. She's fine. She's got a plan. She doesn't need me to stick around.

'Can I stay and do that with you?' I hear myself say. Why have I said that? Yes, okay, the Mormon wives show does sound great and I am absolutely starving, but this woman probably wants me out of her house and I am very clearly not getting laid this evening, not that I need to get laid, but surely I'm wandering into some quite weird territory if I just stay here and pretend to be her like, fake husband for the night?

'I mean…' She looks bemused. 'Sure?'

I really hope she isn't standing there wondering why the fuck I'm not leaving.

Stella

Why the fuck isn't he leaving?

Look, it's not that I dislike Dominic being in my house. It's just… weird. He came over for sex, I decided to cry instead of have sex with him; the obvious thing to do was put his clothes on, suffer through a weird goodbye and then block my number on the walk home. And yet somehow, he's still here. Which, in some sense, is nice. Unless he thinks that I'm going to change my mind and we're going to have sex? Which I guess I could. I might. But it feels unlikely. Very unlikely. Or maybe he's angry with me for promising sex and backing out, and he's waiting to have a go at me? But then he's dutifully chopping the tomatoes I told him to chop, and humming away to the music, so he really doesn't seem annoyed. He just seems… present.

I find a packet of conchiglie at the back of the cupboard – made by a fancy brand, a relic from the time Gavin and I lived here together. Rose was five or six weeks old and the house was stacked with boxes, but I was determined to show everyone I was still fun, I was still a great wife, I could still give Gav a decent birthday. At the end of the night, Rose woke up and I was still getting to grips with breastfeeding, so feeding her involved rolling my tit around for fifteen minutes, so I went upstairs and fed her sitting on our bed, listening to them laughing downstairs and thinking how lucky I was, and how lucky Rose was that she was going to grow up in a house where there were people laughing over pasta and candles and red wine downstairs. Did Gavin know then that he was getting ready to leave? Had he started putting essentials into his gym bag and dropping them to his mum's? Had he run through how he was going to tell me that he was out? Or was he still genuinely happy, and if so, isn't it even more genuinely terrifying that less than a month later, he was gone?

'What's your favourite pasta shape?' Dominic asks, pulling me back to the present.

'Whoa. Huge question,' I say, filling a pot with water to boil. 'Genuinely.'

'I know,' he says, entirely seriously. 'But I am going to need an answer.'

I think about it for a while. 'Okay, well, you need a spaghetti type of thing, for bolognaise, a standard pomodoro, all those classics. And I'm tempted to go tagliatelle, but I'm going to play it safe and go linguine.'

He mocks shock. 'Go on.'

'And then something that does a lot of heavy lifting with sauce, so I'll say a mafalda, and then you need a short pasta, so I'm going for a calamarata.'

He looks bemused.

'Calamarata is like a shorter rigatoni,' I say, by way of explanation.

'It's really lucky that you're not looking for anything serious because, under other circumstances, I think I'd have to marry you for that answer,' he says.

'Yeah, well, bad luck, I'm still technically married,' I say, tipping the pasta into the salted water. 'Can you lay the table?'

He goes through the drawers to find the cutlery and place mats rather than asking me where they are, which I find surprisingly impressive. He even scrounges up a box of matches and lights some candles from the book shelves, dusty because I haven't bothered to do anything so scene-setty for months. Then he picks up a pile of papers from the end of the kitchen table, various leaflets about things I need to do with Rose or don't want to do with Rose or have promised myself I will do with Rose. And then I watch in slow motion as he picks up a piece of paper, turns it over and sees his own name.

'Just put that over there!' I say, my voice embarrassingly high pitched.

'What is it?' he asks.

I try to pull the paper out of his hands, but he's taller than me and holds it sufficiently high that I can't see. '*The Bad Boy, the Romantic* – why is my name on this?'

I go bright red and remember that I can't throw myself off the roof because the windows are painted shut and I have a child to look after. 'It's a list,' I say.

'A list of what?'

'My mantourage,' I say shamefully, looking down at the floor.

Dom bursts out laughing. 'What the fuck is a mantourage?

I try to sound dignified. 'A mantourage, it's actually based on a book by this very impressive American professor.' Okay, I don't think she was a professor, but he might take me more seriously if that's what I call her.

'A professor of shagging?'

'No, professor of… I want to say sociology.'

'That really sounds like a euphemism for shagging.'

'She's not about shagging! Okay, well, maybe a bit about shagging, but basically, she has this theory that if you lack experience and you eventually want to settle down again, you have to spend a predefined period dating a number of men who fit different archetypes, and then when you've spent time with all of them, you can date to marry. And you know, I've done like no dating, I'm a total idiot when it comes to this stuff, so that's what I'm doing. This is like my intensive revision course.'

He nods and then goes back to the paper. 'Which archetype am I? A Bad Boy?'

I really don't know yet. I've barely got to know Dom, and I haven't actually got past the third chapter of Lexie Leung's book because Rose is having a sleep regression and my brain has been melted by mum Instagram and breastfeeding TikTok. 'That would be telling,' I respond, looking up at him and trying to sound coy. 'I put you down as Bad Boy provisionally, okay?'

Dom is elated. 'What makes me a Bad Boy?'

'I don't know!' I retort. 'You were wearing a leather jacket in one of the pictures on your profile.'

'I was dressed up as Danny Zuko for a *Grease* theme night!'

'Well, I didn't know that! You're not even in the mantourage yet; I'm just working it out.'

'Wait, I'm auditioning?'

I sigh, exasperated. 'Yes!

He laughs again. 'This is genuinely amazing. I am going to need you to update me at absolutely every step of this insane plan. I'm going to get into the mantourage purely so I can have a front row seat to what's happening around me.'

I shake my head and drain the pasta, then combine it with the sauce, snow a generous amount of Parmesan over it and put both plates on the table. As the plates touch the tablecloth I realise that I haven't cooked dinner like this, low key, things from the fridge, for one other person since Gav left, and I want to cry all over again but then he probably will leave and it'll be a waste of pasta.

'Where did you grow up?' I ask in a slightly strangled voice.

'Are you okay?' he asks, not ignoring the oddness in my voice like I'd hoped he would.

I nod. He seems to understand that I need to not talk right now. 'Ruislip.'

'Nice,' I say, blowing on a forkful of pasta that I'm suddenly not hungry to eat. 'This might need salt.'

He takes an enormous mouthful. 'It doesn't. And I'm taking it you've never been to Ruislip.'

'I've never even heard of Ruislip.'

'It's the arse end of the Metropolitan line. Lots of pampas grass outside semi-detached "villas". Swinging central in the eighties, apparently. And the high street has three different bed showrooms.'

'Sexy.'

'Exactly.'

'And your parents have always lived there?'

He shakes his head. 'I lived with my grandparents.'

'Why?'

I probably wasn't being invited to ask why, but I've done it now. He looks down at his food, rather than at me.

'My parents split up when I was a kid; they had me super young, so me and my mum lived with them and my dad just sort of fucked off.'

'I'm sorry,' I say. 'That's shit.'

'I mean, it was and it wasn't. My grandparents were pretty great. Apart from watching *The Good Life* when everyone else was watching *Robot Wars*, it was a pretty sweet deal.'

'I fucking love *The Good Life*,' I say, responding to totally the wrong part of this story. 'I wanted to name Rose after Barbara, and he wouldn't let me.'

'What a twat.' He smiles. 'As if I needed to be convinced that he had bad judgement.'

There's a moment. A static moment, with a sort of crackle between us. I could kiss him. I could lean forward and kiss him. We've kissed before, he was into kissing before, it wouldn't be bad or weird or presumptuous. And maybe I won't start crying again this time, maybe we'll go upstairs and I'll get to feel another person's body against mine for the first time in months and months.

He looks at me, searchingly. 'Shall we go and watch the housewives?'

I blush bright red and thank the god I've really gone off believing in that I didn't try to snog him a minute and a half ago. 'Yes!' I say, way too enthusiastically.

We go through into the TV room, which is my favourite room of the house. It's a small one, off the kitchen, made smaller by my insisting on lining it with bookshelves. There's a TV on the wall but other than that, all books. And a squashy sofa I bought from a hotel that was going bust. I wrestled it into a hastily hired minivan by myself just before I found out I was pregnant with Rose and then worried the whole first trimester that I'd somehow broken her by doing it. The walls are a dark red colour in here, so it has a sort of cloistered, comforting warmth.

Dom sits down on the sofa heavily, like he's lived here his entire life, then looks at me guiltily. 'Sorry,' he says. 'I keep forgetting I'm a guest.'

'Fine by me,' I say, sitting down as far from him as I reasonably can, because I'm never getting over the humiliation of nearly kissing him when he just wanted to watch TV. 'If you're not a guest then I can make you wash up.'

I click on the programme, which is about a group of women who are ostensibly friends and ostensibly deeply pious but spend most of their time shagging other people.

'Are those the Mormons?' Dom asks.

'Are you the kind of person who talks over the TV?'

'It's the title sequence,' he says defensively.

'I'm just checking. I need to know what I'm in for.'

'Okay, well, yes, I have occasionally been told that I'm a talker during TV. So are these the Mormons.'

'Yes.'

'I thought they wore long dresses and had plaits?'

I can feel the warmth of his leg radiating out towards mine. Or maybe I'm imagining it. 'That's the Amish.'

'Oh. Right.'

He's silent until the two women are having coffee, less than a minute later. 'Are they married to the same guy?'

'No.'

'But some of them are?'

'No, that's fundamentalist Mormons. These are just normal Mormons.'

'If they're not sister wives then why is this fun?'

'Just wait and see!' I snap.

'Sorry.' He laughs, pretending to pout.

'Wait!' he suddenly says a few minutes later. 'What are they *doing*? That's not her husband.'

'That's what I'm saying. This show is no *Pride and Prejudice*, but it comes awfully close sometimes.'

'The film?'

'The BBC production,' I say. I can't believe he doesn't already know this.

We watch an entire episode. He talks through the whole thing, I pretend to be annoyed by it, and intermittently I think about how weird this is. And how nice it is. And then he moves slightly and his skin brushes mine and I wonder if maybe we're going to attempt to go upstairs again, and then he doesn't and I feel rejected and ashamed again, and it goes round until the end of the episode.

'One more?' he asks.

I have never understood anyone less than I understand this man. But I don't know how to say no, so I refill his wine glass and let the TV start playing the next episode. 'I really think she needs to divorce her husband,' he says sagely.

'They can't, it's fully forbidden, they got sealed in the Temple.'

'Sure, but he's using her for money, she can't stay with him.'

I giggle at his earnestness. I think I lean in to him, maybe? My head is on his shoulder, anyway. And the room is warm, and the wine is red, and somehow, completely by accident, I can feel my eyelashes falling towards my cheeks and I'm letting myself just take two minutes to rest my eyes before we get up and he leaves.

I have always been an amazing sleeper. As claims to fame go, it's a pretty mediocre one, but there you have it.

I've never once had to think about buying a sleep mask or taking melatonin, or any of the things my fellow neurotics have to do. I just close my eyes and bam. Sleep. I can do it in the car, on the train, on a plane. And – apparently – on the sofa of the house I bought with my ex-husband, lying next to a man I've only just met from a dating app.

As is traditional when you've fallen asleep somewhere you shouldn't, I take a moment to realise where I am. Then I unstick my tongue from the roof of my mouth and see the wine glass on the floor at my feet, and want to throw up. There's a body next to me. I mean, not a body, a person. An alive person. Dom. Specifically, Dom is next to me, splayed over the other side of the sofa, breathing gently, with a half-smile. *Fucking hell.* What time is it? Please, please, please, let it be one of those mornings where it's weirdly light at 4 a.m. and there are actually hours and hours left for sleep.

I dig in the sofa to find my phone and, yes, it's 8.30 a.m.

There's a knocking. It's the door. I'm pretty sure that's what woke me up in the first place. Did I order something? I mean, I've always ordered something, that's like, the definitive thing about having a small child, you're constantly ordering things from Amazon at three in the morning, but obviously that's not what's happening here. Which means that the knocking is Gavin, with Rose. It means that my baby is sitting outside on the doorstep waiting for me, while I work out how to hide the man in my house who I absolutely did not have sex with but who it's going to look like I had sex with. Fucking fucking fucking fucking fucking fuck.

I rub under my eyes to get rid of any slept-in mascara and then go to the door, adopting a bright expression and bargaining with the universe to not have Dom wake up. There's one very thin wall between the TV room and the front door, and if he so much as stands up from the sofa, Gavin will see him through the front window.

As ever, seeing Rose for the first time in twenty-six hours is heart-bursting. I drop straight to my knees and unbuckle her from the car seat, noting whether he's made any mistakes on the straps, which to my combined relief and disappointment, he hasn't. I pick her up and she smiles, showing me her little white teeth. I do a half-laugh, half-sob as I drink her in, unable to believe that she's finally back, that I can touch her and feel her, and have her be real in front of me instead of the pictures on my phone that I've looked at every couple of hours since she left. I gather her up into my arms and straighten, still standing in the doorway, blocking Gavin from any ideas he might have about coming in.

'How are you?' I ask him, more by force of habit than anything else. Why have I asked? I need him to leave as quickly as humanly possible so he doesn't see Dom, or, more importantly, so Dom doesn't see him and think he's ended up in some weird suburban divorce swinging situation.

Gavin looks surprised at the question, which is understandable because I very deeply don't care how he is. 'Fine.'

'How did things go?'

'Pretty good. She woke up a couple of times for a feed—'

'That's normal though, around midnight and 5 a.m.?'

Gavin nods. 'Yeah. I did midnight and Mum did 5 a.m.'

'That's good,' I say, possibly snider than intended because the idea that he's taking our daughter away so that he can do fifty per cent of the childcare and have his mum do the rest makes me want to kick a hole in the wall. 'It'd be a lot to do both feeds on your own,' I say sarcastically.

Either he ignores my sarcasm or he doesn't register it. 'Exactly,' he agrees. 'Okay, well, I should shoot.'

'Busy day?'

'Just got to catch up on a bit of sleep.' From the one wake-up he did overnight. I'm tempted to ask how he ever thought he was going to handle the horrors of having a job and a baby at the same time, but then he bailed before there was any chance of having to find out so it would be a pointless question.

Right. I resolve not to say anything bitchy because Rose is going to understand what we're saying to each other one day and it'll be easier if I don't have to suddenly stop being a massive cow overnight. I'm just about to force a placatory goodbye when a shadow falls across Gavin's face. I can feel someone behind me. Fuck.

I turn slightly, still holding Rose on my hip. Obviously Dominic has woken up, and looks like he slept in his clothes because he has absolutely slept in his clothes. Gavin stares. Dominic freezes. Time seems to entirely stop moving.

'All right, mate?' Dom says, after what feels like an hour of them staring at each other.

'This is Dom,' I say slowly. 'Dom, this is Gavin.'

They eyeball each other. Then Gavin turns on his heel and without saying anything walks away. I look at Dom. I look at Rose. I look at the bags and bags of things Gavin brought home with him, things that I'm going to have to launder and put away before doing the whole thing again next week.

'I'm really sorry,' Dom says after a moment. 'I thought it was a delivery.'

'It's fine,' I say, going inside. 'But I'd really appreciate it if you could leave.'

'Sure. Yeah. No, I'll go now, I just wanted to make sure that we were okay – obviously that must have been pretty fucking awkward for you. And this is your kid? She's really cute—'

He reaches out to give her one of his fingers to grab on to and I physically wince.

'Don't!' I yelp.

Dom freezes and pulls his hand back. 'Sorry.'

'I'm sorry,' I say. 'It's not you. I just… I really need you to leave.'

This is so deeply, painfully wrong. On my list of things I was going to do to make sure that this whole dating experiment was okay, no man meeting Rose until we've been together for at least one year was top of the fucking list. It was the number one promise that I made to myself and I've literally already broken it. My inability to get anything right is staggering. It should be studied.

'Okay,' Dom says. 'Sure. Course.'

He shoves his feet into his shoes without undoing the laces and pulls his coat off the coat rack, accidentally taking several others with it. He looks at the coats, the floor, at me, at Rose, and correctly summarises that there's no advantage to hanging them back up properly, and just shoves them back up so they don't fall.

'I'm sorry,' I say, not meeting his eye. 'Really.'

'It's fine,' he says. 'Really.'

There's a long silence. 'Maybe we could be friends?' I ask, like a small child asking if Father Christmas is real.

He smiles. 'We're already friends,' he says. 'You can't watch that much Mormon telly with someone unless you're friends. And I'm serious about helping you with the heavy lifting on the house. I'm bring a drill next time and sort out all those shelves that need to go up.'

I blink back some very embarrassing tears. 'Cool,' I say. 'Always nice to have a new friend.'

'Bye,' he says, as he closes the door gently behind him.

What the fuck was I thinking? In what world was I going to be able to make this work? I had one night to have nice, no-strings-attached sex and instead I had a platonic sleepover with a guy I then introduced to my daughter and ex-husband. What the fuck is wrong with me?

I go to the toy box, unroll the beautiful, expensive playmat that Gavin's sister bought us, and then put out a variety of toys and books. I place Rose comfortably in front of it. Then I go and sit on the sofa, out of her eye line, and I sob.

Stella

It's been six days since Dominic left my house, and I haven't heard from him once. I've stared at his profile picture on WhatsApp. I've watched to see the online status under his name pop up. I've looked at his Instagram (a private account) and his LinkedIn (shortly before remembering that if you look at someone's LinkedIn they can see that you've done it) and found his long-defunct Twitter-now-X account, which has a string of medium-funny jokes about the 2015 series of *The Apprentice*, and a message for Southern Rail complaining about his delayed train. Suffice to say, I am not expecting to ever hear from him again. I don't even need to ask my savvy dating friends to check. I might be a complete dating dummy, but even I know that if you chuck a guy out while you're half crying, having offered him sex and introduced him to your kid and ex-husband by accident, you don't see him again.

Maybe as an act of penance, or maybe in self-preservation, I've also deleted Tangl. No notifications. No messages. I muted and archived the guys I had been talking to and officially shut up shop. No more men.

Luckily there's something else to worry about this week, because my mother has decided to turn her focus on me. My mother is exactly the sort of person you'd want to be friends with. She was in PR, mostly fashion, when I was a kid. A few years ago, after she'd divorced my poor father, she sold her business for an undisclosed (but, we're pretty sure, massive) sum, decided that she was tired of the countryside and moved to back to London, spending her half of the family pot on a one-bed flat in Chelsea where she hosts dinner parties and makes friends with 'interesting people' from creative backgrounds, which is genuinely great for her and probably is, but in real terms means that I can't visit with Rose in case she smashes something and Mum is never available to babysit. Obviously it's great for her and I'd be a complete dick to resent her having a sexy, exciting time in her sixties, but I'd be lying if I said I didn't miss the cosy ex-vicarage where we grew up, or get pangs of jealousy when my friends post pictures of their nice, dowdy mums going apple-picking with their grandchildren.

Anyway, they're coming for dinner tonight because I can't go anywhere without getting a babysitter, so my social life basically revolves around my own kitchen. Earlier this afternoon Rose and I did a long walk in the pram to the Waitrose that I claim is 'down the road' (an A road) and bought all sorts of tiny little foods to try and tempt my mother who eats like a bird and sees weight loss as being akin to getting your PhD. On my wedding day she couldn't think of much to say about the whole thing (admittedly I do now kind of get why) so instead she told me that I looked 'very thin' and it remains the best compliment I've ever had from her.

I've also managed to clean the entire ground floor despite Rose's pathological phobia of the hoover, and

I've washed my hair and put on a pretty white blouse and a pair of jeans that just about fit. Then I wait for everyone to arrive and pretend that I'm not nervous, because how can I be nervous to have my own mother over for dinner?

Gavin took the radio with him when he left. Admittedly, it's one of few things he took, in fact, some of his stuff isn't even unpacked from our original move. But the radio is the thing I've actually been missing, so earlier today, during the big mission to Waitrose, I cracked and bought a new one. It's pale green and vintage-y, the same sort of thing my grandmother had on her kitchen windowsill. I tune it on to some classical music station with intermittent chatting about movements and arpeggios, and instantly the kitchen feels better. Like people really live here.

At 5.30 p.m., I give Rose her tea – half an avocado and some raspberries because she is on a mission to bankrupt us. She summarily rejects the fish fingers I lovingly made from scratch, including my own breadcrumbs, throwing them on the newly clean floor. I pick them up, give them a blow and put them into Tupperware, resolving to try again tomorrow and dismissing the thought that I so deeply wish I had someone to complain about this to.

At ten past six the door opens and Lou lets herself in with her key. 'Hi,' she says. 'Just as a full warning, she has actually got worse. Also, where's my baby?'

'She's on the playmat.' I give Lou a hug, holding a damp tea towel in one hand. 'What? How is that possible?'

Lou swoops in and picks Rose up. I should probably tell her that all the books say you should never interrupt when a child is playing independently but it's too nice, watching the two people I love most, my beautiful sister's dark hair falling over Rose's soft, round body, Rose giggling, Lou fresh with all the energy I used to have for other people's kids.

'Mum didn't happen to cancel, did she?'

'No,' I say, my sense prickling. 'Why? Has something happened?'

Lou sits on the playmat, her legs twisted in front of her. 'Nothing, I was just hoping she might not turn up.'

I laugh. 'Why?'

'She invited herself over to mine last week, turned up two hours late, asked me why my house is "always so cold", showed me pictures of one of her artist friends' kids so I could see how attractive they all are, then asked me to get her an Uber home and magically forgot that I get charged at the end of it.'

Before I can respond that this sounds exactly what I'd expect from Mum, the doorbell goes. I take a deep breath and then answer it. And there she is, my mother. The woman who gave most of my friends their first cigarette.

'Hello, darling,' she says, hugging me. She's tiny, totally birdlike. I must feel like a huge frame of meat to her.

'How are you?'

I go back through to the kitchen and she follows me. 'I'm okay,' I say. 'Tired.'

'Yes, you look it. Is she not sleeping?'

'I mean she's sleeping, but not through the night. She still wakes two or three times, which is developmentally very normal—'

'I don't know how you do it, darling,' she says, taking her coat off and slinging it over a chair. 'When you two were babies, you slept through the night from about six weeks.'

'That sounds really unlikely, Mum,' says Lou, getting up to give Mum a kiss on each cheek.

'Do you not think maybe we were just on a different floor and you didn't hear us?' I ask, opening the fridge to find a bottle of wine.

'Gosh,' Mum says, like she's really thinking about it. 'I mean, I suppose that might have been it. I always thought you were just such good babies.' She pauses again. 'And then I was surprised when you turned into such difficult children. Mystery solved, I suppose!'

Mum goes and sits on the playmat, cross-legged in her expensive jeans. Rose clambers into her lap and looks up at her, then gives her an enormous smile. She's been moving herself around lately, which is so exciting but what a traitor. 'She's gorgeous,' Mum says. 'And she looks absolutely nothing like her arsehole father.'

'Mother!' I say in pretend outrage. 'We can't talk about him like that, not in front of her.'

'Darling, she doesn't understand fuck all, and even if she did, the faster she learns that her father is a dull, little waste of space, the better.'

Officially, I do not approve of this kind of talk. Privately, I'd really like to give her a hug. Of course she goes on to ruin it, almost immediately. 'I did tell you that marrying him was a mistake, if you remember.'

This is technically true. On the morning of my wedding Lou was crouching on the floor, back at my tiny flat in Clapham, hemming my £138 dress, bought from eBay (and only very slightly stained around the hem). Mum came in, still wearing a jumper and trousers, sat on my bed and told me that she didn't think any of this was a very good idea. Which might have been well intentioned but was very deeply too late.

'That's really not helpful, Mum,' says Lou, who's been staring at her phone for the last five minutes.

'I'm not blaming her,' Mum counters. 'Can I have a top-up, please?' She gestures to her glass of wine. 'I'm just saying, I was worried that you might have got married because your father and I had split up, as if you were sort of trying to rebuild yourself a family because I'd buggered off and your father just wanted to be alone with his books.'

Depressingly, this is the conclusion that I'd reached with my therapist in our weekly video calls during Rose's naptime. Apparently, I could have just called my mother and saved fifty minutes a week for the past six months and several thousand pounds.

'See?' Mum says, getting up from the playmat. 'I can see it in your face, I'm absolutely right.' Her smugness is made even worse when Rose reaches up for her. Again, what a bloody traitor.

'I'm going to do bedtime,' I say primly.

'Can't she stay up for a bit?' asks Mum. 'I haven't seen her for so long.'

Whose fault is that? 'No,' I say, biting my tongue. 'She needs her routine. Children do better with routines.' She should be offended by that, because her idea of a routine was keeping the same nanny for more than six months at a time. But she doesn't even seem to notice.

I carry Rose up to her bedroom and switch my brain off while I put her into the bath, wash her with the elephant flannel she likes, as opposed to the pony flannel she's terrified of. Then I give her a massage with oat-based moisturiser (paraben-free, not that I know what a paraben is, or why it's bad). I cuddle her, read her a story, feed her a bottle and put her into her cot with her mobile playing. For a moment I sort of hope that she'll cry when I leave the room and I'll be able to stay here in the warm, pink darkness of her bedroom, smelling her baby smell. But she does a long, deep breath and is very clearly falling blissfully to sleep. So I force myself downstairs, my legs aching on the stairs. Why are they aching? I've done basically no exercise since I got pregnant. Presumably that's why.

Lou and Mum are sitting at the table, having made significant headway into the bottle of wine. I pick up my own untouched glass. 'What did I miss?' I ask.

'It sounds like it's more what I've missed,' my mother says, like she's in a raunchy vintage film. 'You've been a busy girl.'

'I mean I'm trying to get this place finished, and look after Rose, and think about going back to work…'

'Yes, fine, but Lou said you had a date!'

I look at Lou, across the kitchen table. She drops her gaze, clearly not willing to receive the 'I'm literally going to murder you' look that I want to give her. 'Yes,' I say. 'I had a date. And it didn't go well.'

'What happened?' Lou asked. 'You've been insanely vague about it; I need some actual detail.'

I sigh. And then I tell them the whole story, the fact that I couldn't cope with having sex (this is the kind of thing my mother finds extremely normal to discuss with us – I'm aware that sounds insane) through to the wake-up call from Gavin. At which point my mother starts laughing. Properly, genuinely laughing. 'Why is this funny?'

'Sorry,' she says, calming down. 'I just love that Gavin had to see it. Serves him right.'

'Yeah, well, it also completely ruined things with Dominic and humiliated me, and meant that Rose saw some guy leaving our house.'

'Rose isn't even one yet, darling. She barely knows what her hands are. Your father and I were still regularly having sex with you in the same room at that age when we went away for holidays. You girls always came with us and there was no point getting an extra room just for you, you were babies.'

'Mum!' Lou and I say, both viscerally disgusted.

'I always forget how prudish the British are about sex.' Mum sighs.

'You're British,' Lou retorts, through gritted teeth.

'Anyway,' I say, trying to break up what could become a fight. 'It was a disaster and I've sworn off all of it forever. The universe was clearly trying to tell me that I'm moving too fast.'

Mum looks concerned. 'Don't say that, darling.'

Lou starts clearing our plates. I had given Mum a performatively tiny portion of pasta in the hope that she'd have to ask for more, but she hasn't even finished it.

'Sorry,' she says, when she notices me looking at her plate. 'I just don't have such an appetite as you two. Honestly, I envy you.'

Lou is behind Mum's back and looks up to the ceiling mouthing 'give me strength'. I just about manage to laugh. Then she comes back to the table with another bottle of wine and I gratefully accept another glass.

'I have to say,' Lou ventures. 'I don't actually think that date went that badly.'

'I'm sorry? You heard the part where I cried on him? And the bit when he *met* Gavin?'

'No, sorry, just to clarify,' Lou says. 'I mean, obviously you were insane and a total disaster. But I mean him. He actually seems really solid.'

'I agree,' Mum adds. 'He didn't have a tantrum when you couldn't deliver on the sex you'd promised him—'

'That's, like, the bare minimum of consent,' I argue.

'Yeah, I know, but this is London dating on the apps in the 2020s,' Lou counters. 'The bare minimum deserves a fucking parade.'

'That is insanely depressing.' I sigh.

'Come on,' says Lou. 'Get back on the horse. Let me see your profile.'

'Absolutely not.'

'Darling, you really should let Lou have a look; she's always had lovely boyfriends.'

Lou looks aghast. 'Lovely? James who cheated on me? And Alister who used my address to get a credit card and then ghosted me when debt collectors came over?'

Mum rolls her eyes. 'Yes, yes, but at least they were fun. I'm complimenting you – you've got good taste.'

Lou yanks my phone out of my hand, presses 'redownload' on the app store and within seconds I'm cursing our brilliantly fast Wi-Fi. *My* brilliantly fast Wi-Fi. There is no 'our' any more.

'Oh my god,' Lou says, like she's just seen something genuinely horrific. 'Oh, Jesus Christ, Stella.'

'What?' I ask, panicking that I've accidentally uploaded a nude or something.

Lou reads from the screen: 'I'm Stella, I'm thirty-two, I'm newly single and this is my first time on the apps. I'm not ready for anything serious so just looking to make some friends or have some fun. Like all women of my demographic, my interests include Taylor Swift, white wine and really cold Diet Coke. I don't have hobbies because I spend all my time and money going to weddings and hen dos.'

'What?' I ask. 'I thought that was funny.'

A message drops down at the top of the screen, from Dom. Louella looks at it archly. 'There's a message from Dom.'

'Yeah, I can read,' I say, snatching it from her.

My mother is also shaking her head. 'Darling, you put an advert on the internet saying that you wanted to have no-strings-attached sex. You can't let them know that you want that, you have to be mysterious about it.'

'It literally does not say that,' I snap.

'I mean, it kind of does,' Lou counters.

'I'm being honest about what I'm looking for, I don't want to date some guy who's looking for a wife when I'm obviously not ready for that.'

Mum and Lou exchange looks, which makes me angrier.

'I get it,' Lou says, in the kind of voice you'd use if you were trying to calm down a frightened animal, which makes me even crosser. 'But there's an etiquette to these things. It's a negotiation, right? If you want casual sex with a nice guy, you need to look like you're trying to find someone to date.'

I don't want to cry, and there's really no reason to cry, but I can feel tears rising anyway. 'Look, I didn't want to do this, I'm clearly not good at it, and I deleted the app, so this is completely irrelevant,' I say, my voice getting higher. I'm talking too fast.

'I'm just saying,' Lou ventures, and the fact that she's trying to be so gentle makes me more enraged. 'You're new to this. You're naïve. It's not your fault you're naïve, it's just a lack of experience – that's why I took you to the dating seminar. I know you think this stuff is stupid but it's not – it gets you up to speed on the whole dating scene really quickly.'

'Exactly,' my mother adds. 'So next time you try to go to bed with someone you don't start weeping and wailing.'

'I wasn't wailing!' I wail.

'Okay,' Lou says. 'You've had enough of a lecture. Let's just drop it.'

'Thanks,' I say, taking a breath. 'Sorry. Can we talk about something other than me, for a bit? Does anyone else have any news?'

'I got promoted,' Lou says. 'With a pretty decent pay rise.'

'That's amazing!' I say. 'That's way more interesting than my bad date.'

'I've started taking a progesterone suppository to improve my sexual function,' Mum adds.

'That's great too!' I hear myself say.

After Mum leaves, Lou insists on helping me to wash up so that I'm not left to clear up tomorrow morning, then she calls an Uber.

'Hey,' she says. 'I really don't think you should give up on dating. Just make your profile a bit more vague.'

'I have given up,' I say, brushing my toes against the floorboards, following the pattern of the wood.

'What happened to the mantourage thing?' Lou asks.

'That stupid book? From that insane talk? Oh, come on,' I sneer.

Lou points at a pile of papers on the kitchen table, under which is a cream book with a bright pink title on the spine: *The Mantourage*.

'So stupid that you kept the copy you got in the gift bag and read it?'

I stare at the floor and curse Lexie Leung. 'I wanted to see if it was as stupid as it sounded.'

'Sure,' says Lou, giving me a kiss on the cheek and hanging up her tea towel. 'Well, look, I know shit about fuck when it comes to your life, but I think you should do it. What have you got to lose?'

Dominic

I'm not averse to ghosting people. I've got a sort of personal ghosting code, in fact. If we haven't slept together, and it's been fewer than three dates, then it's permissible to just stop replying. Anything more than that, I'll grind out an excuse before muting, archiving and eventually blocking. I know that doesn't sound brilliant, and it's the big crime of my generation, but honestly my pro-ghosting stance is mostly based on my preference for being ghosted. In a world where I've spent time with a woman – having seen the literal best version of me for a couple of hours on a Thursday night, wearing an outfit I look good in, talking about subjects I'm interesting on, really giving it all I've got – and she's decided nope, the sum total of his human existence isn't enough for me, I don't want to know. I mean, if she ghosts me then I'll know, but I don't want to hear why. I don't want an explanation about us not having the right 'vibe' or the chemistry 'not being there'. I just want to walk away into the night and pretend that she's been summoned for military service in a far-off country, or got amnesia, or had an arranged marriage. I want to maintain the polite fiction that I was great, and something else happened to get in the way. Which is why I'm grateful that Stella is ghosting me, and why despite having drafted six – yes, six – messages to her, I've landed on sending nothing. The woman's got a half-finished house and a small kid, the last thing she needs is the emotional labour of writing me a nice long message about why she didn't want to shag me. As if she owes me an explanation. Admittedly I would really like to know what I did to turn her from 'let's have sex' to 'let's open a box of Kleenex', just so I can never do it to anyone else ever again. But we are where we are.

Anyway, onwards and upwards, tonight is my second date with Florrie. I had to message Ed, the younger brother from the stag do and the only one still living in London, to ask for a restaurant recommendation that might impress, in case my favourites had all become TikTok-viral disasters. He's sent us to some Italian place, tiny and pretty, on the edge of Soho. Inside I can see a blackboard of specials and I think there might even be bottles with candles jammed in them.

My phone buzzes, and I assume it's going to be Florrie telling me she's got noro and won't be turning up, but instead it's from Stella. I open it with embarrassing speed.

Huge excitement in SE19, she writes, with a picture of her sock drawer, perfectly organised.

Please stop, I reply. *I thought we'd agreed to just be friends.*

My apologies, she replies. *Thank you for stopping me before I showed you how I'd colour coordinated the wardrobe.*

I don't have a change of trousers so it's for the best.

What are you up to tonight?

Date, I say.

Fun, she replies. *Who with?*

Florrie, I say. It's hard to know exactly what to say about Florrie, because a lot of the things I could say about her make me sound like a bit of a twat. She's six years younger than me, which is just young enough that I am starting to worry about reading a bit creepy, and comprehensively younger enough that she uses slang I don't understand. She was born in the 1990s (a good thing) but after the Spice Girls broke up (a bad thing). Possibly after S Club 7 broke up, though I'm too scared to check. She's also, and I don't want to sound like a massive misogynist, but it's got to be acknowledged, heart-stoppingly fit. Like, I can't believe she's talking to me, has there been some kind of mistake, beautiful. She's five foot ten (she breathed a sigh of relief upon learning that my six foot one is an actual six foot one, not the five foot nine it usually means on apps) with long blonde hair, a tan that has got to have come from a bottle, freckles all over her arms and the prettiest, meanest, poutiest lips I've ever seen in my life. She's Estella from *Great Expectations*, Cathy from *Wuthering Heights*, Sarah Michelle Gellar in *Buffy*. When she turned up on our first date, outside the natural wine bar she'd selected (to my relief – picking venues is clearly not my strong suit) I genuinely couldn't believe that there was any prospect that I might get to touch her. And yet, at the end of the evening, after she'd asked me in enormous detail about my job and seemed genuinely interested in planning restrictions, which I honestly find interesting too but people aren't supposed to know that, she'd kissed me. That way around – I wasn't going to risk trying it on and her suddenly laughing at me for dreaming that I'd be allowed to. We waited for her Uber, then she went on her tip-toes, pressed her lips to mine and told me that we'd do it again.

She seems fun, I say, because I can't work out what else to say. *But obviously until someone invites me for a Mormon sleepover and lets me meet their ex-husband, you'll still be the gold standard.*

She starts typing. Then stops. Then starts again. Then stops. Then Florrie arrives. I look down once more at the screen to see if Stella's replied. She hasn't.

'Hi,' I say, as Florrie parks her Lime bike. I sort of wait for her to apologise for being late, because I've been waiting outside the restaurant messaging Stella for twenty minutes, but there's no apology and I sort of feel like an idiot for thinking she might. It's a Friday night, what's twenty minutes?

She's wearing a pair of low-slung jeans with her midriff on show, her T-shirt stopping just below her tanned waist. She wraps her arms around my neck and looks searchingly into my face. 'I find time management really difficult.'

I note a man walking past us looks at her. Looks at me. Gives me a look of begrudging approval. I want to hate this, but obviously I don't.

'Oh. Same,' I say, following her as she goes into the restaurant.

'This is so cute,' she says, taking out her phone to snap a picture of the restaurant. 'I can't believe we're having dinner – this is so *vintage*.'

Is that good? I really don't know what to say to that.

'I guess that's the perk of dating an older man?' She giggles.

Six years older? Is that an older man? Am I an older man? Oh my god, I'm an older man. Am I going to have to offer her some kind of advice? I'm definitely going to have to pay the whole bill.

The waiter shows us to our table and leaves us with menus. 'Would you like a glass of wine?' I ask. 'Or we could share a bottle?'

She looks at the list and wrinkles her nose. 'Oh. None of these are biodynamic.'

'Ah,' I say. 'Right.'

'Biodynamic wines are made without isinglass,' she explains patiently. 'That's made from fish guts. It makes the wine not vegan.'

'Oh.' I see. 'Oh, okay, I get it. Sorry, I didn't realise you were vegan – are there going to be enough options for you—'

'I'm not vegan,' she says pleasantly.

I decide not to ask any more questions about the isinglass. She orders a vodka Diet Coke and I order a beer.

'So where did you grow up?' I ask her.

'London.'

'Wow. A native, that's pretty rare. What part of London?'

'Godalming.'

Godalming is definitely not in London. You could maybe say London if you were on holiday abroad and a waiter asked where you were from and you were looking for a polite answer, but that's the only exception. 'That sounds lovely,' I say, faltering slightly. I've got no material on Godalming. 'Did you go to uni there?'

'No,' she says. And then she doesn't say anything else. She doesn't ask where I'm from, or tell me where she did go to uni, or what better use of £9,000 a year she found as an alternative to going to uni. Instead, she takes some more pictures of the restaurant. Then she puts her phone down and looks at me, brightly. 'I'm so glad that we're doing this,' she says.

'Me too,' I agree, perplexed.

'So, listen,' she says. 'I just wanted to clarify that I think you seem great and I love the journey that we're on, but I'm not currently open to monogamy.'

Clearly I don't pull a cool enough face because she smiles. 'I know this can be kinda scary to start with.'

'No, no,' I say. 'No, not at all, I just didn't – you didn't – it wasn't on your profile?'

She shakes her head. 'I don't disclose on my profile because men who are in relationships but looking to cheat take that as invitation.'

'Bastards,' I say, shaking my head, because I want her to be very clear that I'm not one of those people. I'm actually genuinely not one of those people. 'So you're, what, into open relationships?'

'Ethical non-monogamy,' she explains. 'I'm open to having ongoing relationships with partners, on a non-exclusive basis. I don't currently see myself having a domestic partner and obviously, no children.'

'Right,' I say, processing this.

'Is that going to be a possibility for you?'

I've spent the last four years accidentally hurting women I really like because I'm not capable of offering them a future, and now this insanely beautiful woman has found a solution to my problem. Do I love the idea of *me* dating multiple women? Not really. But then maybe I don't have to? Maybe I just date Florrie, and she dates whoever, and I've got a whole world of time to sort things out in my flat and work late and see my friends, and I'm not going to end up with anyone crying? Is this a new level of genius?

'That's definitely going to be a possibility for me,' I say.

* * *

After dinner we walk for a while until she picks up a Lime bike and I claim I'm going to walk for a bit when I'm actually going to call an Uber. I kiss her, the bike between her legs, handles pressing into my torso. Her lips are pillowy, her body hard, she smells delicious, like none of the garlic we've just consumed has so much as touched the inside of her mouth. She gently bites my bottom lip, then pulls away and looks up at me through her eyelashes.

I've now got an extremely embarrassing erection.

'I think we could make some really great memories together,' she whispers.

'Me too,' I say.

I watch as she cycles away, not wearing a helmet, taking up half the road, doing everything that makes a cyclist completely unbearable, and I think only about how perfect she is.

Stella

Mum has made friends with a concert violinist from Poland, who lives with a much older man down the road from her, and has lost interest in hanging out with me – those few weeks over so suddenly – and Lou is on a work trip to Stockholm. The girls' WhatsApp group carries on chiming like ever before, and if they've noticed that my replies are muted since the awful dinner at the start of my dating experiment then no one has said anything. I lick my wounds for a few days and then I accept that I'm inevitably going to take Lou's advice, so I might as well download a couple of other apps that aren't overtly hospitable to casual sex. I started new profiles, which didn't mention having kids but also didn't say that I was looking for no-strings-attached fun, and I had polite if slightly boring conversations with nice men about their jobs, their hobbies, their families. It's amazing how much less traction I'm getting now that I don't offer no-strings-attached fun. Before I'd get hundreds of connections per day, and men begging me to go to expensive bars and restaurants that same evening. Now I get maybe a dozen a day and they're vaguely interested in doing something at some point, usually 'a roast' on a Sunday, which obviously doesn't work with Rose.

But I soldiered on. I asked questions about the dogs in various men's profile pictures and eventually, just as I knew I had to, I went on dates. There was an Aperol in the evening sun with Jamie, thirty-six, whose fiancée broke his heart by breaking off the engagement because she wanted to 'travel more'. He cried halfway through the date and we agreed that he probably wasn't ready to move on quite yet. Tom, thirty-four, who ran a fishing supplies company, took me to – I am not joking – a sushi restaurant and told me how much he wanted to move out of London, and Jim, thirty-one, took me to see some stand-up and then told me at the interval that he found some of the jokes 'problematic'. All nice, decent, inoffensive men who I had no desire to see again. After each date we exchanged a handful of messages and then sort of let it mutually peter out. None of these men set my world on fire. But each one of them did give me a reason to put an underwired bra on, blow-dry my hair and leave the house. And with my friends increasingly locked into their long-term partners, Lou weirdly busy with work and Rose gone one night a week, I have to admit it was starting to feel like the closest thing I have to a hobby.

Tonight's victim is Richard, thirty-nine, who describes himself as six foot (though they all do that), and into film, travel and cooking. He lives in Shad Thames, something he seems quite excited by because he mentioned it several times before I googled it and realised that it's a fancy part of London, by the river. Richard didn't initially do much for me. Not 'my type on paper' as people keep saying on their profiles, which is apparently a joke from *Love Island*.

Gavin didn't like reality TV so I have no idea about half the in-jokes these men are using, a bit like I grew up in some kind of cult. Anyway. Richard. He works in finance and seems like he drinks a lot of protein shakes. I was worried that he might be a bit… meaty for my tastes, but Lou was looking over my shoulder when his profile popped up and I was about to swipe 'no.'

'What are you doing?' she asked.

'Oh, come on, he's all muscular and he works in finance.'

Lou looked at me like I'd soiled myself. 'He's stacked and rich? And that's a reason to pass on him?'

'That's not my type,' I whined.

Lou then took a deep breath and explained: 'Okay, remember *The Secret Garden*? The children's book?' I nodded. 'So there are two types of men, and they're both in *The Secret Garden*. Colin, he's the one with the fake disability who lives in the attic and claims to be allergic to sunlight. And Dickon. Dickon is the hardy farmer boy who knows how to, like, raise animals and grow stuff. Now you need to be dating a Dickon, not a Colin. Sadly, most of your previous boyfriends have been Colins.'

'Gavin was tall!'

'It's not physical. Lots of women make that mistake. You can have a Colin in Dickon clothing, don't be fooled by a tan and a decent protein intake. Your type has always been whiny little boys who've been indulged by their mothers, and you need a hardy farmer type.'

At this point I couldn't tell whether she was talking complete sense or if she'd gone mad. I agreed to talk to Richard, and his conversation was pretty okay, so when he asked me on a date, I agreed. Then, this morning, to my literal shock, he messaged me to ask for my address so that he could send a taxi to pick me up. I called Lou, literally unable to process this, and she was enormously approving.

'Give him the address for a house at the end of the street,' she said sagely, 'in case he turns out to be insane, but also I love this for you.'

So in an hour, a car is picking me up and there's a small part of me that thinks he's so too good to be true that he might be going to kill me. But Rose is still in this awful sleep regression and I've been up every ninety minutes, every night, for the last ten days, so, honestly, if he does kill me at least I'll get a bit of a rest.

Rose being gone gives me a chance to go on dates, but it's also a chance to use power tools without the noise freaking her out or it ending like an episode of *Casualty*. I've been meaning to put up a picture in the hall, by the downstairs loo, for about six weeks, but the wall is way too solid to get a picture hook into. Gavin's drill is still in the tool cupboard and, despite having been told several times (by Gavin) that I couldn't and shouldn't use it, I'm completely sure that I can put a couple of little holes in the wall and then (because I'm a modern woman who can have it all) go off on my date.

I get the drill out, then, because I'm sensible, put on a pair of sunglasses to protect my eyes and an apron because I'm already wearing my date dress (Lou convinced me to take a Steve Jobs's black-polo-neck attitude towards dressing for dates and it's been a life-changing time-saver). Anyway, I raise a middle finger to Gavin, who is off at his mum's with my baby, probably talking about how he's going to be a really famous comic this time next year, and then I turn on the drill and press it to the wall. I wince at the noise, but I keep going and a few seconds later I've made a hole. A deliberate hole, exactly where I wanted it to go. I'm a genius. I should start an interior design account. Cheerfully, I drill another hole about 5mm from the original hole.

I step back, then look at my handiwork, ready to go and get some nails to put into the holes for the picture. Then a little dribble of water seeps from the second hole.

Oh.

I don't think that's a good thing?

I sort of dab at it with my apron in the hope that it's going to stop. But, if anything, that makes it angry because the dribble turns into a sort of spray, and now my hallway has a water feature and it's spurting a fine but nevertheless very real, spray of water onto the opposite wall, which I lovingly painted when we moved in.

'Fuck!' I shout.

One finger pressed over the offending hole, I grab for my phone and google 'emergency plumber'. I call three different numbers, all of which ring out. Then I ring Lou, who doesn't reply. I could ring my dad but he's in Surrey, and I know he'd get in the car and drive up here but he really shouldn't drive at night and it's the better part of two hours. I call another plumbing service who say they'll be back tomorrow morning and then I start scrolling down my phone book. Fairly quickly, I pause. Dom.

Honestly, I don't think about it for very long. He lives five minutes' drive from my house and he said he was good at DIY. He's very clearly my best option.

'Hello?' he says, sounding bemused when he picks up.

'Hi,' I say. 'Look, I know this is very weird but you said you were good at house stuff, and my wall is leaking.'

'Your... wall?'

'Yes. My wall is leaking and I need help, and I thought if you were home and you weren't busy you might be able to come over and help me.'

He takes a breath. 'Okay,' he says. 'Sure. Yeah. I'll be right there. Do you know where your stopcock is?'

'My what?' I yelp.

'Never mind,' he says.

Literally six minutes later – and I'm fully aware of how long it's been because I'm standing here holding my thumb to the hole – the door goes. I take my hand off the leak, run to the door, open it and then run back to the leak, pressing my hand back against it so the water runs down the wall, instead of spraying.

'What happened?' asks Dom, who is carrying the kind of toolbox you'd usually see in some kind of period drama.

'I drilled into the wall and then it started leaking.'

'Didn't you use a stud finder?' he asks.

'That sounds like some kind of gay dating site,' I snap.

Dom laughs, then moves my hand away. 'Okay,' he says. 'You've drilled into a pipe.'

'Yes,' I say. 'I had kind of gathered that.'

'Are you going to be this moody the entire time I'm helping you?' he asks.

'I'm sorry!' I say. 'No.'

'I'm going to find your stopcock,' he says. He disappears for a few minutes and goes upstairs. I try to remember if I've left a pair of knickers on the bathroom floor or not, but before long the water stops.

'It's stopped!' I shout.

'Yeah, that was the idea,' he shouts back. 'Some sociopath put your stopcock in the *loft*.'

I smile. It's nice to bicker with someone.

He comes back downstairs looking smug. 'Right,' he says. 'I can probably find something to patch the damaged part of the pipe, and I'll go in via the wall inside that cupboard, so you won't be able to see it much. You'll need someone to come and take a proper look, and patch the pipe with a blowtorch, but this will tide you over long enough not to pay for an emergency plumber. Or I could get a blowtorch and learn serious plumbing rather than just quick fixes.'

'You're a literal angel,' I say. 'And I don't think you should buy a blowtorch. Can I get you anything?'

'I'll take a drink when I'm done,' he says. I must have looked worried, because he looks down at my phone, then my outfit, then puts two and two together. 'Ah,' he says. 'You're off out?'

At that exact moment, a car horn sounds. I don't want to answer it, because I can see from the silhouette that whatever company Richard uses to ferry women around sends a driver wearing a fucking uniform and a hat.

'I don't have to go,' I say. 'I can let my friend know that I've had an emergency – this is literally an emergency.'

'No, no,' he says. 'You're all dressed, you look great, you should go. I can finish this and then let myself out.'

'You absolutely don't need to do that.'

'No, I know,' he smiles. 'But I'm an incredibly good guy. And I like getting a chance to show off my DIY skills.'

I laugh. I think for a moment that I'd really like to stay here. And that it's insane to let him handle this by himself, and irresponsible, and taking advantage. But if I don't, we won't have any water, and when Rose gets home we'll have to go to Lou's or something until I get a plumber to fix it, and that'll probably be hundreds and hundreds of pounds.

'Okay,' I say. 'Well, listen, I owe you a favour. And I hate owing people favours so I need you to actually let me do something for you at some point, okay?'

'Sure.' He smiles. 'Now get going. If he's sending you a driver he must be keen.'

I go bright, deep, painfully red. 'Bye,' I say, staring at the floor. 'Thank you.'

Stella

I think I would probably claim that I wasn't that into romance. Maybe it's an internalised misogyny, trying to be a cool girl kind of thing, but the idea of someone deliberately trying to woo me always struck me as a bit cringey. If anything was going to change my mind about that, it was Richard's take on a first date. Every previous date I've been on has been drinks, or very occasionally dinner. The only other offers I've got have been 'come to mine and I'll cook for you', which even I, the most naïve woman on the internet, understand to mean half a packet of tortellini and a shag. Richard, on the other hand, has been scripted by a woman writing a man to seduce as many women as possible.

The car picks me up on the dot of 7 p.m. and I'm whisked away in air-conditioned silence, into central London and along the river. Waiting outside the Tate is Richard.

He opens my door, kisses me on each cheek and smiles. 'You look great,' he tells me.

Now, initially, I'll be honest, this all feels a bit cloying. He's even better-looking in person and the idea that he's made this big effort to do something I'd like feels sort of queasy-making. Claustrophobic. What the fuck is wrong with me?

'I thought we'd do a gallery late, and then perhaps a drink?' he says, as if he were offering something random and off-the-cuff rather than a date that he's very clearly planned. 'There's an exhibition of works by female artists, and you mentioned that you liked art, so I thought you might like it,' he pauses, sounding sort of hopeful. Then his face falls. 'Though I guess it might also be a bit samey, given that it's what you do for a living?'

'Oh, no, don't worry,' I say, without thinking. 'Interiors is miles away from figurative art, and anyway, I'm actually still on maternity leave.'

The words have fallen out of my mouth before I've given them a second thought. I've got so used to telling men about my 'tiny housemate' on dates that I've stopped being sensitive about it. He pauses, halfway up the steps to the gallery. 'Maternity leave?'

I give him an embarrassed smile. 'I usually buy the first round before I explain all this. But, yeah, I had a baby almost a year ago, I'm going back to work in a couple of months, I split with my husband just after she was born.'

Richard has a serious, furrowed expression, like he's really considering all of this information.

'I'm sorry,' I add. 'I would obviously have told you, I just don't advertise it on the apps because of nonces. Paedophiles. I mean paedophiles.' I really need to stop saying paedophile. 'Not that I think you're a paedophile. I mean, you don't really know if someone is, it's hard to tell, you know, that's sort of the main problem—'

Richard laughs. 'I'm not.'

'Sure.' I laugh. 'Though if you think about it, that's probably what a paedophile would say.'

He looks deeply worried. 'Sorry, I didn't mean—'

'I'm joking!' I say. 'Sorry, bad joke. I make bad jokes when I'm nervous. I'm going to stop talking about paedophiles. Do you still want to go in? I'd really like to see the exhibition. If the kid thing is a problem, I totally get it, I'm kind of new to the whole dating thing so I'm still working out when to mention it—'

Richard looks at me, completely bemused, and I think at this point if he does decide to bail on the date it will have more to do with my verbal diarrhoea and less to do with having a kid.

'I would still very much like to spend the evening with you,' he says.

He opens the door for me, and waiting in the entrance is a short, handsome guy wearing a polo neck.

He beams at us both. 'I'm William,' he says, in what is possibly the poshest voice I've ever heard. 'Delighted to meet you.'

I look at Richard, confused. Is this a double date or something? Richard smiles. 'I don't know much about art, but William came highly recommended via my concierge. He's an expert, so he'll be taking us on a tour.'

Fuck me. I thought sending an Addison Lee was the most indulgent thing a person could do. We follow William inside and he guides us through the exhibition, and then afterwards through some of the galleries in the permanent collection. The galleries are quiet and the light is low, and it strikes me that I've never been here in the evening. In fact, the only gallery I've been to at all in the past year was hosting a Baby Art class where I arrived with Rose, who immediately did a huge shit, fed for twenty minutes and then howled until I took us home. A very long way from wandering through the marble halls following William as our heels click on the stone.

He teaches us how to read a painting – the significance of specific fruits, colours, fabrics, talking unabashedly loud in the hushed galleries, but often telling us such fascinating things that I forget to be embarrassed to be on such a bougie expedition and so clearly on a date. Some of William's tips I remember from studying history of art at school, but most of it is new to me. Any time I bring up something I do already know, William acts like I'm a genius, even though he's obviously just trying to be nice, and Richard looks at me sideways, smiling.

'It's very sexy that you're so knowledgeable,' he whispers to me at one point, while William is slightly ahead of me. I feel a prickle of tension. I'd like him to touch me. He doesn't.

William finishes the tour in front of a self-portrait of Artemisia Gentileschi. It's a picture of her painting. I have a postcard of it on my fridge, half obscured by Rose's 'paintings'. I bought it here, when I'd just found out that I was pregnant. Gavin and I had expected it to take months and obviously, like most women, I'd convinced myself that I was infertile. I'd spent the morning privately freaking out internally about what motherhood was going to mean, about whether I'd ever get to do anything creative ever again. And I'd seen this picture, of a woman painting, and googled her in this total frenzy. It turned out that she'd had five kids and painted through all the pregnancies and the babies. Only one of them lived to adulthood, which didn't totally fit the narrative I was searching for, but still. She did it. So I could too.

I stare at her for a while, thinking about her paintings and her dead children and her marriage, and then I realise I probably look like trying to look like I'm in a film about a woman who likes art, performatively staring at a picture. I break my gaze.

'You were miles away.' Richard smiles.

'I was,' I agree.

I turn to William. 'Thank you so much for that – it really was magical.'

'You're very welcome,' he says with a smile. Richard shakes his hand and I'm fairly sure he presses a wad of notes into the handshake as a tip, but somehow it feels a bit inappropriate to look.

Richard ushers me out into the street where the sun is setting over the river.

'It's a beautiful evening,' I say. 'We could walk down the embankment for a bit and see if we can get a table at Gordon's?' Gordon's is the wine bar by the river that you're obliged to visit at least once a year if you live in London, there's always a bonkers queue and the food is dreadful, but despite all that it's sort of lovely on an evening like this.

'Absolutely,' Richard says. 'Let me just tell the driver to head off.'

'Driver?' I follow his gaze towards the black people-carrier on the street, waiting somewhere that I'm absolutely sure you're not allowed to wait. 'Oh, did you have something in mind?'

'There's a spot I like a little further down. If you're in no rush, I thought we could have dinner?'

Oh. I see. This is a *date* date. He's expecting stuff. Well. Okay. That's fine, he's obviously not buying me dinner because he just wants to hear me yap, but actually that's probably a good thing. Too much time to think about sex is a dangerous thing – this way I can have a couple of big glasses of wine and then rip the plaster off. I showered, I moisturised, I've got those hideous wipes in my bag that make your vulva smell floral and completely destroy your healthy bacterial biome.

'Dinner sounds lovely,' I say.

We drive fifteen, maybe twenty minutes, making gentle conversation. He tells me that he grew up on the outskirts of London and went to boarding school in Kent. I don't make any inappropriate jokes about boarding schools and urban legends about the weird sex games they play, and feel quietly proud of my maturity. We arrive at the restaurant and we're guided to a table on a heated terrace, overlooking the river. The bottle of cava I'd been suggesting at Gordon's, inevitably sandwiched between various gilet-wearing twenty-something stockbrokers, now seems a bit pedestrian. In the car, my phone buzzes.

My heart leaps when I see Dom's name. I should save it to read for later, but I glance. *Started watching original* Pride and Prejudice *and you're right, it's basically PORN.*

I smile.

'What's that? asks Richard. I blush, realising that I'm being very rude.

'Nothing,' I say. 'Just a friend of mine has started watching *Pride and Prejudice*. The really old BBC one. And I'm always saying it's sort of filthy.'

'The period drama? I wouldn't have thought that would have sex scenes?'

I nod. 'I mean, not in a literal sense, obviously, but just like, the vibe.'

'Right,' says Richard. 'I'll give it a watch some time.'

The tablecloths are white linen, there are candles on every table and the waiter places a heavy napkin in my lap. All around us are the clinking of glasses and happy, warm chatter. Everyone here looks expensive and polished. I feel a bit like I've won a competition and at the end of the evening I'll be sent back to where I came from. The waiter (French, snooty, exactly what you want in a place like this) hands me a menu that doesn't have any prices on it. Jesus.

'Is this okay?' Richard asks, possibly misreading my expression for distaste. 'I wasn't sure what kind of food you liked so I thought this would be a good choice, as it sort of does a bit of everything.'

The waiter brings a silver basket of baguette to the table, and a slab of butter. I almost have to smack my own hand away, forcing myself to wait politely to crack into it. The bread is warm and if I had one wish in this moment it would be for everyone else in here to go temporarily deaf and blind so I could eat the entire basket, plus ideally several pats of butter. Instead, I settle for taking one piece and delicately nibbling at it while Richard tells me about his work.

'It's not very creative, not like you,' he says apologetically. 'Honestly, when I left university, I realised that I didn't have that vocation other people seemed to have, so I thought I might as well go into something lucrative, make as much money as I could and then perhaps retire early.'

'Good plan,' I say. 'Pretty much the opposite of my system, which was to pick a terribly paid job in a dying industry, then really compound that decision by buying a house and then divorcing the person I bought it with.'

Richard looks sympathetic. 'What did your ex do?'

'Long story really, I think he sort of checked out when I was pregnant and he realised that it was never going to be properly about him any more. He had a difficult relationship with his dad and I wonder if maybe that was where it started, like he didn't have a blueprint that he could follow.'

'I meant for work,' Richard says, after a brief pause.

'Ah.' I laugh. 'Sorry. Though, that bit is actually equally awful. He used to work in insurance—'

'That's not a bad career.'

'No, it's not. But then he came home one night when I was pregnant and announced that he was quitting his job to become a full-time stand-up comedian.'

Richard winces like I've told him that Gavin lamped me or slept with my sister. 'I'm so sorry,' he says earnestly.

Our food comes – he has the steak and I have the risotto. We watch as boats sail down the river, lights blinking as the sky gets darker. He tells me about his apartment, which is conveniently located mere minutes away. I tell him about my half-finished house in Dulwich and he asks about the plans for the renovations. He seems unsure whether or not he should ask about Rose, and skirts around the concept of her, which I get. I think I'd prefer that, really. Eventually we have coffee, they bring us macarons and we get the bill. Then we loiter outside the restaurant, standing in a pretty cobbled passage between the river and the city. I look up at him, feeling like I'm in every 1990s romcom I've ever watched.

'Thank you for dinner,' I say. I made a half-hearted pretence of wanting to pay for half and was then deeply relieved that he turned me down because my half would have blown Rose's winter clothing budget. 'I had a lovely time.'

'I did too.' He smiles. 'You're very different from the other women I've dated. In a nice way.'

This strikes me as surprising because I'm, broadly speaking, the same as most other women of my demographic – a Diet Coke and Taylor Swift loving, slightly insecure woman with a mild anxiety disorder and too much screen time.

'You know, I have the rest of the night free,' I say, the third glass of wine emboldening me. This is a good story, this is exactly how I want my first time post-Gavin to go. And Richard is a gentleman, so I'm going to need to at least slightly take the lead. 'I don't have a change of clothes for the morning but I'm sure we could work something out.'

Richard kisses me lightly on the lips, then pulls away and signals behind me. The same car that dropped us off is waiting.

'That's a very tempting suggestion,' he says. 'But I don't like to rush things.' The car draws up next to him and he opens the door. 'I'll be in touch this week. I'd very much like to do this again.'

I get into the car because I'm not sure what else to do, and before I can process what's happening, the car is moving, Richard is still out on the pavement and I'm blinking at the street lights trying to work out if I just got rejected for sex.

Dominic

I've done some pretty experimental things in my time. I dated a girl who liked sex clubs, so spent most weekends dressed up in costumes, trailing her around 'dungeons' (usually working men's clubs with dry ice machines) trying to see if I can spot anyone famous under their mask. I've been a very game third person in several different threesomes with both men and women. At university I let a very sweet girl named Alice do a wee on me because, apparently, she'd always dreamed about doing it. And yet somehow, being alone in Stella's house while she's out on a date with another man is making me feel like more of a pervert than any of that ever did.

If I'm totally honest, I was excited when I saw that she'd called and, given that it's Thursday when her turd of an ex has her baby, I sort of assumed she'd say, 'Hey, I know that attempt at a date went really badly but I've had a wine, do you want to come over and rail me?' So getting here and finding her clearly ready to go out, with someone else, felt a bit… humiliating. I'm halfway through tidying up my toolbox (not a euphemism) when my phone rings.

It's my sister.

'I've messed up,' she tells me, without any kind of introduction. 'I left your address logged in on my Amazon Fresh and they've delivered you a load of nappies and wipes. Can you let the guy in?'

'I'm not home,' I say, phone wedged between ear and shoulder while I try to get the toolbox to shut properly.

'Why not?' Georgie demands.

'Because it's nine-thirty on a Thursday evening and I'm a single man in my early thirties so I don't actually have a curfew?'

'Where are you?' she asks. I hear a microwave beep, which means that she's putting a pint of ice cream in to slightly defrost, despite forbidding George or her son to eat anything that's been exposed to harmful rays.

'I'm at a friend's house,' I say. This was a mistake.

'What friend? Why?'

'You are really very rude,' I reply. 'I'm allowed to have a private life.'

'Who is she?'

'She is a friend.'

'I know all your friends.'

'She's a new friend.'

'A date!'

'No,' I say, trying not to sound like I want to smack the phone against the wall. 'She's someone I know who lives locally. She's getting divorced, she has a small child and she needed some help with a plumbing problem.'

'Is that what you guys are calling it these days?'

'That's disgusting and I'm going to hang up on you,' I say.

'Is it your baby?'

'Goodbye, Georgie!' I shout.

'Wait, wait!' she says. 'I'm sorry. That's really nice, I didn't know any of your friends had kids. You're cute to help.'

'Thanks.'

'It's kind of like the beginning of a Hallmark movie.'

'I've never seen a Hallmark movie because my IQ has three digits, but I assure you it's not like that – she's literally on a date with another man right now.'

'Oh.'

'Exactly. I've fixed a pipe she drilled into, and now I'm going to walk home and lie on the sofa in my pants playing FIFA.'

'It's called EA FC now,' Georgie says dolefully. 'George told me.'

'So glad to hear that your marriage is thriving. See you at the weekend. Bye.'

I hang up before she can draw me further into a conversation by asking whether I think the moon landings were faked or pretending that she's having second thoughts about River's childhood vaccinations. Then I pick up the toolbox and head to the front door. On the windowsill next to the front door is a set of keys on a heart-shaped keyring. Presumably Stella's keys. I stop for a minute, working out what to do. It's not really my responsibility to make sure that she can get back in, and she's a perfectly sensible grown-up, she's presumably capable of looking after herself. But if I leave and she doesn't have her keys, and then she's locked out, then that'll be shit for her. I sigh. And then I go and sit on her sofa.

Obviously, the sensible thing to do is message her, so I write a message. *Hey, did you forget your keys? I've finished fixing the pipe but I don't know if you're going to be able to get back in?* I press send, and wait. She doesn't read it. Presumably she's not looking at her phone because she's on a date. I go into the TV room, the one where we fell asleep, and then hunt for the remote. She's got some massively complicated system where I have to press the right button dozens of time to get to the home screen. Someone should really sort that out for her. Eventually Disney+ starts playing a cartoon of two dogs who live in a house in Australia with their parents (also dogs). I try to turn it off, but it's surprisingly funny. So I finish the episode. And then another episode. They're only five minutes long, so it's not like I'm watching that much of it. I try to make that feel true when I realise that I've watched almost half a series. My phone buzzes and I expect it to be Stella, but it's Florrie.

What're you doing?

That is a truly extraordinary use of words. *I'm at a friend's house*, I write.

Friend? Or 'friend'...? She writes back. I feel defensive, which is genuinely insane because this is about the most platonic thing I've ever done and actually, even if it weren't, Florrie has been intensely clear that she's in earnest about this ethical non-monogamy thing. She tells me every time she goes on a date with someone else, and then tells me whether she's slept with them or not. Honestly, I'd probably prefer not to hear about it, because if the date is great then I'm slightly perturbed and if it's terrible or they're not decent to her, I want to kill them. But she says radical honesty is the only way this works, and she's been inscrutable on that front. In fact, I think she might be starting to find me something of a disappointment on that front. She keeps asking whether

I've met anyone, hooked up with anyone or if I'm even making an effort to meet anyone.

Last week we were lying in bed – my bed, she has housemates therefore her house is deeply unappealing as a location for shagging – and she ran her hand over my body. 'I wanted to have a check-in,' she said, her hair soft across my chest. 'I'm concerned that you're not embracing your options.'

I made some excuses about being busy at work and not sparking with anyone on the apps, which she seemed appeased by. Then I stupidly didn't know when to stop and said, 'Anyway, maybe you're enough for me,' which then sparked a long conversation about how if I don't see other people it will create an 'imbalance in our dynamic'. So I promised that I'd do more.

A friend, I type back. Then I pause, concluding that I can probably be totally honest here, while making her feel better about my ability to see multiple women at the same time. *We met on Tangl a while back, and I slept over just before I met you.*

I watch the dots on my screen bounce as she's typing, feeling slightly sick. I've just told a girl I'm seeing that I'm at the house of another girl I met on a dating app. In what world was that going to go down well?

I'm so glad you were able to receive what I said last week, she writes. *Have fun <3.*

The irony is not lost on me that most lying men pretend that they're not seeing other women behind their girlfriends' backs, whereas I'm pretending to Florrie that I am. But whatever. She feels better, I feel better, no harm, no foul. And I guess it's not beyond the realm of possibility that Stella might reconsider our just-friends status. Maybe. Probably not, realistically, but, yeah. It could happen.

Eventually, around half eleven, the door opens and I realise that I still haven't heard from Stella. I jump to my feet and immediately shout, 'I'm still here!' in an attempt to stop her from being terrified that there's a stranger in her house. It doesn't work. She screams.

'Jesus FUCKING CHRIST!' she yells.

'I'm sorry!' I shout. 'I'm so sorry!'

'Why are you still here? You said you were leaving when I left?'

I look at the key on the side. 'I thought you'd left your house key and I was worried you'd be locked out.'

She looks at the key. Her chest is rising faster than usual, presumably because I've just terrified her, but she looks very pretty. 'That's a spare.'

There's a pause. 'I'm sorry,' I say.

'No, no – that was really nice of you.'

'I think maybe it was a bit weird.'

'It can be nice as well as weird,' she says, taking her shoes off and sitting on the sofa. 'Also, you literally saved me with the pipe earlier so, even if you were very weird, I'd still be fine with it.'

'I did message you.'

She looks embarrassed. 'I didn't see it.'

'Oh my god,' I say in horror. 'Did you block me?'

'No!' she says. 'You're just in my archive folder on WhatsApp.'

'What?'

'The archive – it's where you put conversations if—'

'Yeah, no, I know what the archive is. What did I to do deserve that?'

She looks embarrassed. 'I felt, like, a very deep sense of shame about what happened last time you were here and I wanted to pretend that nothing had happened.'

'You? I made you cry when we tried to have sex, insisted on staying all evening and then accidentally met your husband and your kid.'

'Ex-husband.'

'I thought you weren't legally divorced.'

'Yeah, okay, technically you met my husband,' she snaps. 'Anyway. That's why I didn't see your message, not because I blocked you. And for what it's worth I don't think you have anything to be embarrassed about.'

'That's a relief,' I say. 'So. How was the date?'

She looks surprised at the question. 'It was good.' She considers me for a minute. 'Do you want a glass of wine?'

'Sure,' I hear myself say. 'Why not?'

She pours us both a drink and tells me that this bizarre millionaire she's just been out with took her on a private guided tour of an art gallery and then to some mega-fancy restaurant.

'Fuck me,' I say. 'And after all that he still went home alone. Though actually, I've always found that going to dinner is a great way to not get sex. No one wants to start rubbing their bodies together when they're full of chocolate mousse.'

'I did!' she objects, gesticulating with her wine glass. 'I literally offered him sex! The place we had dinner was five minutes from his flat, if that.'

'Maybe he didn't realise you were up for it?' I offer.

'I said that I didn't have to go home and I'd love to see his place.'

'Oh,' I say. Then I do something I wouldn't do with my male friends, but that I feel compelled to do for Stella: I tell her a nice lie. 'Sometimes if you really like someone, you don't want to push it on the first date; it can kind of change the dynamic.'

She smiles, and it looks like a weight's been lifted. 'Really?'

I decide to double down, because making her happy is making me happy. 'Sure,' I add. 'And anyway, he's got to be part of your man entourage, right?'

'Mantourage.'

'I'm not going to say that word, but yes. That. And you need a kind of old-fashioned romantic sort for that, I'd imagine.'

'Yes!' she says, scrabbling for a piece of paper where she's sketched the whole thing out. 'So, he can be the Romantic Traditionalist. God, this is such a relief. I thought I'd completely fucked it up.'

'Not at all,' I lie. 'Leave it a couple of days, play it cool, *don't* message him first and he'll be in touch.'

At least the first half of that is good advice. I know from experience of talking to Stella that she's completely without guile. There are these pigs who live on the beach in the Caribbean and they love humans because they've never experienced predators before, and Stella's dating style has always reminded me of one of those pigs. No idea how bad it can be, and blissfully ignorant that one wrong move could end up with her as pulled pork. Metaphorically. I've lost control of this comparison. Anyway, if she gives him total radio silence then she's got the best possible chance of offsetting whatever the real reason is that he doesn't want to shag her, and if not, that's a problem for the future. It might be nice for her to be single. Maybe. Though I'm not sure why I think that.

I look at her for a moment. 'You've got an eyelash on your cheek.' I lean forward and press my finger to her cheekbone, then hold it up to her. 'Make a wish,' I instruct.

She laughs. 'I don't know where to start on wishes.' But she inhales and blows, poutily, her lips full and pink.

'What's new with you? Other than the new coffee machine at work, which was scintillating, by the way.'

'Almost as interesting as the before and after you sent me of your big sock-and-tight purge?'

She smiles. 'I thought you liked it when women send socksy pictures?'

I groan. 'You're better than that, Stella.'

'I'm really not,' she says. 'But okay. Let's do proper gossip, not socks and coffee machines. What's going on with you? Are you seeing anyone?'

'I am,' I confirm. Does she react to this? I study her face. Maybe. A twinge, between her eyebrows? I suspect she's got Botox there, which makes her harder to read. 'Florrie.'

'That's a pretty name,' she says, pleasant and neutral. So she is bothered. Good. Wait, why is that good?

'It's short for Florence,' I say stupidly.

'I'd have been surprised if it were short for Graham.'

I laugh. 'She's in her twenties and I didn't think six years would be much of a gap, but it's like she's from a different planet. She lives with five other girls. She still wants to go to festivals.'

Stella makes a face and then tries to act like she didn't make a face. 'And,' I go on, 'she's convinced that we need to be in an open relationship.'

'Wow,' Stella says. 'How do you feel about that?'

I shrug. 'It's not my thing, but like I said the other night, I keep accidentally fucking people up by providing the exact level of commitment I always said I was going to provide. So maybe this is a good thing for me.' I finish my glass. 'I'm going to head off.'

'You don't want another?'

'No,' I say. 'I'm not risking another Friday morning snuggle with Gavin.'

'Fair,' she says, getting up. 'I'm going to take all my make-up off and then draft loads of "sorry for being a sex pest" messages to Richard.'

'Do not message him,' I tell her seriously. 'I will be furious if you do.'

She laughs. 'Okay. I won't.'

'Also,' I say, as I go to the front door. 'Whoever put up the shelves in your utility room did it with, like, a spoon and some Vaseline. I need to fix them otherwise I'll never get a good night's sleep again.'

'Okay,' she says. 'I'm not turning down free handyman work.'

'Who said it was free?'

'I'm a struggling single mother.' She pouts.

'Fine. Can I come over on Saturday?'

'Rose will be here,' she says.

I don't really know what that's supposed to imply.

She thinks about it for a moment. 'But I guess that's fine.'

'Cool,' I say. I kiss her on the cheek. 'I'll let you know when I'm heading over.'

I step out into the night and realise that, after all that, I've left the sodding toolbox behind. But then I guess I'm coming back on Saturday, so it doesn't really matter. As I walk home, my phone buzzes. Stella, presumably, thanking me for being her knight in shining armour.

Not Stella. Florrie. *How was your evening/friend?*

I'll reply when I get home.

Stella

The morning after the Richard date, I take Rose for a long walk in the park and on the way home I call Lou to catch her up on the whole thing. After I finish the story, leaving out almost no details about how I threw myself at him and he turned me down, she sighs.

'Okay, well, these things happen,' she says. 'At least you got a nice dinner out of it, and the gallery was a nice touch.'

'Wait,' I say, my hands gripping the buggy. 'You think it went that badly?'

Lou clearly realises that she's mishandled this. She thinks for a minute. 'Okay, well, maybe it wasn't that bad? Maybe you just told it in a way that made it sound worse?'

'If anything, I made it sound better.'

'Oh,' she says. 'Well. Yeah. You offered him sex on the first date, which makes you seem easy; he turned you down, which suggests he didn't fancy you, and you haven't heard from him for twenty-four hours.'

'It hasn't been twenty-four hours!' I yelp. 'It's been, like, eighteen.'

'Oh,' Lou replies. 'Well, that's much better.'

'Really?' I whine.

'Obviously no.'

But, to my complete and utter shock, and honestly, also my complete and utter smug triumph, when I get home there is a box on the doorstep. A box of flowers. They're all white, mostly roses, with tasteful greenery, and the bunch is absolutely massive. I open the card, which reads: *Thank you for a wonderful evening – Richard.*

I send Lou a picture and then a voice note of me half screaming, 'HE DOESN'T HATE ME!'

She replies, *This literally makes no sense, is he insane?*

Maybe he was on his period, I reply. She doesn't reply because she thinks laughing emojis are millennial, even though much to her chagrin she is – by one single year – technically a millennial.

I don't know whether Richard is insane or not, but I message him to thank him for the flowers and he asks if I'm free this Thursday. I should play it cool, obviously, but I don't. I say I'm free and he invites me to dinner at his flat. Only he calls it an apartment, which is what people do when their flat is really fucking fancy. I relay this information to Lou.

'Okay,' she says. 'But let's not get sidetracked. Mantourage, yes?'

She's annoying, but she's right. My monogamous little heart finds the whole idea confusing, but I've made a lot of very big promises about how I'm going to handle my love life going forward and Louella is not going to let me get away with reneging. So I pick up my phone, open Tangl and swipe on everyone who looks like they might be a poet, a thinker, an artist or a dreamer, which results in a stream of men asking me what my star sign is or whether I'm into surfing. But eventually it also turns up Beau, a photographer-creative, who is unbelievably beautiful. He's got blonde curls, blue eyes, a tan that cannot be from living in the UK full time and a dog called Ace who wears a bandana. After exchanging a handful of messages, he asks for my number and while I'm usually pretty fussy about making the transition from app to WhatsApp, I need to prove Lou wrong, so I say yes. He sends me a voice note while I'm washing Rose's bottles and I hit play without thinking, and then stop completely in my tracks. He's got the sexiest voice I've ever heard in my entire life. I literally freeze washing the bottles, and then replay the message.

'I don't know if you're a voice-note person,' he says. *If I wasn't before, I am now, Beau.* 'I feel like it's somehow more intimate? Also, you can't date someone if you don't like their voice. Anyway, I'm thinking we should go out. How's Wednesday?'

Obviously, Wednesday is shit; I can only do Thursdays. I replay the voicemail again, cursing Gavin and the entire universe for this arrangement. Then I do something that I never, ever do. I ring my mum.

She sounds alarmed to hear from me. 'Is everything all right?' she asks.

'Yes,' I say, steeling myself. 'I want to go on a date with a very attractive man I'm talking to on the internet, and he's suggested Wednesday, which isn't Gav's night, and I was thinking maybe you could babysit.'

'Fine,' she says, after a pause that sounds suspiciously like she's dragging on a cigarette. 'What time?'

I'm genuinely shocked that she said yes, but there's no point in lingering and I'll have second thoughts if I think about it too much. I press record on a voice note in response. 'I mean, I really hope you don't hate my voice,'

I say, trying to not sound like I'm trying. 'Because I'd love to hang out on Wednesday.'

In that moment I feel like the fifth character in *Sex and the City*. But when Wednesday arrives, everything about this experience feels painfully wrong. Beau messages me about a club in Brixton where his friend 'likes to play'. I don't ask what instrument, and I'd like to ask what the dress code is, but Beau is surprisingly hard to pin down on anything specific. When the date gets closer, I ask him for various details about the evening and he says he'll 'drop a pin' when he gets there. He says we can go for drinks 'before', but doesn't give me a time, and then redirects the conversation to a dream he had last night where he was a spinning arrow made of coral.

I sort of want to cancel. In fact, I really want to cancel, but then he sends me a voice note telling me that he can't wait to see me, and that he's hoping that he might be able to do more than see me, and, to my total shame, I melt. Look, isn't the idea of the mantourage to experience lots of different things? And if I'm totally honest, I've never had sex with someone really, deeply attractive. Hot guys were never my thing. I've been with Gavin since I was basically a child bride, but even before that I was always more interested in the funny, sarcastic sort of men who had childhood allergies and trauma from being in the bottom set for sports at school. I've literally never seen a body like Beau's (which I'm familiar with both from his profile and the series of semi-nude pictures he sent me this week) in live action. Is it really the worst thing in the world if I want to find out what abs feel like?

On the night of the date, my mum arrives on time, not smelling of cigarettes or overpowering French perfume, which will inevitably get all over Rose and make her smell like a mean Parisian lady. Mum tells me I look nice (which means I must look fantastic, or just slightly thinner than usual) and sends me on my way. Beau hasn't actually 'dropped the pin' yet, but for some reason I can't bring myself to admit this to Mum, so I walk out of the house, marvelling once again at the feeling of leaving with one tiny handbag and no nappies, and I go to the station, not totally sure what I'm doing. I'm going to head towards Brixton, because that's the only concrete location that Beau has mentioned, and happily I know exactly who can entertain me between home and Brixton.

Dom arrives at the pub, on the fancy side of Brixton, looking sleep-deprived. I've already got a bottle of wine and he gratefully pours himself a glass.

'You look terrible,' I say.

'Thanks.'

'Honestly, I have a baby and you look like you've slept less than I have. What's going on?'

'I went for a weekend away with Florrie and her friends and they didn't go to bed until 8 a.m. every night.'

'Jesus,' I say.

'Do you know about "afters"?' he asks.

'Christ, no, what's that?'

'So, you know how we had drinks before we went out, when we were younger? Well, now they do that, then they go out, then they come home and they do more drinking and more drugs, and they call it "afters".'

'You literally could not pay me to be twenty-six again,' I say. 'All the uncertainty and the insecurity—'

'Sorry, aren't we waiting in a pub so that some guy can send you the location for a date that was supposed to start an hour ago?'

'Fuck off,' I say cheerfully.

I'm starting to think that Beau is going to be the first man to ghost me, and while I obviously don't want to get ghosted, the idea of going home after a few drinks with Dom honestly feels like the exact way I'd like to spend tonight. But, lo and behold, a message. He sends me his location, I send him mine, and a quarter of an hour later he's standing outside the pub on a battered bike.

'Hey,' he says, even more beautiful in real life. 'Stella?'

I stand up, kiss him on either cheek, which makes me feel like a great aunt. 'So great to finally meet you,' I say. 'This is Dom, he's just leaving.'

'Nice to meet you,' he says, tipping his head at Dom. 'You can totally hang with us too if you like?'

'No, you're all right, mate,' Dom says, with a slight sneer. 'Where are you two heading off to?'

'I've got friends who are at the Astra, so we're going to join.'

Dom looks shocked, then deeply amused. 'Oh, right. I didn't realise that was Stella's kind of thing.'

'You're open-minded, right?' Beau says, looking me up and down.

Not really, no. I mean, I'm not closed-minded but open-minded would be like, point thirty plus on a list of things you'd say if you were trying to describe me. 'Yes,' I say, smiling up at him. 'I love an adventure.'

'Okay,' Dom says, with his eyebrows raised. 'You realise that you're going to a sex party, right?' he says into my ear as I hug him goodbye.

'Yes, obviously,' I lie. 'I'm not actually as boring as you think I am.'

We wave goodbye to Dom and walk along the street until we reach a run-down-looking pub, all the while I'm frantically trying to remember whether anything Beau said on his messages to me about this evening gave the impression that we'd be going to a sex party. I know I'm naïve about the dating scene but it feels like something you're probably supposed to sense check with your date?

Beau pushes through the door, gives our names to a woman wearing a latex dress.

'I'm sorry, doll, but you can't wear streetwear,' she tells me.

I look down at the dress I'm wearing – an Abercrombie sundress with cherries on it, and I can kind of see her point. 'Oh,' I say, looking at Beau. 'I guess I can't go in.'

Beau grins at me. 'You could just take it off.'

I want to say that I tell Beau to suck it. But he runs his hand down my arm and moves my hair away from my neck, and I want to fuck him so badly that this does seem like a good idea. I'm a grown-up. I'm not a prude. Before I had Rose, Louella made me go to a club in Berlin where everyone was naked and whipping each other. Gav and I didn't really do much by way of experimenting once we'd figured out what buttons worked consistently. Besides, the whole point of this dating thing is to have enough experiences that I don't need to keep having new experiences. If I chicken out now, I'll have to go home to my mother, she'll know that my date was a disaster and when I eventually confess what happens she'll inevitably tell me something horrifying about having been to 'lots of sex parties, darling.'

'There's also the market upstairs,' says the latex woman helpfully. 'You could get something there.'

When I was pregnant, I got something called diastasis recti, where the muscles in your upper torso just sort of banana-split themselves apart to make way for the bump. It's never quite gone back to normal, so my waist looks wider than it once did, and I'm pretty sure that my belly button is actually slightly off-centre from all the stretching it had to do, so this sounds like a better idea. Beau waits downstairs, chatting to the girl in the latex while I go to the upper floor. A man with a blue ponytail and a gold front tooth is selling things to hit people with. To the side of him there's a rack of lingerie and outfits. I tell myself again that I'm not a prude, and that I'm having an adventure. This is a good thing. I'm experiencing everything that I didn't experience in my twenties – these are the kinds of stories I'll be telling when I'm old. Then I pay an eye-watering £65 for a pink mesh 'dress' that doesn't cover my knickers and has a fluffy pink feather trim, which I'm unlikely to get much future wear out of.

As I pick my way down the stairs, I give myself a pep talk. Okay, this isn't ideal. In fact, it's embarrassing, and I sort of hate it, and this was really not the life I signed up for and I feel too old, too fat, too neurologically developed to have let any of this happen, but we are where we are and the purpose of this evening was to get laid so I'm going to wear this for an hour, then Beau and I are going to go back to his place, he's going to blow my mind with the best sex I've ever had, and then I'm going to go home and put all of this behind me. Unless the sex is so great that I want to do it again, in which case Beau (who is going to decide that I'm amazing) will be willing to provide.

In news that didn't surprise me at all at this point, downstairs is a dungeon. I look around and it's exactly like every scene I've ever seen on TV where they're trying to depict sexual degeneracy. There's a balding man wearing rubber pants standing on a cross thing, being whipped by a heavyset woman with a sort of whip. In the corner there's a cluster of more attractive, younger people, all watching everyone else watching them. It's got the vibe of a secondary-school cafeteria, only everyone's wearing fetish gear.

'Do you want to try something?' Beau asks me.

'Um,' I say, trying to sound keen. 'Maybe later? Is there like, another area? Somewhere we can maybe be a bit more… private?'

'Sure,' he says. He guides me into a lounge where there's music and proper lighting and, to my enormous relief, a bar. I pay for our drinks – and try not to mind that I pay for them – and then perch on the arm of a chair, my legs across Beau's lap.

'This is a pretty wild first date,' I say, smiling.

'Sure,' Beau agrees. 'But then it was all on my profile, so I guess you knew what I was planning, right?'

Beau's profile was basically unreadable. It said he was a queer pansexual kinkster looking for GGG and then mentioned a load of clubs he wanted to go to, which I assumed would be music venues and I now realise were fetish venues. So I suppose he has a point. This one's on me.

I pull my phone out to check whether I've got anything from Mum by way of an update on Rose. Nothing from Mum, but there's a message from Dom, which I only see half of. *If you've realised what that place is and you want me to fake an emergency to get you out…*

'Excuse me,' says a man wearing a black leather harness. 'No phones.'

'I'm just really quickly checking—'

'No phones,' he repeats.

'Sure, but my—'

'No phones.'

Beau puts his hand on my leg. 'The phone policy is for everyone's safety and privacy,' he says, like English is my second language. 'I'm a member here, so I have to vouch for your behaviour – please adhere to the rules.'

I consider throwing my phone at him, but I take a breath and try to be reasonable. Obviously, you can't have phones here.

'Come on,' says Beau. 'Let's go explore.'

He takes me upstairs to another room, opposite the one where I bought this hideous outfit. It's a sort of pub function room, only in every corner, people are shagging. Which shouldn't come as a surprise – we're at a sex party – but god, it's really quite arresting. I've never seen someone having sex outside of porn. There's a pretty blonde woman on her knees, going down on another woman. A couple going at it doggy style on the bed. Two men sharing one woman up against the blacked-out window. The music in here isn't loud enough so I can literally hear the noise of the man next to me who is stoically ploughing into his female companion. In theory I'd always thought that coming to something like this might be quite sexy. If Gavin had had any interest, I'd have been up for it. But maybe it's the fluorescent lighting, or the smell of latex, or maybe it's just that the reality of watching people have sex is quite weird? But for whatever reason, this is the least sexy room I have ever been in, in my life.

I think about Rose. I don't want to be thinking about Rose, I don't want Rose to be in any way connected to this half-farcical, half-seedy tableau, but I can't stop myself thinking about her eating tiny pasta shells earlier today and trying to say the word 'cat'.

Beau slides up behind me and wraps his arms around my waist. Then he trails his hand up my inner thigh, towards the gusset of my knickers. He hasn't even kissed me yet and he's trying to put his fingers inside me. 'Do I have your consent?' he asks.

I shake my head and he freezes. 'What?' he asks.

Stepping backwards, I find my way back to the hall. 'Give me a minute,' I say, stumbling away from him.

Beau follows me. 'What's the problem?' he asks.

'I'm sorry, this is just a lot— like, it's very fast, we literally just met—'

'We've been discussing our needs and desires all week?' he says, sounding weirdly annoyed. 'If you weren't into this then you shouldn't have said you wanted to come.'

'I didn't know we were going to a sex club,' I say, exasperated. 'At no point was that made clear to me.'

'You know there were a lot of girls I could have brought here tonight?' he says, increasingly red in the face. 'I picked you because I wanted to be open-minded, and I wanted to experiment with someone older—'

'Older? I'm six months younger than you are!'

He gives me a withering expression. 'It's different, though, isn't it?'

Is that because I'm a woman? I don't have the desire to find out. 'Fuck you,' I say instead, taking my phone out.

'You can't use your phone here!' he yells. I start down the stairs, pulling my dress from my bag, ready to yank the stupid pink thing over my head and change as I head for the door. Then I catch sight of my phone screen and my heart stops completely.

I have seven missed calls. Six from my mother. One from Lou. I've never had more than one missed call from my mother. My mother is the most laissez-faire person I've ever met in my entire life. She calls if she really needs something and if I don't answer...

I race up the stairs, out into the street and dial my mum. It rings and rings and doesn't go through. Then I call Lou. Again, it rings out. I'm calling Mum again when I get a call crossing with the one I'm making and, panicked, I stab my finger at the screen trying to get it to connect. It's Lou.

'What?' I half scream.

'We're at the hospital,' Lou says.

I gag. My hands are shaking so much I can barely keep the phone next to my sweaty cheek. 'Is she okay?'

'I think so,' Lou says. 'I'm dropping you a pin, get in a cab.'

The Uber is thankfully quick to arrive and the driver says nothing as I put my dress on over the stupid pink mesh thing. He drops me at the A&E entrance, briefly making eye contact in the wing mirror.

'I hope all is well,' he says quietly as I get out.

'Thank you,' I say, meaning it.

Then I leg it through the main A&E, to the children's department. In the waiting room, sitting on green plastic chairs, are Lou, Mum and, to my enormous relief, in Lou's arms is a grizzly Rose. I fall to my knees and gather her into my arms. She's sleepy and pink-cheeked in her little white pyjamas, but seems pleased to see me.

'What happened?' I ask breathily, clinging on to Rose.

'She's okay,' Mum says. 'They think she's fine.'

'We're just waiting to be discharged,' Lou adds.

'What happened?'

'Rose had a temperature and she was sick,' Lou says.

'Fuck,' I say. 'Okay, but that's pretty normal...'

'There's slightly more to it,' Lou says, sounding hesitant. Mum is looking across the room, through the double doors out to the rest of the hospital. 'Earlier tonight Mum gave her Calpol, but then she left the open bottle on the side by the cot, and then when she came back to check, Rose had the bottle in the cot and she thinks she might have drunk some of it.'

I feel like I'm going to scream and throw up. 'How much?' I say.

'She can't remember how much was left in the bottle, but she was sick again pretty much straight away anyway.'

Mum still isn't looking at me. 'Great,' I say, staring out of the window. What the fuck was I thinking? That woman doesn't give a shit about me, or Rose, or Lou, or anyone other than herself. Why would I leave her with my child? Only I know the answer to that, and it was to go and try get fingered by some beautiful blonde man with abs. What kind of a parent am I?

'Stella?' Lou prompts. 'I called the NHS 111 thing and they put me through to the poison hotline, and they said that if she was sick straight away and it wasn't more than twenty-four hours' worth of dosage then it's probably fine, but if I wasn't sure I should come to the hospital, so we thought, just to be on the safe side…'

'Yeah,' I say weakly. 'Best.'

A dark-haired nurse in navy scrubs comes into the waiting room. 'Are you Rose's mum?' she asks me.

'Stella,' I say. 'Yes.'

'Right, well, we've done all her obs and it looks like she's all right.'

I squeeze Rose. 'Thank god,' I say.

'You do need to be more careful though, Mum,' the nurse adds.

'My name is Stella. Not Mum,' I snap.

The nurse blinks, surprised at my reply. 'Right,' she says. 'Well, either way, you need to be more careful. It's really not ideal for a little one to get hold of medicine.'

Isn't it? I want to ask. Isn't it ideal? Thanks so much for telling me, I had no idea, I didn't think my child was going to die of progressive organ failure or anything, I haven't been clawing myself apart with guilt for the past hour. 'It wasn't me who was with her when it happened,' I hear myself say.

'Well, yes, but we need to be aware of who we leave the babies with,' the nurse ventures.

Louella gets up, putting herself between me and the nurse, like we're *Real Housewives* and I'm about to swing for her.

'Thanks so much for all your help,' Louella says, in a voice that makes customer service providers quake.

* * *

Mum has the good grace to look miserable in the taxi home.

'I'm so sorry, darling,' she says. There's baby sick on her Isabel Marant top. 'I had no idea she could reach out of the cot.'

'It's fine,' I say, without stopping in the hallway, going straight up the stairs. 'I should have known not to leave you in charge.'

She winces, because she knows that I'm telling her she's not a good grandmother, not a good mother, not a useful, helpful person to have around, that she's always been too selfish to be a real parent.

I carry Rose up to her bedroom. The floor is covered in towels and the air stinks of sick. I can imagine the chaos that must have unfolded when they realised what had happened, how frightened they must have been. I shouldn't have left them. I lay sleepy Rose down on the single bed across the room from the cot, then strip her sheets and swap them for clean ones. I place her gently into the cot and turn to go back to my room, then think better of it.

Downstairs, I hear the front door slam, meaning Louella and Mum have gone. I breathe a sigh of relief. Then I drag the covers and the pillows off the single bed and pile them next to Rose's cot. I lie on the floor with my hand through the bars of the cot, holding on to her, so that if anything changes I'll know. Sleep doesn't come and I don't really want it. I watch the light change. Listen to Rose breathe. Wonder how all of this happened, whether I could convince Gavin to move back here and be a co-parent with me, whether I could just live with him until Rose is old enough to leave home, because he might not love me but the presence of another adult would shore up the foundations and stop me from making stupid, selfish, reckless choices with stupid, selfish, reckless men.

I conclude that Gavin probably wouldn't come back, even if I begged him. He had the most fun, sexy, happy-go-lucky decade of my life and still ultimately decided I wasn't worth bothering with. So that part of the equation is out. But there is a part I can control, the part where I stop looking for fun and distraction and just think about Rose, stay home with Rose, make my life revolve around Rose. Other women seem to manage it, and if tonight has shown me anything, it's that I need to be more like those women.

Stella

Rose wakes around seven and kneels up in the cot, banging her fists. Her cheeks are flushed and her blonde hair is tufty where she's rubbed her head against her mattress.

'Good morning,' I say and smile. She smiles back and reaches her arms up, showing me the three teeth that cost us so many hours of sleep last month. 'I love you,' I whisper, smelling her head.

I have a message from Dom. *How was the sex party?* he writes.

I ignore it.

He follows up with a string of aubergine emojis.

I ignore that, too.

An hour later, while Rose is having her mashed banana and wholemeal toast, I call Gavin. He is very clearly asleep when the phone starts ringing and only half awake when he answers.

'Hi,' I say. 'Do you have a minute?'

'Sure,' he says. I can hear the bedsheets moving.

'Are you still in bed?' I ask.

'No,' he lies. 'I'm on a run.'

'Must be nice to be having a lie-in,' I snark, despite the fact that I should be keeping him on my good side.

'I worked until 3 a.m. in the morning last night, Stella, I needed to restore my reserves.'

'"a.m." means morning.'

'What?' I can hear him getting up, which means I can picture him in his pants, readjusting himself, getting ready to go inside for his mum to probably make him a full English. It's amazing how quickly you can go from loving someone so much that you don't even really mind if they sneeze on you to finding the concept of them repulsive.

'Look, I'm just ringing to say that I don't think you should take Rose this evening,' I say, ripping the plaster off.

'Why not?' He changes our call to a video call.

'She was really unwell last night. And my mum was watching her and it looked like she might have drunk some Calpol. They took her to hospital, to be cautious.'

He looks horrified. 'What the fuck?'

'I know,' I say. 'It was awful.'

'Why didn't you call me?'

I'm taken aback by the question. 'Why would I have called you?'

'Because I'm her fucking father, Stella.' I can count on one hand the number of times he's raised his voice at me, and most them were when I was about to hit something in the car. I'm genuinely aghast. And angry. Angry that he thinks he's got a leg to stand on here.

'Yeah, for eighteen hours, once a week, with your mum heavily supervising,' I snap. His face contorts with hurt. Real, proper hurt. In turn, I flood with guilt. 'Look, it just didn't occur to me to tell you. You don't message me all week, you don't ask about her—'

'If something happens to her, you need to tell me.'

Miserably, I concede that he is right. 'Okay,' I say.

'No, I mean legally. You have to tell me, legally.'

My mouth opens but I'm not sure what to say to that. We don't have a legal agreement. There's never been any suggestion of courts or custody, or any of that. Is he threatening me? The idea that he might suddenly decide that he wants fifty-fifty smacks me in the chest with horror.

'Okay.' Then I force out the words that are appropriate but almost choke me on their way out of my mouth. 'I'm sorry.'

We stand in complete silence for what feels like an age.

'She's eating her breakfast, happy as Larry,' I say, eventually.

'Right.'

There's another long pause. 'So, yeah, just do next week instead?' I ask.

'Uh. No, I think maybe that's not… look, I think we should stick to the plan.'

I press my nails into my fists. 'Gavin, come on.'

'Look, she'll be fine with me, and my mum's here. You just said she's fine.'

'She is fine,' I say, trying to sound bright and cheerful. 'But I don't know if she's going to get worse again and I'd really like to be with her, just in case.'

'That's not how it works,' Gavin says, in a surprisingly gentle voice. 'Stel, she's mine too.'

She's not his too, though. She's mine, almost entirely mine, with the tiniest side order of being his. She's my business and he invested a couple of grand to get it off the ground. He's a committed viewer, he's… I can't think of any more metaphors, but she is not, not, not his.

'Look, I don't want to be heavy about this,' he says. 'But maybe we need a… more, I don't know. Formal, legal arrangement.'

I feel like I might be sick now. 'No,' I say weakly. 'No, it's fine. Come over as planned. We'll stick to what we agreed.' We hang up.

My phone buzzes a minute later, while I'm wiping Rose up and putting her on the playmat. For a second I think Gavin might have had a change of heart and agreed to skip the visit. But it's not Gavin. It's Richard. *Much looking forward to dinner tonight – I've been remiss in asking whether you have any dietary requirements for dinner?*

Shit. Richard.

In the end I conclude that I have to have dinner with Richard. I mean I don't *have* to, I could cancel, but then I'd be sitting at home while Rose is with Gavin, totally alone, thinking about how he might leave a plastic bag in reach of her crib and she could suffocate. I don't want to go for dinner with Richard, but I also really don't want to be in the house alone.

I take a dim view of mushrooms, I reply. *And Marmite.*

No Marmite mushrooms, he replies. *Car for seven o'clock*?

I want to tell him that this car-sending is expensive and indulgent and bad for the environment, but the idea of having to get on the Tube is deeply unappealing. And besides, I'm going to need to take a load of stuff with me because, presumably, dinner means sex.

* * *

I put Rose down for her late-afternoon nap and then watch her sleep for a while before creeping out of her bedroom, yanking the volume up on the baby monitor, then turning on the shower. I strain to hear the faintest noise from her bedroom while I drag a razor over basically the entire surface of my body from below the eyelashes. I pause when I get to my pubes, foaming up a load of shower gel and then washing my vag multiple times.

Gavin appears, a mere ten minutes late. I hold Rose on my hip while I carry all her bags to the front door.

'I can help,' he offers, weakly.

'No, thanks,' I say. 'I'm used to doing things one-handed.'

There's a pause. 'You look nice,' he says eventually.

'Thanks.'

'Are you going out?'

'Yes,' I reply.

'Oh, nice. Great. Anywhere fun?'

'Dinner,' I force myself to respond.

'With the girls?' he asks, still standing on the doorstep and apparently not reading anything into the fact that I haven't invited him in.

'No,' I say. 'Not with the girls.'

He seems to be processing this. 'Right. Well. That's great. Good for you.'

I don't respond, so he picks up Rose's biggest bag. 'Thanks so much for getting everything ready,' he says, as if I don't pack up half her belongings for him every time she goes to stay.

'That's fine,' I say, through gritted teeth.

'I'm going to bring her back on the dot of seven-thirty tomorrow morning,' he says, as if he's being kind. 'I promise.'

I can't summon anything, so I kiss Rose and then watch them leave. Then I grab a bottle of £11.99 wine from the fridge, shove it into my overnight bag and get into the Addison Lee, which has been waiting outside for half an hour.

Richard's flat is exactly what I had expected because it's exactly the flat people get when they have lots of money and neither time nor interest in decorating. It's a penthouse overlooking the river, with vaulted ceilings and beams. The floor is polished concrete, everything is open-plan and the brushed-metal stove takes up half the kitchen. He has an island with stools instead of a kitchen table, and a huge wall-mounted TV. It's basically the least child-friendly space that I've ever entered, and it looks a bit like a set designer built a flat for a stereotypical bachelor.

'This is lovely,' I say, not totally truthfully, as he shows me around.

'Thanks,' he says. 'It's a bit neutral, but I don't have great taste in interiors so I thought better to err on the side of caution. Plus, I think the view does a lot of the work.'

He's not wrong there. The entire front of the flat is glass, and the river is like a moving painting. Boats, people, bridges, the sun slowly making its descent. It's beautiful. 'I could stand here for hours,' I say, as he pours a buttery Chardonnay into a huge, sparkling-clean wine glass.

My phone buzzes. It's Dom.

Is he finally going to put out??? he writes.

I pounce, turning the screen over before Richard can catch sight.

'I frequently do,' Richard agrees.

Richard produces two steaks from the fridge, which come wrapped in white paper so presumably came from some deeply expensive butcher rather than the supermarket.

'Who taught you to cook?' I ask.

He looks a little embarrassed. 'When I moved to New York, I took one of those cooking classes for total idiots because I honestly couldn't make so much as a sandwich.'

'I didn't know you'd lived in New York.'

'Five years,' he says, grinding pepper onto the steaks. 'I moved back last year.'

'How come?'

'I had a break-up, my lease was up, it just felt like time to leave.'

'I get that,' I say, pulling out a stool and sitting down at the island. 'Why'd you break up?'

He looks surprised at the question. 'I'd rather not discuss it.'

'Oh. Sure. No, that makes sense. Of course,' I stammer, embarrassed to have accidentally asked something that clearly pressed on some tricky territory for him. 'I guess I'm used to talking about my ex all the time because he's still in my life.'

Richard looks up at me, pausing his chopping. 'Because of your daughter?'

'God, yes. I'd prefer never to see him again, but he has Rose one night a week. Hence me being here.'

'I see. Well. That sounds like a good thing, I suppose? That she has time with him?'

I nod, privately thinking that it's not a good thing at all. 'Yeah.'

'And as she gets older, do you imagine she would see more of him?' Richard asks.

'I guess,' I say. 'I don't really know what we're doing to be honest. Just kind of finding our way as we go. We agreed some ground rules, like she doesn't meet anyone we're dating until it's long term, and we keep each other in the loop about any major life events.'

'That sounds sensible,' he says. He moves around the island and looks down at me, brushing my hair away from my face. 'I think you've done an amazing job in how you've navigated all of this with such grace.'

'Thank you,' I say, breaking his gaze and looking down, flushed. 'I'm not sure I am really, but I'm trying.'

We go back to small talk, about the process of buying the flat and the process of buying my house, and trying to sort my house out. He cooks the steaks and produces some matchstick fries he prepared earlier, then chops a green salad.

'I don't know how you managed this and did a whole day of work,' I say, as he plates it up. The cutlery is like new, in fact, everything looks new. I almost want to ask for the details of his cleaner and then beg them to come to Dulwich. 'When I was working, I just came home and made noodles most nights. God knows what I'll be like when I go back to work.'

'You're going back?' He looks surprised.

I nod. 'Yeah, they let me take an extra month of mat leave because of everything with Gavin; my old boss is terrifying but has been weirdly incredibly kind about all of this stuff. But once Rose is one she'll start nursery and then I'll be in the office a couple of days a week, and writing from home the rest.'

'Do you want to go back?'

This strikes me as a very weird question, so I stop eating. 'Yes,' I say. 'I can't wait.'

He nods. 'That's good, then.'

'You seem surprised,' I say.

'No, not at all,' he counters. 'I had just assumed you'd be at home with your daughter for longer.'

'I mean, I have to earn a living.'

'Of course. I misspoke.' He refills both of our wine glasses.

'Most women do go back to work, you know,' I add. I don't think he meant to say something hurtful but anyone who's ever had a baby and a job knows how dangerous this territory is, how there are landmines under every inch of this conversation.

'I know, I know,' he says. 'And if you love what you do then, of course, that's right. I think I had always had it in my head that I'd want to provide enough for any family I had that my partner could work or not work, but have it be a choice. If that makes sense.'

I nod. I'm being overreactive here. That's a nice thing to say. He is a nice man. 'That sounds like a great plan,' I say. 'Do you want children?'

'Yes,' he says. 'I feel it's a bit of a failure that I haven't managed it yet, but I very much would like a family. Ideally a large one.'

'Large?' I laugh. 'How large are we talking? Football team? Rugby team?'

He laughs too. 'No, I think three would be wonderful. Though I'm aware you can't really plan for these things entirely.'

'I always wanted three,' I agree. 'My sister and I were always desperate for a brother, but my mum had us within a year of each other and, understandably, she was very much done with the baby thing.'

'And you?'

'Me?'

'Are you done? With the baby thing?'

I look at him, and at his beautiful flat, and I think about creepy Beau trying to put his finger up my crack and my mum crying because of the Calpol, and shunting Rose between two houses. 'No,' I say. 'I'm not.' I take a breath. 'I think one day I'd like to do it again, and have it work the conventional way. Where you don't get divorced.'

Richard nods. 'I think that sounds lovely.' He takes a breath. 'To that end, I wondered if we might discuss something. This is rather American of me but I do prefer clarity. And I wanted to say that I very much enjoy your company and I'm not currently seeing anyone else. I'd like to focus my attentions on getting to know you better. To the exclusion of anyone else. And I wondered if you might be interested in doing the same.'

Gosh. My first reaction, which probably isn't the absolute ideal reaction to a nice, handsome man asking me to be exclusive, is to wonder why he sometimes talks like he's been written by AI. Oh god, what if he prepped for this conversation by asking ChatGPT what he should say? I try to smack the idea away. He is not using generative AI to ask me to be exclusive. He's a good person. A good man. A good prospect, if we're going to be a bit Jane Austen about it, and yes, okay, it's quicker than I'd planned and it's not the period of wild exploration I'd claimed to want, but am I really going to turn down something perfect because of the timing? When I left uni, before I moved to London and met Gavin, I got offered a job at a printmakers down the road from my parents' house, literally the ideal job. But I wanted to go to Ibiza with my mates for a month, so I turned it down, and then a year later I was still temping and applying for jobs even tentatively related to interior design, which taught me a pretty salutary lesson about assuming chances will come back around.

I've never had the exclusivity chat before. Gavin and I just spent all our time together so there wasn't anyone else to shag, and then by the time we lived together it sort of seemed implied. I've had friends agonise over how to raise it, when to raise it. I thought in the brave new world of app dating this was supposed to take months and months. And the whole idea was that I wasn't going to date anyone properly, that I was going to do the mantourage and fill my roster. Only I tried that and it wasn't exactly a raging success. So maybe...

'I'd like that,' I hear myself say. 'Very much.'

Richard smiles. He toasts me, then leans over and kisses me. I'm paranoid that I taste of steak, but I kiss him back, and feel warmth spreading through my body. I look up at him, through my eyelashes, the wine warm in my blood.

'Do you want to show me the bedroom?' I smile.

He kisses me again. 'Eventually,' he says. 'But I don't want to rush you. I know you're not like that.'

I kiss him back. Like what? I'm not like what?

Two hours later, after a lot of snogging but literally nothing more than snogging (and, eventually, a slice of Basque cheesecake that he'd bought from some very bougie bakery), I call Lou.

'You will literally never guess what just happened,' I say, as she picks up the phone.

'What?' she asks.

'I went to see Richard—'

'Which one's Richard? The rich one?'

'Yes. I went over for dinner and he lives in like, a penthouse, and he cooked me a steak and then asked me to be exclusive—'

Lou sighs. 'If you're going to ring me late at night to tell me things, they need to be gossip or drama, not things that are going to make me jealous of your life.'

'My life is still a disaster,' I counter. 'After he told me he wanted to be exclusive, he then refused to have sex with me because he didn't want to rush me.'

'Did you find this man from some kind of magical wishing tree?'

'Lou! No, look, I know this sounds insane and, when I say it out loud, I get how it sounds, but I actually… I feel a bit weird about it? Like why does he want to be exclusive? Why doesn't he want to shag me?'

'Because he likes you and he wants to snap you up.'

'But why?' I whine.

I can hear Lou rolling her eyes at me. 'Look, you're being insane – this is good news. Not all men are scabby losers like Gavin. And you can just take it slow and enjoy him.'

'He said he wouldn't want his wife to have to work after she had kids.'

'Oh my god, he's a monster, we should call some kind of hotline.'

I sense I'm losing my audience. 'I'm just saying, isn't that a red flag? It's old-fashioned?'

'You have a handsome, rich boyfriend who can cook and wants to provide for his future family. That is the dream. Stop being ungrateful. Goodnight.'

Lou hangs up. I stare at the phone for a while. Then I do something that feels surprisingly disloyal. I voice note Dom.

'Hey,' I say. 'I realise that you're not employed officially as my dating spirit guide but I need your wisdom. I had dinner with Richard, and it was great, but he asked me to be exclusive. And then he didn't want to shag me because he doesn't want to rush. What the fuck is going on?'

I send it.

He's not online. Probably out having a nice time with someone prettier and less needy than me. I hope so. He deserves that.

Dominic

Earlier this week, Florrie asked me to come to a poetry reading. We were lying in bed together and she looked up at me, the pillows stacked under her chest, her hair a curtain on either side of her face, and adopted an expression I hadn't seen before – something akin to being bashful. 'I'm doing this reading thing,' she said, not meeting my eye. 'It's in Peckham, and I was thinking you might come?'

I'd have gone however she asked me, but something about the way she asked – perhaps coupled with a recent conversation about her parents never turning up for anything her entire childhood – meant that I answered with an enthusiasm I couldn't usually muster for a poetry event.

She is, in fairness, actually really very good at writing poetry. And songs, and blog posts about things that are wrong with the world. Unfortunately, a lot of the people who are ahead of her in the queue to read at this thing are dramatically less talented. I arrived on the dot of 7.30 p.m. – before Florrie herself had even showed up – which meant sitting through an acknowledgement of privilege (we were all invited to close our eyes – or do whatever felt safe as an equivalent – and reflect on the factors that might have prevented someone from being able to attend the event). Around this point I started to wonder if that thing about getting more right-wing as you age was true.

Around 8.30 p.m., after I've checked four times that she told me this time and this date at this venue (as if there would be another poetry open-mic night going on), Florrie arrives. She's perfection, in a white sundress that she probably found in some French market or an estate sale at a dead Hollywood icon's house. Literally half the heads in the room turn to look when she pushes through the pub doors, which isn't ideal because the person on the stage is doing a rhyming thing (I want to say rap but he's so white it really doesn't feel accurate) about being bullied in primary school. Apparently unbothered by interrupting, Florrie stands and watches the poet finish, then claps with an enthusiasm I don't think anyone could fake. Then she makes her way to my table, where I'm relieved to finally no longer look like a weird freak who came to a poetry thing full of students on his own.

'You look beautiful,' I tell her. 'Can I get you a drink?'

'Just water,' she says. 'I want to be sharp.'

We sit through several more acts, Florrie's attention rapt on the tiny stage, mine wandering to whether I can walk home via the chip shop and trying to work out which neighbour's hand is in the picture that Amazon sent me of my delivery earlier. Eventually it's Florrie's turn.

She goes to the stage, her legs long and brown between her cowboy boots and her white skirt.

'This piece is called *Getting Fucked*,' she says, her voice husky and delicious.

She reads. And it's clearly about someone she's slept with, and the desire to be fucked in a way that made her feel like she didn't exist. And I listen, because she's brilliant and the only person here who should ever be trusted with a pen again. But also, I can't help wondering when she wrote it. Who's it about? I watch her eye line to see whether she's looking at anyone else in this room, whether she's reading it for the direct benefit of a man – or a woman – who's listening right now.

She finishes and everyone claps. I'm irritated that they only clap at the same level as they did for the previous guy, when she's dramatically more talented.

Eventually, just as I've fully lost feeling in my left arse cheek, the whole poetry thing is over. Despite my moderately well-disguised horror at some of what I've just seen (including a guy with a cut-glass Eton accent doing a spoken word performance about being misjudged and knowing what prejudice is) there were a couple of quite moving pieces. I'm sort of excited at the prospect of walking home with Florrie and quizzing her about her piece, and her thoughts on the rest of them. Hopefully we can have a laugh at the stupider ones and she can explain the ones that I'm too thick to have understood.

The applause dies down and everyone throngs to the bar to get drinks. I get up embarrassingly quickly so I'm at the front of the queue. I turn back and search the crowd for Florrie.

'What do you want?' I half yell at her.

'Tequila lime soda,' she says. 'And a Neck Oil for Bash.'

Bash is, I assume, the man standing next to her. He looks like a young Johnny Depp, sort of sallow but painfully attractive and standing really very close to Florrie, who is, as far as I understand it, my girlfriend. I get a round, navigate through the hapless poets trying to queue for a drink, and hand over two of the glasses.

'Thank you,' says Florrie.

'You're welcome.'

I look at Bash, sort of expecting he's going to say 'thank you' too. Not that it's a big deal, I've just bought him a drink that cost seven quid, not offered to be an organ donor.

'Hi,' I say, after an uncomfortable pause. 'I'm Dom.'

'Bash,' he says, establishing that I didn't mishear his name and he really is going about the world using a noise as a moniker.

'Unusual name,' I say. 'Is it short for something?'

'Sebastian,' Florrie says, putting her hand on his forearm. 'After Sebastian Flyte, from *Brideshead Revisited*.'

'Ah,' I say, taking a sip of Guinness. 'The gay alcoholic?'

No one laughs.

'So, I was thinking dinner?' I say eventually. 'There's a nice-looking Indian place round the corner with good vegan options.'

Florrie's eyebrows pinch together. 'Oh, that sounds so lovely, but Bash and I are going to some drinks thing with a friend of his.'

'Oh,' I say, high-pitched, trying to sound really absolutely fine and not at all surprised, also trying to shake off the searing embarrassment of getting turned down for a date by a woman I'm already romantically involved with, in front of Bash who I already hate. 'Okay, great. Cool.' I draw out the 'o' sound in cool which is, ironically, the least cool thing I could do.

Florrie catches up with me outside the pub as I'm leaving. I said polite goodbyes but obviously I didn't do a great job of acting like I was really fine with this.

'Hey,' she says, holding my forearms with her smooth, cool hands. 'Are we good?'

'Of course,' I say. 'I just misread the vibe for tonight.'

'Okay,' she says, seemingly relieved. 'I'm really glad that you came.'

'Me too,' I lie.

'And honestly, I would love to go to dinner with you, but Bash is feeling really raw about having me read that poem about him, and I owe him some aftercare.'

The poem was about Bash.

I nod. 'Absolutely,' I say. 'Aftercare. A warm down. A warranty, a purchase guarantee…' I'm just saying words now. I pull myself together and kiss her on the cheek. 'Let's do something later this week,' I say. Then I stride off, with no idea whether I'm getting any closer to the station or not, putting as many paces between me and them as possible.

I get to the Overground and my phone pings. It's a voice note, from Stella. *I don't have headphones*, I type my reply, *so I can't listen to this right now, but if there's any chance it's an invitation to come to your house and complain about my terrible night, then I'd bite your arm off.*

She's typing. I have – confusingly – got butterflies.

See you in twenty? she replies.

'You seem very sober for a woman who had a romantic dinner with her new boyfriend,' I say, as Stella pours me a glass of wine and fills me in on her evening, which I have to admit is flummoxing me. I'm starting to wonder if this bloke she's seeing is signed up to some kind of internet-bloke online dating scam where they teach you to not shag women because it's a power trip, or something like that.

'I know,' she says miserably. 'It's the wine he buys. It's all so expensive and delicious, and he decants it and puts it in lovely glasses, and then you have to sip it and enjoy it.'

'What a monster.'

'I know.' She laughs. 'Shall we get a bit pissed?'

I'm still smarting over Florrie, who hasn't messaged me since I've been here. 'Yes,' I say. 'Go on.'

We open a bottle of cava because it's all she's got in the fridge and then we knock it back while positing increasingly less likely reasons that Richard might not want to shag her.

'Maybe he's impotent?' I suggest.

She shakes her head. 'Nope. When we were kissing he was very not impotent. Against my leg.'

I screw my face up, involuntarily. 'Maybe he's religious? Like when the Jonas Brothers all wore those purity rings?'

'I mean surely he'd have mentioned that by now? Right?'

'You'd think,' I agree. 'Why don't you sack him off?'

For some reason, I'm very much hoping that she's going to say this is a great idea and ideally she'll message him right now to tell him to piss off.

'I can't.' She laughs. 'He's perfect.'

'How is he perfect?' I ask, resting my hand on my chin. The chin slips. Or maybe my hand slips. Something slips and she laughs at me.

'He's... I don't know. A grown-up. A good man. He wants a family.'

'Everyone wants a family!' I retort, picking up the bottle and refilling our glasses.

'You don't!'

'I don't know if I do.'

'Okay, but Richard does. He wants a house in Richmond and lots of kids and an SUV and all the stuff that you need to be a proper family.'

I scrunch my face up. 'You and Rose are a proper family.'

'We're two people. That's not a family.'

'Of course it is,' I say. 'That's ridiculous.'

She shifts in her seat and twists her hair away from her face. 'We always talk about me; let's talk about something else. Let's talk about you – how's your love life?'

I don't know why I don't tell her about Florrie. Actually, I do know why. Because I would have to tell her about the open relationship and because Stella is too grown-up and battle-worn to pretend that she thinks it's a good idea, and I don't want to do any of that.

'It's fine,' I say. 'Nothing major to report.'

Stella makes us crumpets, which are technically Rose's, and then lets me have two Babybels from the fridge.

'I love people who have kids,' I say, feeling really very pissed now, with crumpet in my mouth. 'No one else I've ever dated has ever had Babybels in their fridge.'

Eventually, we decide that it's time to go to bed otherwise we're in danger of a repeat performance of meeting the arsehole ex-husband.

'Time to go,' I say, heaving myself up.

'Thank you for cheering me up,' Stella says, as we stand by the front door. There's an orange street light coming in through the window, across her face. Her lips are so heart-shaped and full. She looks up at me. She parts her lips slightly and I'm pretty sure she's getting closer to me. Is she about to kiss me? Is that okay? Am I going to tempt her into a drunken mistake that ruins this thing she's got going with No Dick Rick?

'Do you feel better?' I ask, swaying slightly, trying to ascertain how much of a gentleman I need to be right now.

'No,' she says, smiling. 'I just don't get it. I thought he fancied me.'

I look down at her again. 'I fancy you,' I want to say, to cheer her up, because she should be cheered up. 'I think about you when I'm having a wank sometimes.'

'What?' She looks shocked.

Oh. I said that bit out loud. The wrong bit. Shit.

She laughs.

I laugh. 'I'm pissed,' I say. 'I'm going to go home. Sorry. Jesus.' Was that sexual harassment? 'Bye.'

I get into my Uber. The driver is on the phone to someone else, but tactfully rolls down the windows and I breathe the cool, sweet summer air in, focusing on a fixed point on the headrest in front of me so that I'm not sick in the back of this bloke's car. Then I get home, eventually get the key into the lock and collapse into bed.

Around 3 a.m. I get a message from Florrie.

Hey angel, she writes. *What are you up to?*

I want to tell her that it's 3 a.m. so obviously I'm asleep, only I'm not asleep so I can't. So instead, I do something that I haven't done since I was a teenager: I try to make her jealous. *Just got home*, I say.

Oh, fun, she replies. *Would you like to share more?*

How is she so sanguine? Are people born like that, or has she trained herself into it? It's driven me mad all night to think of Bash licking her neck and talking about his start-up or theatre troupe or whatever bullshit he does with his life, and she's apparently totally insouciant at the idea that I could have been anywhere with anyone.

Just back from Stella's place, I say. Which is completely true. Just not in the sense that she thinks it is.

The phone rings – she's calling me now. 'Oh, cute,' says Florrie, in a voice that suggests she doesn't find it cute.

'Did you have fun with Bash?' I ask, trying to sound sober.

'It was nice.' She sighs. 'Though he couldn't come because he feels guilty about how he's treated me in the past, which is always sad, but otherwise nice. How was Stella?'

'Good,' I say, trying to process the fact that the girl I'm seeing is casually telling me about having sex with another man. Worryingly, I'm not sure I'm very upset about it. I can hear Florrie breathing and I realise that she wants more information from me, but that she doesn't feel she can ask what Stella and I have been doing. And I figure that it's probably easier for everyone if I don't say anything. I don't want to lie – that would violate the strange sort of moral code that I've invented for myself where I let her think that I'm seeing Stella, and then keep seeing Stella but don't start shagging Stella, even though obviously I'd really like to be shagging Stella, because if I do that I'll fuck it up with her like I have with everyone else I've ever tried to make it work with.

'I'm really tired,' I say in earnest. 'Is it okay if I call you tomorrow?'

'Sure,' she says. 'Goodnight.'

Stella

I've never been a cheat. Literally never. I'd slept with two people before I met Gav and I was painfully aware when we moved in together, and again when we got engaged, that if I stuck with him then I'd never see that number increase, and I thought it was a perfectly sensible compromise to make. And yeah, occasionally I thought about what it would be like to get railed on a one-night stand, or snog the yoga instructor on a hen weekend away with my mates, but for the most part, monogamy always made sense to me. There was no one I'd ever met who was appealing enough that they'd be worth swapping my home, my future and the fact that I shared my bed with the guy who'd seen me in every season of my life, met all my grandparents before they died, spent the night in my childhood bedroom before my mum sold the house, all the stupid, banal, essential stuff that ties you together into one unit instead of two people. So monogamy it was. And it wasn't even especially difficult, honestly.

Probably stupidly, I'd always assumed Gavin was the same. It had never occurred to me to track his phone or wait until he was asleep to go through his messages. I reasoned that if I woke up and found him reading my messages to my university friends, where they detailed their break-ups and work dramas and fertility woes, I'd have considered him an absolute psycho. So why would I have done it to him? It wasn't like I thought he was hiding anything and I was too scared to know, I just blithely assumed that he probably felt the same as I did. That screwing someone else was an intermittently appealing idea but ultimately not worth it, in case it ended our marriage. And I suppose I was half right. It wasn't another woman, it was the prospect that he was secretly brilliant at something that he'd never had a chance to pursue. Or maybe it was the idea of a totally different life that didn't have me in it, that barely had Rose in it. Or maybe he had a sort of anaphylaxis at the way that having a child changed our life. I don't know. I guess all of those are a kind of cheating, a choice of something else over me. Over us.

I take a left turn to do another circuit of the park, pushing the pram slowly to keep Rose asleep.

There probably will be another woman, I realise. I'm already seeing someone else. So he will be too. Probably someone younger than him, possibly someone younger than me. And maybe I'll feel differently when it happens, but right now I just feel sad for the fictional other woman, that she's going to have to follow him around telling him how brilliant he is, like I once did.

I've tried to put the almost kiss with Dom out of mind. It's been almost two weeks and I've kept communication with him as light and non-committal as I can. When the washing machine broke, I paid a man £350 to come and fix it for me, rather than summoning Dom. When I see an amusing meme or read an interesting article, I send it to

Richard, not Dom. Because for all the guilt I feel about the nearly cheating on Richard a mere four hours after we'd become exclusive, there's nothing I can do to change any of it, and realistically the only sensible thing that I can do is focus my efforts on Richard. Richard sends flowers every Friday, following our Thursday nights together. He still insists on a car to pick me up, though these days we sometimes also have dinner at the French place down the road from my house while I get a babysitter for Rose. It's nice. Sufficiently nice that I try not to let myself acknowledge that we're approaching our tenth date and we still haven't done much more than snog.

Dom noticed my coolness and, characteristically blunt, called me out on it, over a WhatsApp. I fobbed him off with some excuse about Rose going through a tricky stage and needing some time to focus on her. I felt bad for lying. But he's got Florrie, the new girlfriend, so we're both doing what we should be doing.

Whether he believed it or not, he left me to my own devices until a couple of days ago, when the sun was out and the local park was heaving with pale, semi-naked people.

'I miss you,' he said. 'Come on, let's bunk off and go to the pub. Bring Rose, we can give her a vape and a pint of Guinness.' And my god, was I tempted. Not the vape, but the idea of having a friend to sit with and yap at, outside a pub on a warm early evening, the thought of finding somewhere with a grassy bit at the back so Rose could crawl and maybe toddle about and pull daisies out of the ground while we talked about the mindless murder show we've been watching or my impending return to work, it all just seemed so normal and lovely and right.

But I promised myself and everyone else that I was going to give Richard a proper chance and sneaking off to the pub with someone who I nearly snogged while white-girl wasted a few weeks ago is not that. So I said no. And then I walked Rose home past a pub and, to my shock, felt tears pricking behind my eyes when I looked at groups of people having fun together. Stupid. Completely stupid, to be having FOMO at my age is genuinely tragic. But there you have it.

Tonight, I've caved to Louella's pressure and agreed that she can meet Richard. We're having dinner – at my house. He's barely ever been there, just to pick me up if we're doing something in this direction. I don't – if I'm totally honest – relish the idea of him being here. But that's stupid, and probably just because the time I had Dom over for a date was such a complete and utter disaster. This evening is going to be different.

I decide against another loop of the park. If I have to see the same ducks again, I think I might scream. Instead I take the risk and push the pram into the supermarket, wandering the aisles and trying to decide what to cook while I watch Richard be dissected by my sister. Roast chicken?

Stella

'What are you making?' Louella asks, sitting on my kitchen sofa, cross-legged. She sniffs the air appreciatively.

'Roast chicken,' I say.

'Oh my god, divine,' she says, lying back. 'That is my favourite news. Remember before you had a baby and your life blew up, and you used to make us amazing food all the time?'

'Yes,' I say, hunting through drawers for a potato peeler. 'That must have been really hard for you.'

'Thank you!' she says with enthusiasm. 'People were really focused on you and the baby, and there was very little support for me.'

I laugh. 'Okay, so some things you should know about Richard,' I start. 'He's—'

'Really rich,' Luella interjects.

'Yes,' I agree. 'He's really rich, but also he's quite a gentle soul. Like, slow burn, more of a listener than a talker—'

'Rich man who doesn't talk much? Absolutely ideal,' says my mother, coming in from the garden where she's been smoking and sulking because I won't let her smoke in the house. She hadn't initially been invited to dinner, but she's staying with Louella this week while she has some repair work done on her own flat (because Louella has time to procure fresh flowers for the spare room and no screaming 6:30 a.m. wake-up call) and she got wind of it. So now, rather than a casual evening where Richard meets Louella over a glass of wine, he's meeting my mother and my sister.

'Mum,' I say. 'Please, please don't say things like that in front of him.'

She rolls her eyes. 'I won't, obviously. Is your father not joining?'

I shake my head, wanting to point out that I didn't invite him this evening in much the same way that I didn't actually invite her. 'He's got a parish council meeting.'

'They have those every fifteen minutes,' my mother says, shaking her head. 'Surely he could have missed it. He should want to meet your partner.'

'He's not my partner,' I almost whimper, the word landing horribly hard. 'He's someone I'm dating. We haven't even—' I stop myself before I tell my mum that Richard and I haven't had sex yet, because that's the kind of thing she's liable to bring up over dinner. 'He's someone I'm dating, and that's it. Okay?'

'Well, he should want to meet someone you're dating,' Mum insists, refilling her wine glass.

'He's driving Lisa from down the road,' Louella says archly. We both know that Dad is shagging Lisa (or whatever slightly religious people in their sixties do when they're dating). Mum is in denial about this.

'He's such a pillar of the community,' she says grandly. 'She's very lucky to have him. Honestly, living in that village in the middle of nowhere and not being able to drive, it's utter madness, I'd go mad. But then I need more social and cultural stimulation than someone like Lisa.' She says the name like it's a skin disease and the doorbell goes before Louella can fire any more shots, much to my relief.

'Hello,' I say, looking up at Richard. He's tanned and handsome in a white T-shirt and chinos, and he's carrying four bunches of flowers.

'That's a lot of flowers,' I say. 'Did you take them off a lamp post?'

He looks confused. 'They're for your mother and your sister,' he explains.

We reach the kitchen and Lou and my mother are obviously in raptures over this. 'These are for you,' he says, handing Louella a bunch of peonies. 'Your sister mentioned that you like them.'

Louella is literally blushing, which I've never seen her do before.

'And these are for you,' he says, handing Mum a bunch of white roses. 'I thought you might like a classic.'

'I always like a classic,' says Mum in an insanely saucy voice that I never want to hear again. 'These are yours.' He smiles, passing me a bunch of tulips, which admittedly I do love.

'Who are those for?' Louella asks, pointing at a bunch of tiny tea roses.

'Ah.' Richard looks bashful. 'Probably silly, but they're for Rose. I didn't want to leave her out.'

'That's incredibly sweet of you,' I say, feeling a smile spread across my face. 'Thank you.'

'You should give them to her,' Louella says. 'We can get her up? Right?'

'No,' I say, flatly. 'She's only just gone down.'

'She probably isn't asleep yet,' Mum ventures.

'It's not that,' I say, trying to make this conversation go away as quickly as possible. 'Richard hasn't met Rose yet. But she'll love these – thank you. I can't wait to show her in the morning.'

'Why haven't you met?' Mum asks, looking confused.

'Can I get anyone a drink?' I ask. Richard indicates that he'd like me to open the bottle of red he brought and I look for a corkscrew, grateful for something to do.

He asks Louella about work, my mother about living in Chelsea (her favourite topic), and they chatter away. At one point I think my mother might actually be fluttering her eyelashes at him. Eventually, he goes to the bathroom and they both round on me.

'I love him,' Louella says.

'He seems like a very good sort,' Mum agrees. 'Lovely manners. Very clean fingernails.'

She is absolutely right about that, I have never seen Richard with anything less than pristine nails. He comes back from the bathroom and picks up the wine. 'Can I top anyone up?' he asks.

'They were talking about you while you were in the bathroom,' I say, putting potatoes into a pot of boiling water and salting the water liberally.

'Oh!' Richard says. I think he might be blushing. 'Right. Well, I guess that's to be expected.'

'She's so indiscreet.' Mum tuts. 'We were just saying how lovely you are. And I was about to say that I think it's very modern that you don't mind about Rose, or about Stella having been married before. I think a lot of men would be—'

'Thanks, Mum,' I interject.

Richard studies the tiles on the kitchen floor. 'I think Stella seems wonderful,' he says, clearly absolutely and completely out of his depth in this conversation. 'And we've all got our pasts, right? Everyone's got their baggage.'

I bristle at the word 'baggage', a word that I've consciously avoided when describing myself and especially when describing Rose. It's such a hideous expression, and I know it's fair. It's actually very accurate. A lot of the time having a baby does feel like I'm dragging a suitcase around behind me and I'm not allowed to put it down or leave it at left luggage. But still.

'Sure,' Louella adds. 'Exactly. And Rose isn't baggage, anyway. She's a bonus.'

'Quite.' Richard nods.

'Dom always calls her my tiny housemate,' I say, 'which I quite like.'

'Dom?' asks Mum.

'A friend of mine,' I reply, blushing in what I hope isn't enough of a deep red that anyone notices.

'Which one is Dom?' Mum asks. 'The one who doesn't shave her armpits?'

'No, Mum.' Louella sighs. 'That was Lola, and she went through a very brief phase of not shaving in 2015.'

'Did Rose take to you?' Louella asks Richard, shifting in her chair. 'No judgement if not, she cried every time I came into the room for the first three months.'

'They haven't met,' I say again. Louella knows that they haven't met because she'd have grilled me for details about their first meeting, which means she's deliberately testing the water with him. Annoying, but equally exactly what I would do.

'Stella has been very cautious about introducing anyone into her life in a more meaningful capacity,' Richard says. 'Which I think is admirable and deeply pragmatic.'

'Hear, hear,' Mum says, raising her glass.

I mash the potatoes, take the tenderstem broccoli out of the oven when it's sizzling and charred in the skillet but not cremated, and everyone sits down at the table. The evening is still so warm that we have the doors open and even though the garden is a ramshackle mess, the air smells so sweet and the weeds I keep promising to tackle are in flower so it manages to look quite pretty.

'Has Gavin said how long he's willing for you to keep living at the house?' Mum asks, after we've sat down and everyone has made noises about how delicious the chicken is. Louella rolls her eyes at the question.

'Mum.' She sighs. 'That's not a question for now.'

'It's fine,' I say. 'I'm perfectly happy for Richard to hear about it, it's not a secret.'

Richard looks interested; he refills my water glass, studying me. 'Your ex still owns part of the house?'

'We agreed that because he left, he'd keep paying into the mortgage, I'll keep living here, instead of him paying child maintenance. And then once I finish fixing it up I'll sell it, and we'll both take back what we put in.'

'Wow,' says Richard. 'That's rough. Still having to have so much connection to someone who's hurt you so much.'

Mum and Louella nod in agreement. 'Sure,' I say. 'But then, we share a kid so I guess we'll always be connected.'

Richard nods but doesn't reply. There's an embarrassing lull in conversation.

'What about Rose's birthday party?' Louella says, throwing the perfect, easy distraction into the conversation. 'Excited?'

* * *

Mum gets a cab back to her hotel; Louella is delighted to see that the Lime bike she arrived on is still outside on the street (as if anyone living in the suburbs of Dulwich is biking anywhere at ten-thirty on a Tuesday night).

Richard waits until they've gone and then wraps his arms around my waist. 'I think that went well,' he says.

'It literally couldn't have gone better,' I agree. 'If we break up my mum will never forgive me. Even if it's you who does the dumping.'

'Why would we break up?' Richard looks stricken.

'I'm joking!' I say. Which is mostly true, I am joking. But also, the sense of relief from my mother was genuinely palpable. I think she might have looked at me with Richard and seen an immediate fix to all the damage from Gav and the break-up, a cure to Rose growing up in a broken home, a sort of emotional Gorilla Glue to provide a life that looks like the one she wants for me. And I get that. I feel it myself, sometimes. 'I just mean, they really liked you. They'd be sad not to see you again – I was just being silly. Do you have to head home or do you want to stay for a while?'

'I'd like to stay,' he says, running his hands along my back, underneath my top. He kisses me and I try to work out whether my mouth will still taste like chicken or if the wine will have taken the edge off. I tighten my muscles, trying to pull in my stomach.

'I'd like that too,' I say.

We kiss on the sofa for ages, like a pair of teenagers. He seems sanguine about my refusal to let him go upstairs, a strange sort of rule I've created which makes me feel safer about Rose, or like I'm doing something less badly behaved. I figure I'd have men down here for dinner if they came over as friends, or as boyfriends of friends, so having a man down here and making out with him has to be fine. Right?

He runs his hand up my inner thigh and it sends shivers down my whole body. He – to my absolute shock – presses his leg between mine, making me whimper. 'I like that noise,' he says breathily into my ear.

'I like that feeling,' I say, trying to make words into sentences. It has been so fucking long since I had sex. So fucking long since I had the weight of another person on top of me and that blissful, glorious sensation of another body pushing into mine.

'Should I get a condom?' I whisper.

He pulls back. 'I should probably head off,' he says.

I honestly think I could cry. I know I shouldn't mind, I know he's entirely within his rights not to want to sleep with me, and I know that there's nothing less acceptable than expecting sex from someone else. But fuck me (or, in Richard's case, don't), I'm so frustrated right now that I could genuinely scream. Did I do something wrong?

I inhale, trying to work out whether there's any chance that despite a shower, perfume and deodorant, I might actually smell.

'Okay,' I say weakly. 'Cool.'

He gets his jacket and finds his keys, all the while I'm thinking that the second he's gone I'm going upstairs, finding a vibrator and praying that it's got enough battery power left to get me off.

'There's just one thing that I wanted to mention.' He drops his gaze. 'I feel a little concerned about your ex-partner having so much control, in terms of the house.'

'I know,' I say. 'It's not my favourite, but we are where we are. And he has actually been pretty reasonable, giving me the year to get myself straight, and when we do sell it then at least I'll have a small deposit so I can get a little place with Rose, still in the area. It could be worse.'

'I just wondered whether it might be easier if I were to pay into the mortgage, rather than him.'

I look aghast. My brain was mostly focused on how badly I wanted to get myself off, so I was only sort of half concentrating, and now I'm worried that I've misheard. 'Sorry?' I say. 'You want to pay Gavin's half of the mortgage?'

He nods. 'I looked at what you paid for the house, and based on what I assume you'd have put down for a deposit, it's not a prohibitive sum.'

I feel myself bristle. He looked up how much my house was worth? He did a financial assessment about how much my mortgage must be, based on profiling me? But then, how often do I look up someone's house after I visit them? And that's not because I want to help them. It's because I'm being nosy. At least he's trying to do something nice here.

'You could return it when the capital is released at the point of sale, or we could just regard it as a gift,' he goes on.

'A gift?' I say weakly. 'A gift is like, a necklace. Not a mortgage.'

'It's only a suggestion,' he says. 'But we could have paperwork drawn up so that it's all watertight and you weren't at risk. And it would mean that you didn't have so much tie to him. I will entirely understand if it doesn't appeal, but it seemed a more elegant solution than your being obliged to him.'

'Wow,' I say, trying not to think about the fact that he talks like a badly-written romantic hero in the kind of book my mum reads in the bath. I shouldn't be a bitch. He's being incredibly nice. And obviously, I'm going to say no. I have to say no. I can't just let this man that I've known for less than three months start paying to keep a roof over my child's head. 'Richard, that's insanely generous. Emphasis on the insane. And I love that you offered. I think you know that I can't accept, but really, thank you. It means a lot.'

He kisses me again and the raging arousal is back, instantly. Then he's gone, and I can't face the hunt for a vibrator; I'm face down on the sofa with my hand between my legs within seconds of him leaving. I've almost certainly come before he's got his seatbelt on. Afterwards, I lock eyes with a Peppa Pig stuffed toy, lying on the floor, looking mournfully at me. 'Sorry you had to see that,' I say. Time for bed.

Dominic

Have you ever watched one of those films, intended to be amusing, where the main character makes a series of agonising blunders while you're shouting, 'No one would ever do that, you fucking idiot,' and it makes the whole thing borderline unwatchable? That's exactly what's happened in my real life this week. On Tuesday I realised that it was Stella's kid's first birthday party on Saturday afternoon. And while I don't have any huge yen to hang out with a baby, I haven't seen Stella much since our night at hers and I miss her. She's been half-hearted over messages and I want to catch up. Plus she's about to go back to work so who knows when she'll be around to hang out again, and I want to see if her sister is as great as she sounds because maybe that'll be the one woman who can convert me to commitment. (Joking, mostly.) So, I write *STELLA BIRTHDAY PARTY* on a Post-it and put it on my fridge, which functions as my diary.

On Wednesday, Florrie came over. You can see where this is going, I'm sure. She arrived on my doorstep carrying a bunch of tiny white flowers, wearing denim shorts so short that they were basically pants, and I almost melted. We went inside and shagged for two hours, at which point she was understandably parched and went to the fridge to get a bottle of water, while I was half asleep and gloriously post-coital.

She came back to bed and slid herself under my arm, breathing gently, smelling like maple syrup and vanilla. 'When's Stella's party?' she asks.

If she had asked literally any other question, I could have got out of it. What kind of party? Where's Stella's party? Is it Stella's birthday party? Any of those, easy. But when is a complete nightmare. I rack my brains trying to work out whether there's a day she's mentioned some unmissable plan so that I can pretend I think it's then, and then backtrack later. But with Florrie, nothing's ever concrete – she's a human manifestation of a summer breeze.

'It's on Saturday,' I say, my chest contracting.

Florrie says nothing. She's not stupid. I mean she's literally not stupid, she's got a degree in French and Spanish from UCL, but she also takes courses in psychology from the Yale distance learning program and reads lots of books about how people's brains work so I assume she knows that silence is a powerful tool. I also know that silence is a powerful tool and yet it works on me, completely.

'It's on Saturday,' I say, the words spilling out. 'It's not her party, it's actually for her daughter.'

'She has a daughter?'

'Yes,' I say, realising that I've been really very parsimonious with the data. 'She's called Rose and she's going to be one on Saturday.'

Florrie wrinkles her nose. 'And you're going to the party?'

'She's having a load of friends along; first birthday parties are usually more about the parents than the kids, honestly.'

'Oh,' she says. And then she asks the question that I knew she was going to ask, that I was completely and utterly dreading. 'Can I come?'

I try to say no. In fact, I do say no. The first thing I say is, 'No! Florrie, you'll hate it. You're far too...' And then I trail off, trying to find a better word than 'cool', and totally fail. 'It's not your scene,' I venture. 'You don't seriously want to go to a kids' party?'

I realise that asking the question is my major mistake, because now I've basically given her the option.

'I want to go where you go.' She smiles, running her hands over my chest. This obviously isn't really true because she wanted to go to a squat rave last week where I very much wasn't. But there's clearly no way through this. I'm going to have to say yes, then just cancel at the last minute.

'Sure,' I say, my voice several pitches higher than usual. 'That would be great.'

To make things worse, my cancelling-last-minute plan is scuppered when she stays over the night before and wakes up next to me. I consider suggesting that we sack the party off, but that would let Stella down. And I consider faking an illness, but that's getting into a new frontier of deceit that I just can't bring myself to broach. So that's how I found myself in the back of an Uber, Florrie wearing a sheer, pink cotton dress, which entirely shows both of her nipples, me holding a huge, pink unicorn toy with a bow on it.

'Hey,' I say, as we turn onto Stella's street and I've left it until the absolute last possible moment. 'Just to say, I don't think her friends and family know that we're occasionally...' I search for the word. 'I think her friends and her family think she's not…' I'm really hoping Florrie is going to jump in at some point. 'No one knows that she's been seeing me, so can we just keep things really light and not mention it?'

Florrie looks worried. 'That's so sad. Why don't her family know?'

'Because she's just had a baby and she doesn't want them judging her for getting laid, I'd imagine.'

She looks even more worried. 'I really don't like bringing deception into my dynamics.'

'I know that,' I say, as we pull up outside the house. There are balloons on the door and the front lawn has been mown. She must have hired a gardener. I'd have done that for her, if she'd asked. ''I know that,' I say, feeling like I'm negotiating with a terrorist. 'But we have to do no harm, right? Our dynamic has to stay transparent, but she hasn't consented to being outed as open, so we should respect that, right?'

Using ethical non-monogamy babble seems to work so those TikToks I watched have clearly paid off.

'You're right,' she says. 'We should uphold her right to disclose as she feels ready.'

I breathe a sigh of relief and tap my phone to give the driver a massive tip as we approach the door.

'Dom!' Stella says, opening the door, obviously shocked to see us. She's wearing a blue dress and she's got Rose on her hip. Rose looks bigger. How can she be that much bigger in six weeks? 'Hello!' she adds, obviously trying to pretend that she knew I was coming. 'And this must be Florrie?'

Her recall is impressive. She goes to give Florrie a hug, and Florrie half flinches as Rose reaches out one, probably sticky, hand to touch her hair.

'Baby!' Rose says.

'Sorry.' Stella laughs. 'She can only say "baby" and "dog", so that's actually a compliment.'

I look at Florrie, waiting for her to respond. She doesn't. She looks at me, then at Rose, then at Stella, then at me again.

'How was the journey?' Stella asks.

'Fine,' says Florrie.

'Good,' I say. 'I mean we should really have walked, it's like twenty minutes, but, you know.'

'Sure,' she says. 'I'm going to get some ice for the Pimms, everyone's in the garden, you know where things are – Florrie, the loo is that way – and help yourself to anything. There's a beige buffet but there's other bits in the fridge if you're hungry, plenty of vegetarian and vegan stuff.'

'I'm not a vegetarian. Or a vegan,' Florrie says sharply.

'Sorry!' Stella says, flushing. 'I must have confused you with someone else.'

We go out into the garden and I take a beer, grateful that Stella's the kind of person who serves alcohol at a children's party. Florrie pours herself a very large glass of rosé and puts her hand into mine, for the first time ever. Is she nervous? She's never struck me as socially inept before.

'Are you okay?' I ask.

'Yes,' she says. She takes out a pouch of tobacco and starts to roll a cigarette. A group of other parents standing at the far side of the garden look at me. 'I don't know if this is a smoking— I mean, I'm not sure you can…'

'We're outside?' she says, with ice in her voice.

'I know but there are kids everywhere,' I say, once again feeling like she's about to blow up a building if I don't say the right thing. She puts the rollie back into her bag.

'I don't like kids,' she says.

Right. I'm not really sure what to do with that statement because we're at a child's birthday party, which she specifically asked to attend. 'I get that,' I say. 'I'm not, like, a huge devotee of them myself.'

She looks up at me, the freckles on her nose starker because she looks paler than usual. 'Can we go?'

I look around. 'I don't think we can leave right now. Why don't we do an hour and then we can go? There's a really nice pub up the road; I'll buy you an ice cream on the way.'

She half smiles. 'Okay.'

A woman who looks a lot like Stella, and weirdly also nothing like Stella, approaches us with a plate of snacks. 'Do you guys want one?' she asks, holding them out with a flourish. 'They're all organic and kid-friendly with no salt so they're obviously horrible.'

I laugh. Florrie does not.

'I'm Dom,' I say. 'Are you the sister?'

'I am,' Louella says. 'Nice to meet you. You must be the handyman! We love you – you've saved Stel a fortune. I don't suppose you make house visits a bit further afield? I've got a picture that needs hanging…'

'Sorry,' I say. 'Needy single mums are the only clients I take on.'

'Classic,' Louella replies. 'That bitch gets all the luck.'

I laugh again. Florrie doesn't, again, which seems to alert Louella to her being there.

'Sorry, I'm so rude. I'm Louella, most people call me Lou. Are you Dom's girlfriend?'

'Yes,' Florrie says.

'Dom's been such an angel to Stella,' Louella says. 'You've got a good one.'

Florrie says nothing.

'I love your dress – it's dreamy.' Louella soldiers on, unbothered by carrying the conversation apparently. 'Where's it from?'

'It's vintage,' Florrie replies.

'Love that – where did you find it? I feel like all my go-to places are so barren for good stuff at the moment, just like wall-to-wall old Zara.'

'I don't really like to share where I source my pieces,' Florrie says, smiling. 'Otherwise they get too popular.'

I might not have two X chromosomes but even I can tell that this is a bad thing for one woman to say to another woman.

'Right,' Louella says with a smile. 'Well, I should try to force these horrible snacks on some other victims. Have fun.'

I watch Louella go and wish I'd made a better impression, or at least any impression.

'Who is that?' Florrie asks.

'Stella's sister. Rose's aunt.'

'Oh.'

Florrie surveys the party with a look of distaste. 'How long do we have to stay?'

I try to look like I don't think this is a staggeringly rude question. 'Uh, another half hour or so.' I want to add that I'd imagine everyone is probably going to be keen for us to leave because we're standing in the corner talking to each other and being rude to anyone who does attempt to make conversation with us. But I don't. I increasingly think this might be my final date with Florrie so it's probably incumbent upon me to see it out with good grace, so she doesn't pay an internet witch to put a curse on me, or start an Instagram account about what a bad man I am.

At the other side of the garden, Stella is sitting on a striped rug, eating a cupcake messily. She laughs and wipes her hand on the rug, then feeds Rose a tiny bit of icing. They're in their own little world, those two. I'm not sure it would much matter if any of the rest of us weren't here and yet, somehow, I'd really like to be sitting on that rug with them.

Stella says something that I don't hear and everyone laughs, and I wish I knew what she'd said.

Twenty minutes later, we've had a stilted conversation with another couple who've brought a baby. They met Stella and Gavin through something called Bump and Baby, which seems to be a sort of training programme for new parents. They talk about Gavin as if he died in a terrible accident instead of bailing because he's a twat. Florrie answers questions about what she does for a living (student), all of which make her sound like she's about twenty-one and make me sound like a complete pervert.

'Shall we go?' I ask Florrie.

'Sure,' she says.

I hug Stella tightly as I say goodbye. 'You've done an amazing job.'

'Turns out kids' parties are a doddle, just balloons and unlimited carbs.'

'I meant more generally,' I say quietly. Florrie is waiting by the front door and it's unreasonable to keep her waiting. 'This whole thing, your mum-ing. You're a rockstar.' I kiss her on the forehead and then follow Florrie out into the street. She starts striding in the direction of the nice pub I bribed her with earlier.

I barely talk on the way there because I'm replaying the party and the weekend, and also trying to convince myself that I don't have to break up with Florrie because I could probably just be busy and avoidant, and let her get the message at a distance. But then she surprises me.

We sit down outside the pub. I get her a glass of wine and me a pint, and she rolls a cigarette. 'I'm sorry,' she says.

'For what?'

'For being shit, at the kids' party.'

This is a genuine surprise. 'You weren't that bad,' I lie.

'I was rude. Or at least, I seemed rude. I find stuff like that really hard, I can't work out what to say to people like that.'

'People like what?'

'Kid people.'

'Oh,' I say, processing this.

She shakes her head. 'I don't like kids, don't want them, and places like that freak me out. I don't know what to ask and it's just like, standing inside this whole life that I really, deeply don't want to have, and I freak out that I'm going to tell someone how much I hate it, so I say the wrong thing. Or I say nothing and then everyone thinks I'm horrible.'

I want to tell her that she didn't seem horrible, but we'd both know that was a lie. 'Why did you want to come?' I ask gently.

'I wanted to meet Stella,' she says, fiddling with her lighter.

At this point I feel very, very bad. Because I should now tell her that there was a misunderstanding, and Stella and I are just mates who've snogged once and nearly snogged a second time.

'I get that,' I hear myself say. 'That makes sense.'

'Maybe we could all get dinner together sometime,' she says. 'Talk about non-kid stuff.'

The idea of telling Stella, even if we were in some mystical polyamorous set-up, that we couldn't talk about Rose over dinner makes me feel weirdly defensive of her.

'Sure,' I say. 'At some point, let's talk about doing that.'

She looks happier, which makes me feel less guilty, even though it absolutely shouldn't.

'Do you want another one?' She gestures at our almost empty glasses. It's the first time she's ever offered to buy me a drink and it feels churlish to refuse.

'Sure,' I say. 'That would be lovely.'

Stella

It's the last week of mat leave, before I head back to work. My boss, Charlotte, has, without exception, been exemplary. After I told her what happened with Gav she sent an email, all lower case, no punctuation: *what a shit leave it with me.* And a few weeks later I got a bemused email from the HR department who said they were extending the paid portion of my mat leave to the full fifty-two weeks. I've never entirely understood how they managed to do it, or why, given that she openly dislikes children and calls marriage 'modern slavery', and it's not like I was some golden-girl wunderkind of the office. For whatever reason, she did, and I was inordinately grateful to her. But even I have to accept that right now, it's time.

Rose is bored at the baby classes I drag her to, and if I'm totally honest, the idea of buying an overpriced lunch from Pret and then eating in total silence at my desk is starting to feel incredibly appealing. I've found a childminder down the road, a blissfully kind but surprisingly firm Spanish woman named Anna. It's in a big, bright, Victorian house on a quiet street, with a shady garden and five other happy-looking children of various ages. Anna gave me a long list of rules to follow and things to bring, all of which terrified me, and then explained about the settling-in period, which is where I leave Rose with her for increasingly long windows so that she gets used to it. Obviously leaving Rose, who has been attached to me (sometimes literally, by my nipple, though I basically stopped breastfeeding way back in spring) for almost a year, felt like having a limb amputated. But to my relief, she didn't seem especially bothered by any of it. She waddled towards Anna on day two with a gummy smile and then wrenched a toy out another child's hand.

After I drop her off each morning, I come home and stand in the house and try to decide what to do. I work through my wardrobe, cobbling together work-appropriate outfits from the things that still just about fit me. I throw away piles of clothes from my pre-pregnancy life that are never going to fit or have a purpose in my wardrobe again. I sand and paint the woodwork in the spare room, strip the hideous wallpaper from the upstairs hall.

On Thursday, Richard comes over – a new compromise on our step towards him being in my life in a more formal capacity. I make us a bolognese and he tells me about his trip – he's just got back from Dubai, bringing a beautiful and very expensive-looking doll for Rose, and a beautiful and even more expensive-looking pair of earrings for me. I light candles, lay the table properly, revel in having someone come to the house to justify making things nice, instead of shoving some food in a bowl and eating it while I mindlessly scroll the internet. We sit at the table, him tanned from his trip, me tired from my day, and it feels nice.

'How was the party?' he asks as I dust Parmesan over our food.

'It was good,' I say, which was true. All our old friends, the ones who'd known me and Gav through baby classes, turned out in force. Though, I suppose they're more my friends now than 'ours'. I doubt they're talking to Gav, now he's not in the WhatsApp groups where we trade questions about our kids' poo and rashes. Many of them fled London the second their babies breathed in a whiff of pollution. A handful of my school friends came with their babies. Gavin had the good grace to have a 'gig' that afternoon (again, I'm really not sure who's going to see comedy on a Saturday afternoon), and obviously Louella was brilliant, if a bit hungover. 'We had a lovely time.'

'Who was there?'

I run him through the guest list. 'Though, my friend Dom brought his new girlfriend and Louella said she was a complete dick.'

Richard looks amused. 'How so?'

I recount how unfriendly Florrie was, and her vintage showdown with Louella who is the patron saint of not gatekeeping.

'Maybe she's threatened.' Richard smiles.

'By Lou?'

'By you. How do you know her boyfriend?'

'We matched on an app ages ago,' I say. 'When I was dating.'

Richard's demeanour changes. 'He's an ex?'

'Not an ex, no,' I explain, twisting a strand of spaghetti around my fork. 'We went on one date, then he came over here for dinner and it was a total disaster.'

'I thought you didn't let men meet your daughter.'

It feels weird that he still calls Rose 'your daughter' but maybe this isn't the moment to raise it. He also seems oddly bothered about something that I've so easily explained to him. 'Yeah, anyone I'm romantically involved with, sure. But I'm not romantically involved with him.'

'But you were.' Richard has put his fork down and is looking at me searchingly. 'Right?'

'For a bit,' I say. 'But like I explained, we worked out pretty quickly that we're better off as friends, and now we're just friends.'

Richard says nothing. He goes back to eating. I'm completely unsure how to approach this. Gavin never had the slightest whiff of jealousy about him. I'm assuming this is jealousy, anyway. So I don't know exactly how I'm supposed to handle it. Presumably it would be best to reassure him. I know there's nothing to worry about, obviously, but he maybe doesn't? Louella has gone to Korea for work and she's hooking up with a guy from the office out there, so I've resolved to give her a break from my stupid questions about dating. I could message my uni friends but – and I know this is pathetic – they enjoyed the divorce so much, I just know how this would go down and I can't deal with days of questions about whether we managed to resolve this terrible situation. So I should just follow my instincts. I have good instincts. I mean, not with men, historically, but more broadly. At work, people think I do, and with the interiors for the house.

'I could not have Dom around Rose again,' I say tentatively. 'If you think it feels like a double standard.'

Richard nods. 'I think that sounds sensible.'

'Cool,' I say. 'Let's do that.'

I go back to eating, assuming that this will shift the weird, moody cloud that's settled over the room, but it doesn't.

'I think,' Richard says after a few minutes of silence, just the music and our forks on our plates, 'if you don't mind, I would feel more comfortable if you stopped seeing him entirely.'

On a flight back from Italy a few years ago a woman accidentally knocked an icy gin and tonic into my lap while having a row with her husband, and it's a similar sensation to this, a sort of cold shock. 'Stop seeing Dom?'

'I mean he's a new friend, right? It's not like you go back a long way, or anything?'

He's right, technically. And I don't know how to explain that because Dom found me when I was this squishy broken shell-less snail of a person, and he was the only one I could properly talk to in that weird moment, it feels like we bypassed all the temporal limitations of becoming friends and skipped to having known each other for years. 'He's important to me,' I venture.

'I understand that,' he says, not looking at me. 'But…' He trails off.

'But what?'

He gets up, going into the kitchen. He takes the water jug as if he's going to refill it but I'm not sure who this pretence is for. When he comes back, he takes a deep breath then sits down again. 'I was in a long-term relationship. Before we met.'

'Yes,' I say. 'You said.'

'She cheated on me,' he continues, halting, like he's hardly able to get the words out. 'With an ex-boyfriend. Someone I always had a bad feeling about.'

'I'm so sorry,' I say, suddenly understanding. 'That's awful.'

'Now I know,' he adds, 'this isn't entirely rational and I am working through it. But my therapist has told me that if I have a boundary, I need to ask for that boundary to be respected. So for now, while I'm still very hurt from what I went through, I have to ask if you'll consider not being in an active friendship with any exes.'

He's not an ex. I want to reiterate that he's not an ex. But I get it. I wouldn't date someone with a blazing but unspent need to try stand-up comedy, in case they did what Gav did to me. And maybe this is just exactly the same thing?

'Okay,' I say. 'I'll stick a pin in the friendship with Dom, and we'll check in and see where things are going a bit further down the line. Cool?'

I don't like saying it. The words feel wrong as they leave my mouth. I know what Louella would tell me. I know what I'd tell Rose if someone asked this of her. But Richard is sweet and respectful and successful, and he wants me despite all the complexity of my life. He's made huge compromises in how we date, coming to my house rather than going out, my only ever going to his place on a Thursday night, him never being allowed to go upstairs at my house. Those things are huge. So really, is it such an enormous deal if I make one sacrifice in return, for him?

Stella

It's been less than a week since I told Richard that I'd stop spending time with Dom, and he's currently on his way over to my house.

Just as I've never been the kind of person to cheat on a partner, I've also never been the kind of person to lie. To a fault, actually. If I went to dinner with my friends and one of their husbands had been fired or they were sporting new filler in their lips, I'd come home and tell Gavin straight away. I always took the view that 'don't tell anyone' didn't include Gavin because he mostly didn't care. Only he was actually a huge gossip, so he very much did care and I shared secrets that, on balance, I probably shouldn't have, including my own. I told him what I'd bought him for his birthday before he'd even seen the wrapping paper, I ruined every surprise I ever tried to plan, I even told him that I knew he was going to propose because I'd seen a chunky charge on his credit card statement. Lying just isn't my thing.

So this morning, when I saw three missed calls from Dom, I knew that I was going to have to lie to someone and I felt deeply, painfully ill-equipped to do so. Rose was on the floor, playing with some tasteful wooden animals in a Noah's Ark that one of my uni friends bought her. I open my phone and I swear I'm about to message Dom to tell him that I can't talk, when he calls again. Four calls in a row is not nothing, so I answer.

'Hello?'

'Hi,' he says, sounding absolutely dreadful. 'How are you?'

'I'm fine – what's wrong?'

'Nothing,' he says, once again sounding truly dreadful. 'No, nothing. Just… Have you got a minute?'

I should say no, but I don't know how, and it would be such a complete and utter lie. If I was busy then I could say that I'm busy, but realistically, I don't just have a minute, I have an entire day. Richard and I are having dinner tomorrow night. I've promised to make a roast because he said he misses a home-cooked roast so badly. But until then, it's just me, Rose and a booking for the slightly shit local zoo.

'I've got ages,' I say. 'Do you want to come over?'

'Yes, please,' he says. I want to feel guilty but his tone is too strangled and I'm too worried about him. What could it be? Maybe he and Florrie broke up, but he didn't seem that attached to her so I doubt he'd be devastated about a split there. Could be someone in his family, but surely he's got closer people to call for that?

'Florrie's pregnant,' he says the second he walks through the front door.

I nod. 'I kind of thought that might be it. Tea?'

He nods and I make him a cup of tea because that's the sort of thing you're supposed to do when someone's having a crisis.

'This tea is horrible,' he says, sipping it.

'I know,' I say. 'I don't drink tea; those teabags are probably three years old.'

He takes another gulp. 'Fuck me,' he says, sounding dazed. Then he looks at Rose, who is throwing all the balls out of the mini ball pit that I deeply regret buying her. 'Sorry.'

'I don't want to ask an inappropriate question,' I venture. 'But she's sleeping with other people, right? It's an open relationship?'

Dom nods.

'So if she were pregnant, would it be, you know… yours?'

He looks down at the mug. 'I'm the only person she's had that kind of sex with in the last month, apparently. She doesn't always "do" penetration with her lovers.'

'Bet that makes you feel special,' I say, marvelling at how Florrie can be five years younger than us and yet from a different world.

He laughs. 'Very.'

'Does she know what she wants to do?'

He shakes his head. 'She said she needed to be alone, and then she left, and she hasn't replied to any of my messages.'

'If she wants to be alone, then that's fair,' I say. 'Finding out that you're pregnant is terrifying, even if it's on purpose and with someone you know really well. Finding out like this, it's pretty much every woman's worst nightmare.'

Dom looks blank. 'I've been having sex for nearly twenty years and this hasn't ever happened to me. We were being so careful, like, literally using-condoms-and-she's-got-the-implant careful.'

I shrug. 'These things happen sometimes.' There's a pause and then I say the thing that I know I really need to say. 'You've told her that it's her choice what she does, right?'

'She knows that.'

'Dom, seriously, it doesn't matter if she knows it, she needs to hear it. From you. She needs to know that you're not going to judge her if she decides to get an abortion.'

He looks over at Rose, horrified.

'Dom, she's one, she doesn't know what the word "cow" means, let alone what "abortion" means.'

Dom sort of laughs. 'I'll send her another message and I'll make sure she knows.'

'Good,' I say. 'Now what are you going to do for the rest of today?'

'No idea,' he says. 'Wish it was a weekday so I could go to work and take my bad mood out on other people. Go home and wait for Florrie to call me and tell me whether we're having a baby, I guess. Watch TikTok until my eyes bleed.'

I sigh, knowing that I'm about to turn my little lie into a much bigger lie, and not feeling great about it. 'Come to the zoo with us.'

'Really?'

'Absolutely.'

He finishes the horrible tea and half a packet of Hobnobs while I pack an enormous bag of spare clothes, nappies, wipes, snacks, books, toys and a blanket, and shove it all under the pram. 'How long are we going for?' Dom snipes.

'If you don't have absolutely everything then you might as well have nothing, baby rule number one,' I say.

'I can't think about babies right now.'

'Bollocks,' I say. 'You might be having one of these, whether you like it or not, and you're in your thirties, you've got a good job, you own a nice flat, you're perfectly capable, so you might as well at least try to see some of the positives of having a kid.'

We put our shoes on and walk towards the station.

'Okay, tell me one thing that would be fun about having a baby,' I demand.

He thinks about it for a minute. 'Parking in the really good parking spaces, right near the big Sainsbury's.'

'Yes!' I agree. 'That's a great one! What else?'

He thinks for a while longer. 'Paternity leave? Like an extra holiday?'

I decide not to tell him that paternity leave is to holiday as prison is to hotel. 'Sure!'

'I could work on a kid-friendly house,' he says thoughtfully. 'Like, I could try to work out what the absolute perfect house for a family would be. And design it, and maybe one day I could build it.'

I want to stop and hug him, but I settle for an encouraging nod. 'Exactly!'

He helps carry the pram up the stairs at the station, saving me my least favourite step of dragging it backwards, filled with terror that I'm going to drop Rose. On the train we look out the window into other people's gardens and I keep pointing out the benefits of child rearing. 'Loads of snacks,' I say. 'There's never not a digestive biscuit in my handbag.'

'Nack,' says Rose.

'Snack!' I yelp back. 'Rosie! That's a new word!' I beam at her, soaking up her brilliance, drinking in the roundness of her face and her total bemusement at my excitement. I scramble to give her one of the squashed blueberries I've decanted into a tiny Tupperware, because I need her to understand how amazing I think she is and her love language is mostly just fruit at this stage of her life. 'That's another magic one, when they start talking and suddenly they're people instead of really needy pets.'

'Yeah,' Dom admits. 'That's fun.'

We wander around the zoo, showing Rose the animals. Dom hoists Rose up so that she can see the lizard hiding in the rainforest section, and again standing behind a queue of boys violently shoving each other by the monkey cages. I try to not let myself think, even for a moment, how much more fun this is, how this was the plan, how this was exactly what I wanted life to look like. After Rose has lost her mind at seeing a real-life sheep (arguably not a zoo animal, but this place isn't famed for its biological diversity) she then starts whining. I put her back into the pram and pull the visor down, and within seconds she's snoring gently.

'I'm desperate for a wee,' I say. 'But if she hears a hand dryer she'll wake up, she's a psycho about them.'

'I can stay with her,' says Dom haltingly, clearly not sure that this is a good idea. But I want a wee without an audience for the first time in several days, so I slip into the loos and leave him gripping onto the buggy handle. When I've finished washing my hands in the monkey-themed sink, I come out and find Dom talking to a similarly trendy thirty-something, also tall and handsome and also holding on to the exact same pram. They look like they came off the production line at the same Trendy Dad factory.

'I met a pram twin.' Dom smiles as I return.

'Isn't it amazing off-road?' the man says earnestly.

I have never taken the pram outside of Zone 3 so I take his word for it. 'Yeah,' I say. 'Amazing.'

'I'd better get on, my other half's got our twins in the reptile house. Nice to meet you.' He heads off and Dom looks at me, astounded. 'That man thought that I was a *parent*.'

'You're holding a pram in a children's zoo. If you're not a parent, he should really have called security.'

'But still!' he says, and I don't want to dent his excitement. 'Okay, what next?'

'Pub?' I suggest.

He looks shocked. 'With a *baby*?'

'With a *sleeping* baby.'

Rose will reliably nap for another hour, so we walk slowly through the park and up to a pub by the river, looking out over the water. It's warm and the light is sparkling, even through the river is sludge brown. I get a Pimm's, the silliest drink imaginable, and eat all the fruit out of it with my fingers, getting sticky juice on my top.

I briefly look at my phone and realise that I haven't messaged Richard all day, so fire him off a picture of me from the zoo, Rose cropped out. *See you tomorrow, can't wait,* I add. It's sort of true. I mean I can wait, but no one ever means 'can't wait', it's just a sort of thing you say, isn't it?

'Anything from Florrie?' I ask.

He shakes his head. 'Nothing. I'm worried for her.'

'Did she seem in a bad way?'

'I mean, she was pretty cut up. She came over last night, when she first worked out that her period was late, and then we couldn't even look at the test. We went to bed and we didn't even look at it until the next morning.'

'What?' I say, a sunrise of hope starting in my chest. 'You didn't look at the test for eight hours?'

'More like twelve,' he says. 'What? Why are you smiling?'

He is such an idiot.

Dominic

Stella looks at me like I'm the stupidest man in the entire world. 'Did you read the test instructions before you took it?'

'Obviously we didn't read the instructions, it's a pregnancy test. One line means pregnant, two lines means not pregnant.'

Stella sighs. 'How strong was the line?'

'Really light,' I say, not wanting to relive it all. 'I could hardly see it, but it's there.'

'You realise it could be an evaporation line?' Stella says, like she's pulling a rabbit out of a hat.

'A what?'

She sighs. 'You have to read the test within five minutes, otherwise the result is invalid. Was it a blue dye test or a pink dye test?'

She sounds absolutely insane. 'How would I know?'

'Were the lines on the test blue or pink?'

'How could that possibly matter?'

She stops the pram, abruptly. Rose giggles. Stella does not. 'Dominic, I spent two hours a day on the fertility and pregnancy testing forums when I was planning to get pregnant with Rose. I know everything there is to know about pregnancy tests and I'm telling you that it makes a difference. Blue dye is way, way more likely to run and cause an evaporation line.'

I'm too dazed to really process this. 'Uh. Blue. The lines were blue.'

'Go and find her,' she tells me. 'And take another test. Pink dye. Superdrug or Boots own-brand are the most reliable. Go on!'

We reach the station and I carry the pram up one set of stairs, then go back down, around and stand on the platform at the other side. We face each other, both sort of half laughing at the awkwardness of it. The sun's starting to slowly set. She must be cold, wearing a summer dress and no jacket. I watch as she pulls the blanket over Rose and think how much I'd like to pull a blanket over Stella, on a beach or by a campfire in the woods or somewhere like that.

Her train arrives. She whips the pram around and reverses it on, then waves at me through the window. And then she's gone.

I take the train to Peckham and then get an Uber to the bit of Camberwell where Florrie lives with all her friends. Then, feeling like a bit of a stalker, I ring the doorbell. One of her friends, who is either called India or Octavia, answers. 'Is Florrie in?' I ask, once again feeling like a complete stalker.

India/Octavia seems bemused but leads me through the dark hall with patterned tiles into the garden, where they're sitting outside on kitchen chairs, drinking bottles of San Miguel.

'Dom!' Florrie says, getting up. 'I didn't know you were coming?'

'I messaged you,' I say, trying not to sound defensive.

'Sorry,' she apologises, stubbing out her cigarette. 'I just needed a bit of a break from my phone so I turned it off.'

'Sure,' I say. 'Can we have a quick chat?'

I follow her up the many, many stairs to the top of her house where she has the attic bedroom. It's a really great place, with a sloping ceiling and huge windows looking out over the gardens of Camberwell, but we don't spend much time here because she's (gloriously) loud in bed and her housemates don't always appreciate it.

'I think we need to take another test,' I say, trying not to sound out of breath from the stairs. 'Apparently, sometimes, if you don't read it quickly enough, it can be a false positive.'

She shakes her head. 'No, I don't. I took a bunch more when I got home; they were all negative. It must have been an evaporation line.'

'How does everyone else in the world know about evaporation lines apart from me?' I say, louder than I intended and drowning in a confusing cocktail of relief and something that feels a tiny bit like disappointment. 'Why didn't you tell me?' I ask. I know I shouldn't make this about myself but I can't help feeling like this is information I probably could have been given, over a WhatsApp if nothing else.

'I didn't think it made any difference,' she says, sitting down on the bed. She crosses her long, tanned legs. 'We both knew what I was going to do if I was pregnant.'

'Sure,' I say. 'Yeah, I get that. But there would have been a discussion, and being pregnant and then having an abortion is a pretty big deal—'

'No, it's not.'

I try to process this. It's her body, and it would have been her choice, and I don't deny that for a second. But I think I'd have found it a big deal, to watch her go through that, to find out what actually happens, to know that we'd made a decision to not become parents. Not that I'd have objected, of course, and I wouldn't have had any right to voice it even if I did object, but it's okay to think that it's significant, right? Like, as a plot point in my life, in her life, it's meaningful, right? 'Okay,' I say. 'Well, look, I'm so glad you got the result you wanted, and I'm so glad we don't have to think about this again. At least not for a long time.'

'A long time?' She cocks her head to one side.

'Well. I mean, this is all very, very hypothetical, but I guess I'd like to have kids at some point, one day, so if we stayed together then maybe we'd talk about it—'

'I'm not having kids.'

Oh. 'Right. Okay. Well, that's also totally fine…'

'Kids ruin your life.'

I think about this for a moment. 'I get that it might seem that way, but I think a lot of people would argue that they change your life rather than ruining it, so as long as you're on board for those specific changes, then it's more—'

'It would ruin my life,' she says, getting up.

'Okay,' I say. 'Totally your call. I'm not pitching to have a load of babies right now, just open to the idea. In the future.'

She gives me a look that could reasonably be described as withering. 'You're in your *thirties*.'

I mean, yeah, I'm in my thirties. That's a normal time to think about kids. I mean normal for a man. And yeah, that's not fair, I get that. My sister, Georgie, was shipping her blood to companies she'd seen advertised on Instagram to get her 'levels' checked from the day she turned twenty-nine. Sure, it's a luxury that I've got bollocks and my sperm don't start getting problematically old for longer, but we all know my entire life is easier because I'm a man, and I'm aware of that and I try not to do anything evil with whatever good fortune I've got. This doesn't feel like the most opportune moment to start talking about unearned privilege.

Florrie swallows, and stands up. 'Honestly,' she says. 'If you want babies then you should probably go do that with someone who has already given up on having an exciting life.'

'Right,' I say, getting up. 'Okay. Well, I'm glad we talked about this and I'm going to head home; it's been a head-fuck of a day.'

'For you? You weren't the one who thought they were pregnant.'

My calm is running out now. 'I mean, I thought that I'd got you pregnant for about nine hours longer than you thought that you were pregnant, because you couldn't bring yourself to write me a three-word message.'

'You're centering yourself in my pregnancy scare now?' she snaps.

'I'm not "centering" myself. Anyway, I'm just saying, typing "I'm not pregnant" wouldn't have been that much to ask.'

'You're being so demographically clichéd,' she fires back.

I open the bedroom door and start down the many flights of stairs until I hear her footsteps behind me, presumably because she's decided to apologise.

'Dom,' she calls.

'Yes?' I reply, stopping on the stairs.

'How did you know about the false positive thing?' she asks. I look upwards and she's standing above me, pale and furious, not sounding at all like she's about to say she's sorry.

'What?' I ask.

'The evaporation line. Who told you about that?'

I sigh. I know exactly how this is going to go down. 'Stella told me,' I say quietly.

She flushes pink. 'So you told her that I was pregnant before I'd even had a chance to process it? You thought she should know that extremely personal news about my life before anyone I'd actually told?'

'I needed someone to talk to,' I argue, my voice harder than I'd intended it to be. 'I was worried. I didn't know if you wanted to keep the baby. She's had a kid, she knows about this stuff.'

'You knew that I was struggling with my feelings around her and you went to her instead of talking to me.'

'You'd turned your bloody phone off!' I snap.

She picks up her phone and throws it across the stairwell, down the stairs. It hits the wall behind my head and the screen cracks, then it hits the stairs and bounces down to the landing, where it lands precariously between two spindles. 'I needed a break!' she yells as she throws it.

I look at her. At the phone. Back to her. She bursts into sobs, tears streaming down her face. What I would really like to do right now is go downstairs, without looking behind me, slam the door on this house and all the privileged, entitled women who live in it, and never speak to her again. But before I've got the strength to do it, I look up at her one more time. Her eyes are navy blue against the pinkness of her eyes, still streaming with tears.

'Will you hold me?' she says, in a tiny voice.

'Of course,' I say.

I traipse back up the stairs, wrap my arms around her and then lift her up, carrying her back into her bedroom. I lie down next to her and stroke her arms and shoulders and hair as she cries.

She twists around and presses her face into my chest. 'I'm sorry,' she says. 'It's been such a horrible day.'

I nod. 'It's okay. We all have our moments.'

Eventually her sobs subside and she looks up at me. Her cheeks are swollen and her lips are fat. 'Can I ask you to do something for me?'

I nod. 'Sure.'

'Please will you stop seeing Stella?'

Everything Florrie has ever told me about her take on ethical non-monogamy (which is a lot) has focused on how having 'a veto' (aka the right to ask someone to stop seeing someone else) is not fair. She's described it as unreasonable, immature, even once as controlling. So it's hard to take this complete about-face in my stride. But she looks sad. And young. Her face is pinched and she's looking up at me through her fringe and I don't want to hurt her feelings, at all.

So I think about it for a moment, wondering if this could be a neat way out of the incredibly stupid situation I brought upon myself. 'What if Stella and I were just friends?'

She shakes her head. 'You have chemistry; it doesn't work like that. I need you to stop seeing her. Completely.'

I hold her a little tighter for a moment. Then, for once in my life, I don't say the easy thing that will make the other person feel good enough that I don't have to feel guilty. I say the hard thing, the thing that I don't want to say, the right one. 'I'm sorry,' I whisper. 'No.'

Stella

When I pictured going back to work, I pictured the bit where I had a coffee in my hand, took part in an interesting discussion, pointed out some amazing new colour trend that everyone liked, and then sat alone at my computer getting to use my brain for the first time in months. I did not, stupidly, give any thought to the process of getting there. This morning I woke up at quarter to six, a calculated move in order to get ready before Rose woke up. Rose then woke up while I was in the shower, meaning that I had to skip the conditioner and go and feed her. She had her bottle while I dripped on her, the floor and everything else, then she played on my bed while I rejected the outfit I'd planned the night before in favour of three other outfits, all of which looked dreadful, and eventually settled – you guessed it – on the first outfit. I then wrestled Rose into the First Day of Childcare outfit I'd picked, took a load of pictures of her, fed her some breakfast, changed her into a new outfit because I'm a rookie who fed their tiny child porridge without a big enough bib, and then I wrestled her into the pram. I walk fifteen minutes to drop her off, then ten minutes in the opposite direction to the station where I narrowly miss a train and wait on the platform, cursing the fact that it's drizzling and grey despite ostensibly being the summer. By the time I arrive at the office, coffee in hand, I have been awake for four hours and I feel like I've run a marathon. It dawns on me that when I finish work I'm going to have to leg it back to collect her, then do her tea, her bath, her stories, her teeth and her pyjamas, then settle her down to sleep and then do the whole thing again tomorrow, and the next day. That I'm going to have to do this basically every day for the rest of my life (or at least until she's older, if I'm being a bit less dramatic). How the fuck do people do this?

'How are you finding it?' Liz – a colleague who started at the magazine around the same time as me – asks, as we take the same lift down to the ground floor at lunchtime.

'It's an adjustment,' I say, through gritted teeth.

'I know,' she says. 'It's really tough. Let's go for drinks after work next week and I can run you through the top tips on survival.'

'That's so sweet,' I say, meaning it. 'But I've got to do pick-up in the evenings.'

'Ah,' she says, smiling. 'You've got to get hubby doing half the pick-ups and drop-offs – that's what makes life work. At least twice a week I make sure that I get home after Alex has them in bed – there's a life hack for you.'

I nod and realise that I haven't told anyone what happened while I was on mat leave, about Gavin or the divorce or, well, any of the huge life I lived while they were still here, still doing the job that I used to see as the central bit of who I am as a person. 'That's a good tip,' I say, because I don't know what else to contribute. So that's how everyone else is managing this. Sharing the load.

By the time Rose is in bed, the prospect of cooking anything is unappealing so I pour a bowl of cereal and watch things on my phone that make me angry: women giving opinions about parenting, men giving opinions about women. It's all so irritating that I turn it off and sit and spoon the cereal into my mouth in silence. Then I look at my phone. Look at the clock. Try to convince myself that I want to tell someone how awful it all is, and decide against it. It's 7.45 p.m., and I go to bed.

The next morning, I wake up at six and accept that I'm not going to be able to have great hair and make-up for work any more. I pull on a pair of jeans and a clean shirt, which is what I would have worn before I was trying to convince everyone that I'm still the same person I was pre-kid. I smear tinted sunscreen into my face as I feed Rose her porridge (this time in her pyjamas) and on the way to the childminder, I find a shortcut along a side road, which shaves a full three minutes off the trip. I try to convince myself that this means things are getting better, especially as Rose decides that this morning is the first morning she really does mind about being dropped off.

She starts wailing when she sees the front door at Anna's, and she clings to me. I have to physically peel her off me and place her on Anna's chest.

'It's fine,' Anna assures me. 'They all do this – every single one. She will be playing happily in five minutes. Just go.'

I go. I miss the train again and spend fifteen minutes sitting on a cold, metal seat on the platform, thinking about all the ways that Rose could be injured at the childminder's, even though I'm fairly sure that Anna is a much safer and more expert child wrangler than I am. As the train pulls into the station, my phone pings and it's a photo of Rose, red-eyed and puffy from crying, but smiling and playing with a plastic horse. I burst into tears at how brave and resilient she is, and how guilty I feel and how completely unerringly shit this situation is.

For the first time in my entire life, I don't want to go to work. I mean, I've had days where I don't fancy it and I've very occasionally phoned in sick when I could have made it in, or made a last-minute plea to work from home because of a hangover. But for the most part, I've liked my work. It's been close enough to what I actually wanted to do that it's fun. The people I work with are nice. I mean, we write about wallpapers and lampshades – it's hardly a coal mine. Only, despite having said I was bored at home, despite having been really ready to go back, I'd rather go and walk around the same park I've been walking around for almost a year, having a one-sided conversation with Rose.

At the office I try to join in our morning meeting about What's Hot right now, but obviously I don't know What's Hot. I could suggest that leaving your baby at childcare when they're screaming for you isn't hot, but that's sort of the opposite of what anyone here is interested in, and, let's face it, every woman who's already had a kid will tell me that they've been there, done that and my discovering it is actually quite boring for everyone else.

The week wears on. I get the morning routine down, Rose screams at drop-off then cheers up after I leave, I miss the train, do an average-to-poor job at work, come home, eat a ready meal or breakfast food, and then go to bed at an appropriate bedtime for a nine-year-old. On Friday morning, Dom messages me. He's been quiet, since the announcement that he'd (thankfully) parted ways with awful Florrie.

Let's go for a drink tonight, he writes. *Don't say no and don't be boring.*

I can't, I reply. *Sorry.*

Boring, he writes. I turn my phone over and look at the article that I'm supposed to be editing. I've read the same paragraph three times and it doesn't make sense, but I'm concerned that it's because my brain has gone to mush rather than because it's badly written.

My phone buzzes.

Boringggggg, he writes.

It pings again a few minutes later.

I put it on silent.

At lunch, I open WhatsApp and Dom has sent three sleeping emojis and then other emojis intended to illustrate how boring I am, which I would probably have found funny a few weeks ago, back when I had a personality. Then at the end, there's a plaintive, earnest message. *I have actually been feeling really down and obviously don't want to let any of my male friends know that I've got a soul, but if you could face me popping over for a glass of wine tonight that would mean a lot.*

I am still very much supposed to not be seeing him any more, as far as Richard knows. But Richard is in Dubai again and has been giving me a tastefully wide berth while I readjust to the working schedule he doesn't think I should have. And I do want a glass of wine. And a chat. And to do something that isn't work and childcare followed by more work and more childcare. *Okay*, I write back. *But I am going to be in bed by 11 p.m.*

Deal.

* * *

Dom arrives carrying a six-pack of beer, which I have no interest in drinking. He sits on the kitchen sofa, clicking the can in his hand in an annoying, repetitive way, and I pour myself a glass of wine.

'What's for dinner?' he asks, grinning.

'I don't know,' I say, from between my gritted teeth. 'Did you bring anything? Are you planning to cook?'

He rolls his eyes. 'Okay, angry, I can order us a take-away if you want.'

'I don't want that,' I say. 'I need to eat something with a vegetable in it, otherwise I'm going to get scurvy.'

'Okay…' He trails off. 'So being back at work is great, then?'

I look at him, and behind him I can see my reflection in the mirror I stupidly hung at that end of the kitchen. I've got purple shadows under my eyes so dark that I can see them from across the room. My skin looks completely dull, matt, like I'm made out of wax. The shirt that I'd hoped was sort of cool and slightly boho in an Isabel Marant way is straining across my chest because it's from the pre-Rose days where I had sensible-sized tits, and the whole outfit is giving middle-aged mum at a middle-class sports day. I'm filled with desire to take the lid from the casserole dish I'm currently holding and hurl it across the room, smashing the mirror. Obviously, I don't do it. But I wish I could.

'It's shit,' I say, trying to keep it together. 'I'm doing a bad job with Rose because I'm exhausted and a bad job at work because I'm exhausted. I have to be two people every single day and I hate it.'

'That's shit,' Dom says flippantly. 'I hate that for you.' He leaves a gap for a moment, presumably for me to ask how things are going with him. I start chopping an onion instead.

'So Florrie blocked me on everything,' he ventures. 'But also sent me a thousand-word WhatsApp message about how I'm not emotionally mature enough to be in a long-term relationship, which, in fairness, is very much how I advertised myself from the beginning.'

I realise in that moment that I haven't registered my single-person discount for council tax, and I was supposed to do it months ago. I put the knife down on the chopping board, wipe my hands and go to find a pen to write this down so that I don't forget again.

'Are you okay?' Dom asks.

'No,' I say. 'I've been really clear about that, I'm in a shit mood and I'm having a shit time, and I know that you and Florrie broke up and I'm really sorry about that, but she was awful and you didn't really like her, and I don't have the emotional energy to pretend that I feel really sad for you because it's not an actual problem and nothing actually sad has happened.'

Dom looks surprised, but also sort of impressed. 'Wow,' he says, shifting on the sofa. 'I mean, first of all, ouch. And secondly, yeah. I guess, fair. Ouch, but fair.'

'Sorry,' I say, going back to the chopping board. 'I'm being such a bitch.'

'It's fine, I think I actually quite like it.'

I half laugh, and tip the onion into the pan. 'Why did you actually break up? I'd assumed you'd do that typical man thing where you were just half-hearted and cold until she got the picture and ended things with you.'

He laughs. 'I mean, that is my usual style, but no, on this occasion I didn't need to. She broke up with me.'

I pause while I'm looking for the tomato purée. 'Really? She seemed very into you.'

'Yeah, but she wanted things I couldn't agree to.'

'Like what?'

He opens another beer, looking uncomfortable suddenly. 'She wanted me to stop seeing you.'

My hand slips on the cupboard handle. 'What? Why?'

'Long story, but basically she thought we had a romantic thing going on, not just a friendship, and it suited me to let her think that because she'd been in open relationships with guys who didn't see other people and apparently that didn't work, and I don't want to date loads of people at the same time, and I figured it would be a great deal if I could have like, half the week to play FIFA and get work done, and do some more work on my flat, and she could just think I was shagging other people.'

'Right,' I say slowly, trying to understand. 'So you were pretending to cheat on her?'

'Well, she wanted an open relationship, so it wouldn't have been cheating.'

'This is insane.' I laugh. 'And what, she found out?'

'No,' he says, looking guilty again. 'She asked me to stop seeing you.'

I'm confused now. 'But surely given that we're not actually seeing each other, you could have just agreed to that?'

'No,' he says. 'She wanted me to stop seeing you at all. Like, socially, as a friend, full stop. And I couldn't do that.'

I cross the room and he stands, and, without thinking about it, I wrap my arms around him and rest my head on his chest, hugging him like I'm a small child who's fallen over in the playground. The force of it knocks him backwards slightly, but he recovers his footing and I feel the warmth of him, the solidness, the softness. He squeezes me, hard. The nicest hug I've had in a while. The only hug, actually. He told Florrie that he wouldn't stop seeing me. He picked me over Florrie. Beautiful, sexy, fun Florrie. I'd have picked her over me every time.

I'm going to have to talk to Richard. If Dom, who might change his name to Avoidant by deed poll, wouldn't agree to cut me off, what was I thinking considering doing that to him? And realistically, where did he get off asking me to stop seeing one of my friends?

'That's really nice of you,' I say, into his chest. 'Not to dump me.'

He makes a gruff noise, which implies that for once in his life he doesn't have anything clever to say.

'I think it might have finished me off if you'd taken this week to cull our friendship,' I go on.

I pull away and realise that I've left tear splotches on his jumper. I didn't even know that I was crying.

'Right,' he says. He puts down his beer and takes off his jumper, pretending to not notice the tear stains. 'Sit on the sofa. I'm going to finish dinner.'

'No,' I protest. 'You'll do a shit job.'

'I mean, maybe, but at least this way you'll get to sit down for more than five minutes today, okay?'

I nod, sit down, let him top my wine glass up, and then sit with my knees hugged to my chest, watching him cook. He's the only person other than me who has ever made anything in this kitchen. He's even fairly good-natured when I shout instructions and tell him off for using the wrong knife on the wrong chopping board.

He plates up a perfectly passable pasta and we sit on opposite sides of the sofa, shovelling it into our mouths. 'How's rich Richard?' he asks.

'Fine. In Dubai.'

Dom makes a face. 'Why?'

'Making money.'

'Makes sense.' He considers me for a moment. 'Do you see yourself falling in love with him?'

I think about it, though it's a question that I've tried quite hard to avoid. 'I don't think I want to fall in love again,' I say.

'Oh, come on—'

'No,' I say. 'I mean, I'd like to be in love again. But I don't want to fall into it. I didn't pick anything with Gavin – it just sort of happened around me. If I'm going to be with someone again, I want to consciously, sensibly step into it and then let it develop. And, yeah, I know you think I don't have strong enough feelings for him, but he's so decent and so kind, and we have a nice time together. He takes me seriously, he wants good things for me – there's so much about him that makes sense. So if I'm going to have a life with someone again, I think I want it to be with someone like Richard.'

Dom shrugs. 'Real shame we didn't record that, would have been a perfect speech for your wedding.'

I feel pricked by this. 'I'm not just one person any more, I can't just pick a hot guy who has great throwdown and makes me laugh, and then hope that he's going to be a decent stepfather. I've got to be smart about this, much smarter than I've ever been, and Richard is probably that.'

Dom shrugs. 'Whatever you say.'

There's a long silence. 'What are you doing this week?' I ask.

'I've got a meeting on Monday with a guy who wants to construct a building with no fire doors, looking forward to that, and then on Tuesday, I've got a job interview.'

'Oh, cool,' I say. 'I didn't think you wanted to move? You like your job.'

'Yeah,' he agrees. 'But I thought I might want a change of scene. Location-wise.'

'The interview's not in London?'

'No. It's in Dublin.'

'The interview is for a job in Dublin?'

'No,' he says sarcastically. 'The job's in Reykjavík so we're meeting in the middle.'

'Dublin isn't in the middle of London and Reykjavík,' I snap.

'It was a joke,' he snaps back.

Right. So he's going to get a job in Ireland and then move there, and then I'll see him twice a year for a forced drink for the first few years and then eventually not at all, and we'll just send each other WhatsApps saying, *I miss you, friend!* until one of us dies. I'm so glad that we invested all this time and emotional energy into building this weird friendship for it to completely disappear overnight.

I lied to the man I'm seeing in order to keep in contact with Dom. Not that Dom knows that, and technically he didn't ask me to, but I lied – and I never lie – because I care about him and he's my friend, and hanging out with him is important.

'What's the job?' I ask, attempting to sound interested.

'A bigger firm, in the city centre. They're trying to build some affordable housing because everything in Dublin is mad expensive. It's a really good project.'

'Sounds like it,' I say, stabbing a piece of pasta. 'And I guess it'll be an exciting new start. Do you have any friends there?'

'Orla, the girl I was seeing back last year. Remember her?'

Obviously I remember Orla – the first time he told me the story about her I went home and went through his Instagram followers. 'So maybe you'd get back together with her.'

He shrugs. 'I mean, I couldn't make it work before, so probably not this time.'

'Doesn't seem to stop you though, does it?"

'What's that supposed to mean?'

'I mean, you keep dating, even though you know you can't actually give anyone what they actually want. Orla, Florrie—'

'Hang on, I broke up with Florrie because she wanted me to never see you again—'

'That's pretty convenient though, isn't it? You're probably never going to see me again anyway if you're moving to Dublin, you just used me as an excuse so that you didn't have to do your own dirty work and break up with her like a grown-up.'

Dom looks at me like I've slapped him. 'Right,' he says. Then he gets up. 'Look, we said we'd keep this evening brief, we're both tired—'

'No, I'm tired, I get four hours sleep a night and work full time from an office – you can do whatever you want literally all the time, you're not tired—'

'You know other people can experience things, not just you, Stella? You know you don't actually have the monopoly on being unhappy? Yes, your husband left you and that was shit, but it was also a long time ago and a lot of bad things have happened to other people in that time.'

'I am fully fucking aware—'

'Tell me one? Tell me one thing that's happened to your mum, or your sister, or any of your uni friends?'

Obviously I know the answer to this but I'm strangled with how angry I am and I can't force any words out. So instead I say, 'Fuck you, Dom. You just don't like that I told you a hard truth about the immature way you live your life—'

Rose cries, I hear over the baby monitor and from the top of the stairs. I head for the bedroom.

'I'm leaving,' Dom says simply. 'Bye, Stella.'

'Good!' I shout back, marching up the stairs two at a time. 'Great!'

When I come back down from settling Rose, good as his word, he's gone.

Stella

Richard returns, once again, from Dubai. He brings presents for both me and Rose, and seems genuinely pleased to see me. I feel guilty about having seen Dom twice while he was away, and miserable that neither Dom nor I have made any kind of contact since our massive argument. But I'm determined to put on a decent show for Richard, who has managed to ignore his jetlag to come over for dinner. I make a risotto and we sit down at the table, him full of stories from his meetings, me keeping one eye on the clock to work out when we can go to bed. Or rather, when I can go to bed, because he still hasn't been upstairs at my house and despite having been dating for almost three months, we still haven't gone any further than kissing.

Almost as if he's read my mind, he puts down his fork. 'I have a surprise for you.'

I try to look enthusiastic. I love surprises. Surprises are my favourite thing. I just also can't stop thinking about the fact that I've got to wash my hair, which either means washing it before I can get into bed tonight, or getting up extra early tomorrow and hoping that the clunking of the boiler doesn't wake Rose. The other day I tried bringing her into the bathroom while I was showering and she almost got the loo brush into her mouth before I noticed. Suffice to say, no part of any system I try to put in place is working at all well so far.

'That's exciting,' I say, trying to inject enthusiasm into my voice. 'What is it?'

'I booked us a holiday.'

A holiday? As in, a holiday for me and him and Rose? We'd need multiple bedrooms, and he hasn't even met Rose. How am I going to get up with her for her middle-of-the-night feed (which I absolutely have to stop giving her at some point, but can't face dropping right now)? How on earth is a holiday going to work?

I must look as confused as I feel internally, because he explains. 'I mean, I've booked us two nights away, at a hotel.'

This doesn't really answer any of my questions. 'That's amazing,' I say. 'But Gavin only has Rose one night a week.'

Richard smiles. 'I spoke to your mother and she agreed to come and look after Rose for the Wednesday night, so that we can have a proper break.'

I fix a smile on my face. This is a nice thing. It's thoughtful. It's kind. It's a way for us to have the kind of mini-break a normal couple without a complicated baby-and-ex-husband situation would be able to do. If I were dating someone who had a child, I'd want to go away with just my partner sometimes.

Two nights does feel like such a long time, though. 'I need to check if I can get the time off work,' I say, haltingly. 'I've only just gone back so they might think it's a bit of a piss-take for me to take days off.'

'I'm sure it'll be fine,' Richard says. 'And you could always work from there if you need to. It's a lovely place in the Cotswolds,' he explains, getting out his phone. He shows me the website for a hotel that I've seen various influencers on social media go to. 'They'll have great Wi-Fi and places to work if you need to. Though I thought you could spend some time by the pool, get a few treatments, that sort of thing.'

I won't lie, the idea of lying on a massage table while someone pounds the knots out of my back and rubs me with a nice-smelling oil sounds like the kind of bliss I can hardly imagine. 'This is so kind of you,' I say. 'Let me know what I owe you for the booking.'

He smiles and shakes his head as if the idea of me paying is so silly it's not worth engaging with. 'I'm excited to have a longer stretch of time together,' he says. 'I know I've been a little old-fashioned, insisting on taking things so slowly, but I'm entirely sure that it's going to be worth it.'

To my surprise, work is completely relaxed about me taking three days off only a few weeks after going back.

'You need a bit of R and R,' my boss says when I put the leave request in, half hoping that she would tell me that I can't go. 'You seem burnt out.'

I try not to engage with this, but she's not wrong. My ideas are blunt, my skin is terrible and I'm exhausted all the time.

Similarly, I sort of hope Mum might back out, but no, she's full steam ahead. We don't talk about the Calpol incident but she assures me over and over again that she will be careful, and so on the Wednesday morning I find myself packing the only pair of semi-sexy pyjamas that I own, and then going through the tagged photos at the hotel to work out what other, more stylish people have worn there and then trying to create copies of those outfits using my existing wardrobe, which is entirely made of clothes from M&S. And before I know it I'm kissing Rose and squeezing her and trying to blink back tears as we get into the car. She's going to be with her childminder today, with my mum tonight, her childminder tomorrow and then with Gavin. So realistically, tonight is the only time I'm actually missing with her. And she'd be asleep then anyway. I repeat this inside my head as the car leaves London, pulling onto the motorway. Then I think about what would happen if we died in a car crash and Gavin got full custody of Rose. I've got a will, but suddenly I think I should probably make a book of things he'd need to know if he was going to look after her all the time, like how she likes it when I sing her songs from *Cabaret*, or how she wants her milk cold in the afternoon but warm at bedtime.

'What are you thinking about?' Richard asks. He's sitting across from me, a driver in the front to get us to the Cotswolds. I'm starting to think that maybe Richard can't drive, which is obviously totally fine but feels like the kind of thing we should have talked about. Does he know that I failed my test four times before I passed? Probably not.

'Nothing,' I say, smiling. 'Just how much I'm looking forward to this trip.'

'Me too.' He smiles.

The hotel is divine, even if I do keep sneaking into the bathroom to play videos of Rose on my phone. Our room is a cottage on the property, a short walk from the main house where there are huge drawing rooms with squashy sofas to read books on, and surrounded by sloping lawns and blossom-heavy trees.

'This is incredible,' I say honestly as we're unpacking. He puts all of his clothes away into the wardrobe and I realise that I haven't shared bedroom space with anyone since Gavin. Usually I'd just leave my suitcase on the floor and pull out the stuff I need, but I sense Richard wouldn't approve of that, so I unpack properly, my clothes looking very shabby and crumpled in the enormous wardrobe.

Just as I've finished unpacking my toiletries, Richard is behind me. I look up into the bathroom mirror and smile at him. 'Hello,' I say, bashful. I have a feeling I know where this is going.

'Hello,' he replies.

He takes my hand and guides me into the bedroom, and then lays me down on the bed. He kisses my neck, strokes my hair and runs his hand up my thigh. In an ideal world I'd really like to have showered because it's been twelve hours since I've washed and I feel like I've got car smell on me.

He kisses me again and I giggle slightly, pulling away.

'Are you okay?' he asks.

'Yes,' I say, trying to smile.

Memories of the time Dom tried to touch my thigh come flooding back. The tears, the hotness in my chest, the way he wrapped his arms around me and let me sob into his chest. The solid softness of his body. I shouldn't be thinking about Dom right now.

'I'm just a bit nervous. It's been a while,' I say, dragging myself into the present. Richard seems – weirdly – to really like hearing this. He guides my hand to his crotch and invites me to feel how hard he is. And in fairness, he's very hard. 'Wow,' I say, in earnest. He strips his clothes off, then pulls my jumper over my head, unbuttons my jeans and yanks them off. 'You're so beautiful,' he says, looking down at my body. 'You can't even tell.'

I think he might be making an oblique reference to my having had a baby, but I'm not going to press on that because I'm about to get laid for the first time since Gavin left and, at this point, I would have sex with pretty much anyone, so the prospect of this handsome, muscular guy is almost too good to be true. 'Tell me again that you're nervous,' he says, kneeling between my legs.

'I'm nervous,' I say. 'But I'm turned on too, I want you.'

He presses his finger to my lips, kissing me, his breath sharp with mint. After a couple of minutes of kissing, his body hard against mine, he pushes me down onto the bed. He puts on a condom, pulls my knickers to the side, pushes himself inside me and I whimper with pleasure at the feeling of finally being filled up, at the weight of him on top of me. 'Yes,' I whisper. 'Yes.'

He finds a rhythm, an odd, bumpy one, and I remind myself internally that I'm used to Gavin and no one other than Gavin – the two men before Gavin were so long ago – and this is probably just as legitimate a way to have sex as what I'm used to.

He moves against me in the same bumpy manner for a few minutes before he starts to pant. 'Good girl,' he says. 'You're such a good girl.'

I wince slightly at the expression but it would be a bit rude to call him out for it when he's about to come. Seconds later, he does.

'My good girl,' he whines into my ear. I try very hard to pretend that I haven't heard it, hoping that the lack of reaction might send enough of a signal that he gets the message and never says it again.

He rolls off me. I start to slip my hand between my legs to finish myself off, like I did with Gavin when we were feeling lazy. He looks perplexed. 'What are you doing?'

I smile. 'I was going to… you know. Finish.'

'You didn't orgasm?'

I shake my head.

He looks aghast. 'Are you sure?'

I can't help laughing. 'Yes, I'm sure. But it's fine, most women don't come from penetration alone. We can work on it later.' I kiss him. 'No biggie.'

I sort of expect him to come back to bed, to kiss me, possibly to initiate getting me off, to laugh the awkwardness away. But instead he gets up and I hear the shower running, apparently not coming back and apparently very much not interested in finishing what I was about to start. Any residual arousal I was feeling evaporates into embarrassment at him having seen me like that. What was I thinking? Maybe what I was doing is weird? Do other women not do that? Gavin and I always did it that way, but that doesn't mean that it's actually normal. I bury my face in the pillow and let out an embarrassed whimper, wishing I could rewind and take that last part back.

After his shower, Richard returns with a towel around his waist, seemingly in a better frame of mind.

'What shall we do now?' I ask. I should finish the conversation about sex, I know that. But it's too embarrassing. And it's not like I actually want an orgasm at this point. 'There's a nice walk through the woods apparently?'

'I've got a work call,' he says apologetically. 'Why don't you go to the spa? I block-booked you some treatments.'

He doesn't have to tell me twice. Within minutes, I'm down in the wine cellar, which serves as a spa, filling out a form to confirm that I'm not pregnant and haven't been breastfeeding in months so I want the deepest deep-tissue massage a woman can get.

By the time we get to dinner, I'm feeling better. I miss Rose, but knowing that she's in bed (and my mum sending me a picture every half hour all day long) helps. Plus, for the first time since my mat leave ended, I'm moving slowly and it feels blissful. I put my swimming costume on at a glacial pace, enjoying the complete novelty of not rushing. I wander back to our room, carrying my shoes, grass between my toes, and find Richard sitting at the desk, typing. He's concentrating so I wash the massage oil off my skin and double shampoo my hair. I blow-dry it and get changed, and we walk over to the main house for dinner.

'How was your work thing?' I ask, as we sit down and look at the menu.

'Oh, very dull,' he says, smiling. 'I won't bore you with it. What do you think you'll have?'

I scan the menu, trying to decide. 'Very hard to pick,' I say.

'I doubt any of it will be as good as anything you cook,' he says, taking my hands. 'That's one of the things I love about you – you're such a woman.'

I'm slightly bemused by this. 'Thank you?' I reply. 'I think?'

He laughs. 'I just mean, I've been out with quite a few girls who haven't got the first idea how to cook, or run a home, and I think it's wonderful that you're so adept.'

'Thanks,' I say, once again very much unsure how to respond. I order a cocktail and he has a glass of wine, then we order our food and make small talk about the hotel and how our weeks have been. 'Did you get up to anything interesting while I was away?' he asks.

I swallow, deciding that this is probably the moment. 'I'd meant to tell you, actually. I ended up seeing a friend.'

Richard's head jerks slightly. 'Who?'

'Dominic.'

Dominic

I consider carefully before I message Orla. The things Stella said when we last had dinner had stung, and they stung because they came with a side order of truth along with a much bigger main course of being really unpleasant. But she's not wrong. I have been a coward, and I've let people like Orla take the brunt of that, and that's really not the kind of person I want to be. So when I message her, as I get on the plane, I'm careful. I tell her that I'm in town for an interview and that I'd love to catch up. No suggestion of anything else. Then I turn my phone off, and when we land at Dublin Airport I turn my phone on and wait to see whether she's replied. She has, with the name of a restaurant and a time – 8 p.m.

The hotel I'm staying at is basic, but fine. I chuck my bag into the corner of the room, then realise that I've got a job interview tomorrow morning so I should probably do the right thing and hang some stuff up. I take a long shower to get the plane off me, then I walk slowly over to the restaurant Orla picked. It's a sweet, romantic sort of French place with pleasingly rude waiters. I order a beer and a glass of Pinot Grigio for her, and then I wait.

When she arrives, she's undeniably gorgeous. Her hair is dark and shiny, her skin is pale with a sort of luminous quality like whipped cream. She's wonderful.

'This is a surprise,' she says as she sits down without saying hello.

'Do you like surprises?'

'No.' She smiles.

We order various specials to share and a bottle of red, and she tells me about her promotion, her new flat and her impending girls' trip to Zante. And once she's told me about all the brilliant, exciting, challenging things that she's doing with her life, she draws breath, sips her wine and asks, 'And how about you?'

'I'm here for a job interview,' I say.

'So you're moving to Dublin?'

I shrug. 'Only if I get the job.'

'Do you want to move?'

It's a great question, but not one that I feel like answering. 'I think it'd be a bit of a sticky commute.'

We finish our food, and then we order a chocolate mousse to share, and then coffee, and by the time we've finished those the waiter is practically putting the chairs on the tables. I can't bear the idea of going back to my hotel room, alone, and spending the night trying to guess what questions they're going to ask me at the interview and wondering what Stella is doing right now. Her Instagram stories suggested that she'd gone to the countryside to some swanky hotel with Richard. I muted her account after I saw a smug video of a boating lake.

'What now?' Orla asks, as she finishes her coffee.

I don't want to be alone. I can't be alone. And I doubt she ordered a double espresso at 11 p.m. because she thinks she's about to go home for a nice long sleep.

Her flat is beautiful. It's up at the top of an old Victorian building and she's painted it in pale pinks and dusty blues. She's collected all these things, clearly from her travels all over the world. It's like walking into a scrapbook of who she is.

'This is beautiful,' I say, earnest in my assessment. 'Really.'

'I know,' she says. 'I've got great taste.'

She pours us another drink and we sit on the sofa, legs touching.

'So,' she says. 'You've come a long way to hear me talk about the hen dos I've been on and the prospect of making partner.'

I laugh. 'I'd have gone twice the distance to hear any of it.'

She puts her hand a little higher on my leg. 'Liar,' she whispers. Then she leans in to kiss me. She tastes like the chocolate mousse and the coffee. I kiss her back. We kiss, and I wait for the rest of my body to get the memo about the kissing. But it doesn't happen. She runs her hands along my body, and nothing. I put my hands under her top and find her nipple, hard under the lace of her bra, some of the nicest nipples I've ever had the fortune to look at, and still, nothing. She straddles me, one thigh either side of my lap, grinding against me in a motion that would, the last time I saw her, have sent me seeing stars, and still absolutely fucking nothing.

'Are you okay?' she whispers.

'I'm so sorry,' I whisper back. 'I don't know what's going on...'

She sighs and gets off my lap. 'Can I be plain?'

'Are you ever anything other than plain?'

She nods. 'Fair cop. But look, you look terrible. You don't seem yourself. And now you're suddenly trying to move to a different country. What's going on?'

I laugh. 'There's nothing going on! I just got off a plane. I'm tired.'

'The flight is less than two hours.'

'I've had quite a lot on. At home.'

She looks concerned. 'Like what?'

And then it all comes spilling out. Florrie, the pregnancy scare, realising that I want kids, realising that I've left it pretty late to realise that I might actually want to have kids. Stella. Our date, the almost shag, meeting her husband, hanging out with her kid. The fact that I think about her all the time, that she broke my fucking heart when she called me out the other day, the whole horrible messy, miserable business.

'You're an idiot,' she says, smiling. 'But I think even you know what the answer is here.'

I shake my head. 'What if it's not that I have feelings for her? What if it's just that, right now, I think I want kids and a marriage, and she's the fastest way to get there, and then as soon as I've got her, if she'll even have me because she's in a relationship with a really rich guy whose name is literally Richard – what if I break that up, and then I get bored and I break her heart, and what if I even fuck up Rose's life?'

I look at Orla, at the flush on her chest and her unbuttoned top and how gorgeously pretty she is. 'I'm sorry,' I say. 'I shouldn't have taken up your evening when I'm so messed up.'

She kneels up and kisses me gently on the cheek. 'You're going to be fine.' She smiles. 'And I'm going to find someone who's a bit like you, but much less trouble.'

I pause, because my phone is ringing and basically no one ever calls me. I look at the screen and do a double take. 'It's Stella,' I say. 'Why would Stella be calling me?'

Orla shrugs. 'It sounds like you should pick up the phone.'

I answer. 'Hello?'

'Hi,' Stella says, her voice low. The skin on the back of my neck goes tight. Something is wrong.

'What's wrong? Are you okay? Is it Rose?'

'I'm at a hotel with Richard and I told him that you came over last week, after he'd asked me to stop seeing you, and he's angry. Really angry.'

'Where are you?'

'I'm in the bathroom, I just told him I needed a breather. Listen, if I go in there and I call you, can you just tell him that nothing happened? That it was purely platonic?'

'Jesus fucking Christ, Stella! This is not normal – he can't—'

'I know,' she snaps. 'Please, I just need your help with damage limitation, okay? I lied to him, I shouldn't have lied to him, I just need to—'

I look at Orla. 'I'm sorry,' I mouth.

'Go into the other room,' Orla tells me. 'Talk to her. I'll make some more coffee.'

Stella

From the moment I say the name 'Dominic', I realise that it was a mistake to tell Richard. I mean, arguably it was a mistake to agree to not see one of my best mates, but we're several mistakes on from that now. Richard is sitting across the table from me, our untouched plates of food getting cold as he stares at me.

'Dominic?' he repeats coolly.

'Yes,' I say, trying not to get flustered. 'Dominic. The friend I went on a date with a while back? You'd asked me not to see him any more, but circumstances conspired and I ended up having him over to dinner the other week, and I thought I should mention it, just in the interest of honesty.'

Richard picks up his fork. 'So, just to clarify, I asked you not to see him again and you invited him to your house?'

Something sparks in my chest. 'Yes,' I say. 'My friend. And I was wrong to say that I would stop seeing him, that was disingenuous of me. I should have explained that he's a good friend who's been there for me over a really hard period of my life, and that I don't want to cut him out.'

Richard cuts up his steak. 'I see,' he says.

Dinner is frosty. I try to keep a conversation going while Richard gives me one-word answers. Part of me thinks that I should tell him to grow up, that I was honest with him eventually and that I've apologised, and that I shouldn't really have to apologise for spending time with a friend, even though I should have been honest about it. But what if he breaks up with me? I can't afford to get my own room at this place, if they've even got one available that I could book. I could go back to London, but it's late and I don't know when the last train is, or how I'd get to the station. Visions of waiting at reception until a rural taxi can be summoned to take me for the 5 a.m. train fill my head.

'Room for something sweet?' asks the waiter, hovering by our table and apparently not picking up on the absolutely terrible vibe emanating from us. 'Would you like to see the dessert menu?'

Richard shakes his head.

'No, thank you,' I add.

Richard signs the bill, which I want to pay for, given that my admission ruined the evening, but I'm not sure this is the moment to try.

We walk back to the room through the grounds. The air smells sweet and there's dew on the grass. We get back to the room and he closes the door behind him, then he takes a deep breath.

'I don't want to fight,' he says resolutely.

'Me neither,' I say, pleased, surprised at his change in tone.

He stretches up, like he's trying to release the anger from his body. 'So, we just agree, you don't see him again, I forgive you for what you did, we move on. Okay?'

I look at the floor. 'I don't think that's a compromise. That's me doing what you tell me to do.'

He looks aghast. 'You're not serious?'

I mean, it's very clear that I'm serious. 'You should meet him,' I venture.

'I don't want to meet the man who was fucking my girlfriend. What kind of a cuck do you think I am?'

'We haven't ever fucked!' I shout back. 'I've told you that. Multiple times.'

'Yes, and your honesty throughout this entire saga has been faultless,' he snaps.

'I wouldn't have needed to be dishonest if you'd been reasonable,' I fire back.

'Do you have any idea how lucky you are? To be with me?'

I recoil slightly at this. 'You're a great guy and you're very generous, I know how fortunate I am—'

'You're damaged goods,' he says. 'You realise that? Most men wouldn't be able to look past that, but I thought – you're attractive, you're mature, you know how to run a family – I thought you'd understand how lucky you were. I thought you of all people wouldn't do what Sophia did.'

Sorry, *damaged goods*? Damaged fucking goods, what is this, the eighteenth century? Having a child doesn't make me damaged. I go to storm out of the room but he's between me and the door and he doesn't move. I wait a moment, assuming he'll give way, assuming he won't want me to feel trapped. But he doesn't. He stands, steadfast, in the way, not letting me past. Shit.

I retreat, realising that this might be more of an inflammatory situation than I'd previously thought. I pretend to start to cry.

'Give me a minute,' I say, going to the bathroom, playing for time.

Almost on autopilot, my shaking fingers reach to dial Dom. He doesn't pick up on his usual fourth ring and I'm about to hang up when he answers.

'Hello?' he says, surprised to hear from me.

He starts saying something but I just spill it out, turning on the extractor fan so that Richard won't be able to hear.

'I just need you to tell him that there's nothing between us and there's no problem, and then I can get out of here and get home, okay?'

I hear the sound of a door closing on the other side. 'Call the fucking police,' Dom says, his voice low. 'Stella, I'm not joking, call them.'

'No,' I say, doubting myself even as I say it. 'It's not that bad, it's just… please?'

Dom's voice sounds strangled. 'Okay,' he says.

Then I go out into the bedroom, brandishing my phone. 'It's Dom,' I say quietly. 'I thought you might want to hear it from him, okay?'

My heart thuds. Was this a good idea? Is this just going to make him angrier? I thought maybe talking to another man rather than to me might appease him, but his face is expressionless. I can't tell if I've actually just spectacularly fucked it up. But at least this way, I think darkly, Richard knows that someone knows where I am and who I'm with. I have witnesses, if he does anything… I shut the thought down. I'm going to be fine – this is going to be fine. We're having a row and we'll fix the row, and then I'll calmly tell him that I'm not ready for a relationship, which is patently fucking true because every man I get involved with turns into a complete psycho. Right?

Richard takes the phone from me. 'Hello?' he says, his tone even.

I can't hear what Dom's saying down the other side. But Richard sounds calm. Friendly, even.

'I get it,' he says. 'I just think, well, you know what it's like. We're possessive, aren't we?' He even manages a little laugh. 'All right, well, look, maybe we'll have a drink when we're back in London. All right. Good night.'

He hangs up the phone and I hold my breath, waiting for him to turn and smile and apologise. But he doesn't. He just looks at me. For what feels like hours. He stays completely still, staring at me. Then, without breaking eye contact, he raises my phone, throws it across the room, at the wall, where it hits the pretty Cotswolds stone and smashes, glass splintering from the screen, and lands the floor. My first thought is for all the pictures of Rose that I've taken and not backed up, the ones of her licking the spoon while we baked, rolling around in the garden, pulling up daisies.

I stare at him, dumbstruck, expecting him to apologise for his loss of control. But he doesn't. My skin feels tight, every single fibre of my body is telling me that I need to get the fuck out of this room.

'What was that?' he asks, slowly, quietly, in a tone far more menacing than a shout.

'I thought it might help for you to hear it from him. I knew you didn't believe me and I thought—'

'You thought I'd want to talk to him? Are you fucking stupid?'

I don't know how to answer this but he's getting closer and there's nowhere for me to go, no door between us, no exit route.

'I'll ask again,' he says, closer now, far too close. 'Are you fucking stupid?'

'Richard, I don't think you mean to but you're scaring me right now, can we just take a beat? Just get some air maybe? I might go for a quick walk—'

I try to push past him but he's too quick and he's got me against the wall, not exactly pinning me but somehow trapping me.

'Richard, please,' I try again, unable to comprehend that I've ended up in this situation. 'Please?'

He's looking down at me, almost smiling now, and I'm trying to work out if I can push my way past him, or knee him in the balls, or scream, when there's a knock at the door.

'Security!' a man's voice shouts. 'Everything all right?'

'Just fine,' Richard calls back, putting his finger to his lips, telling me to stay silent.

'I need help!' I yell, sounding stupid and pathetic and mad. For a second I don't know if they've heard me. There's no reply from the other side of the door.

All I can see are Richard's eyes blazing with anger and all I can think about is that I'm fairly sure he's going to hit me – and I've never been hit by a man before – and all I can hope is that he'll stop hitting me before anything serious happens.

And then the door clicks and two men push their way in, and Richard jumps backwards away from me. I'm across the room in seconds. The two security guards look at the smashed phone, my flushed face, Richard still fixed to his spot.

'Is everything okay?' they ask again.

I shake my head.

'Do you want to come with us?'

I nod.

'This is ridiculous,' Richard says. 'I'm not paying nine hundred quid a night to be treated like a criminal.' He storms out of the room.

No one seems quite sure what to do. So I pack my things while the two blokes, both very nice, middle-aged men who apparently haven't ever had to break up a fight between a couple in all their years of working at the hotel, help me pack. My hands are shaking so Glen, the bigger one, unzips and rezips my suitcase for me. I shove in everything I can, then pick up my phone. Only then do I start crying.

'They'll be able to fix it, I'm sure,' Bill, the smaller one, adds.

'Do you think I'll be able to get my photos back?' I say, between sobs. 'My photos of my baby?'

Both men look horrified. 'You've got a kid with him?'

I shake my head and, for the first time in a long time, am very grateful for Gavin, who is a shit, but not a shit who has ever scared me, even for a minute. 'No, not with him.'

They both seem mightily relieved.

When I'm packed, they escort me to reception where the manager is waiting. She's a no-nonsense eastern European with poker-straight, blonde hair and perfect make-up.

'I can call the police,' she tells me, as we sit in a room behind reception. 'Or I can have him removed from the hotel, or both.'

I say that I can't bring myself to make any more of a fuss and she seems to understand. She insists on getting me my own room for the night. 'In the morning, I'll have a car waiting for 7 a.m. It will take you to the station before your...' She pauses for a moment, considering the right word. 'Before he has checked out.'

Security guide me up to a room, an enormous suite in the main building, our footsteps muffled on the thick carpets as we walk. I try to make as little imprint on the room as possible given that I'm not paying to be here and I don't want to make more work for housekeeping. Without changing or taking my make-up off, I slip between the cold sheets and begin to cry. I cry for Rose, and the fact that this happened to me and it might happen to her one day and the idea that if security hadn't arrived at just the right time, Rose might have ended up without me. I cry for myself, all the versions of me who tried so hard to get everything right, to build a normal, happy, safe life and still ended up in this absolute fucking mess. I cry until the hotel pillow is soaked and then I roll over to the empty, cold side of the bed, where other people who sleep in this room find the warm body of their partner, and I stare at the fuzzy ceiling, waiting until morning.

I get home before 10 a.m. on Thursday, the traffic mercifully quick on the way home. I pay the driver, wincing at the cost of a taxi all the way from Oxfordshire, not that a train ticket at peak time would have been much better. Rose is already at Anna the childminder's, and Gavin is picking her up directly this evening for his night with her. I could, in theory, go to work. But I don't know if they'd let me claim the day back and I don't really feel very much like I can be in a room with other people right now.

I'm slightly nervous that Richard might turn up on my doorstep and my broken phone means that if he's tried to get hold of me, I haven't heard about it. I double-lock the front door and make sure all the windows and back door are locked, wondering how I've managed to get myself into a situation where I'm securing the house I live in alone with my child from a man I was dating. What the fuck went wrong? How am I so uniquely talented at getting things wrong?

I realise that I didn't date much, that I'm naïve, that I'm inexperienced, but this can't happen to everyone. Other people must be able to date without getting themself into an endless series of dangerous, humiliating fuck-ups. Did I just use up all of my luck in the first thirty years of my life when I had a good job and a healthy baby and a husband who came home to me at night?

I unpack. Change the sheets on Rose's cot and tidy her room. Change my own sheets. Take a long and very hot shower, scrubbing my skin until it's red and every last trace of the weekend is gone from it. I keep remembering him on top of me, the noises he made, the feeling of his skin on mine, the way he called me a 'good girl'. I want to have him exorcised.

Then I message Louella from my laptop, giving a brief overview that Richard turned out to be a psycho and I'm home for the night if she happens to want to come over and hear all the gory details. I don't much want to see her, but I don't want to be alone either and I know she'll insist on knowing what happened.

At a loss for something to do, I try to remember how I used to fill my time before I had Rose. On Saturdays, I'd usually beg Gavin to drive me to some antique market in the middle of nowhere so I could buy furniture that would hardly fit in our flat. Saturday afternoon would mean stripping and priming on the patio, and on Sunday, I'd watch *Pride and Prejudice* or some other period drama that I'd seen a hundred times. I'd show Gavin my work from the day before, triumphantly, while he was reading the newspapers and he'd praise me endlessly, even if he thought the whole thing was a folly, and then act disappointed we couldn't keep the piece because I'd sold it on Etsy.

It's been months since I've picked up a brush for more than five minutes. So I take a box of paint samples and start stencilling flowers on the wall in Rose's room, something I've wanted to do since we first moved in. I paint ivy along the walls and roses branching off them. Eventually I look up and it's lunchtime. There's paint on my hands and my arm is aching, but it looks lovely. I'm proud of it. I reach for my phone to take a picture and show someone what I've done, but I don't have a phone. So I just look at it.

After lunch I wash my brushes and marvel at how long the day feels without anyone else to take care of. I go to the spare room and excavate my sewing machine. There's a bag of fabric scraps from various projects that I've never finished and a packet of stuffing, so I resolve to make a cushion. Deeply uncomplicated work – a child could do it. But it's finished in less than an hour, so I stitch pom-poms around the edge and it looks nice on my freshly made bed. I'm halfway through searching the fabric bag to find something else to sew when the doorbell goes.

I freeze. If it's Richard, I'm really not sure what to do. Would I call the police? Actually, I literally can't call the police because I don't have a working phone, which is only occurring to me in the moment. If it's not Richard, I need to stop dicking around enjoying craft time and go to the nearest Vodafone and get one. But if it is... I keep still and hope that the person outside will go away, but they don't.

They knock again. And then I hear a voice – a voice that, thank god, doesn't belong to Richard.

'Stel?' it calls.

Standing on the doorstep, holding a suitcase, is Dom. He looks exhausted and there's a coffee stain down the front of his T-shirt. 'Thank fuck you're here,' he says. 'Can I come in?'

I pull the door open further and he puts his case down in the hall, heading into the kitchen. 'Am I allowed to be here?'

'Allowed?' I ask, perplexed.

'Richard? He wasn't wild about you seeing me?'

I half laugh. 'Richard doesn't get a vote any more.'

'You broke up?' He looks relieved.

'We did,' I say, going to make us a coffee with the fancy machine. 'Well, I didn't literally say the words "we are over" but I think the bit where you called hotel security on him and I fled the room—'

'I was worried it was an overstep—'

'No,' I interrupt. 'It wasn't, he was about to hit me when they came in, I think.'

Dom blanches. 'You're not serious.'

'I mean, I don't know,' I say, backtracking. 'He might not have done, but he had me against a wall and I didn't feel great about the direction things were going in.'

'I'll kill him,' Dom says. 'I'll absolutely fucking kill him.'

I hand him the coffee, as if he needs to add caffeine to this situation.

'Thanks,' he says. 'Jesus, Stel, I am so fucking sorry.'

I shrug. 'These things happen.'

'They shouldn't. Not to anyone. Especially not to you.'

'Well, at least I figured out who he was pretty early on.'

'You really can pick them, can't you?' he says, half smiling. He's teasing, and he doesn't mean to be mean, so I try not to let my face show quite how much his comment hurts, or quite how true it feels. Because while I'm not one to victim-blame, it does seem like my track record is quite staggeringly bad, and the only thing that all these men have in common is me. When I started dating, I was determined to move onwards and upwards from Gavin and instead I managed to spend time with blokes who, to greater and lesser degrees, made Gavin seem like an okay option.

'Yeah,' I say, trying to keep the choke out of my voice. 'My taste is absolutely unparalleled.'

He shakes his head. 'Why didn't you tell me what happened? Not to make it about me, obviously – sorry, I'm not trying to be a dick – but I've been going insane. All the way here, on the flight, I just kept thinking, fucking hell, what if he killed her or something?'

'He smashed my phone up,' I say, trying to keep my tone at least a little bit light. 'So I couldn't get in touch. I'm sorry, I would have told you, obviously. I'm really grateful that you called security, and they were great too, so thank you.'

He gets up and wraps his arms around me. I rest my head against his chest and he strokes my hair, rocking me slightly, and I want to stay like this for the rest of forever. He smells so familiar, so warm and clean.

'Wait,' I say, pulling away. 'You were in Ireland?'

He nods. 'I was.'

'How did you get back?'

'Well, I had planned to come by sea, but in the end I decided to go on one of those brand-new flying machines that they've invented.'

I roll my eyes. 'You had a job interview? Today?'

He shrugs. 'I wanted to get back.'

'So you flew to Dublin for a job interview and then you flew back less than twenty-four hours later without going to the job interview?'

For the first time in the entire time that I've known Dom, who has historically had the kind of effortless brass neck that I'd pay my life savings for, looks bashful. 'I got an earlier flight, and I skipped the interview, because I wanted to see you.'

I smile. I don't know what to do with this information, but I still smile.

'I was with Orla, you remember? Orla who I was—'

'Shagging before we met, yes.'

'We had dinner and we went back to her flat.' He pauses, and I try to look like this is a totally normal thing to hear him say and not bothering me at all.

'Cool,' I say, my voice way too high-pitched.

'And then you called. And she… she was the one who told me to get security. I was just a complete mess, absolutely freaking out about the whole thing, but she said she'd known men like that before and there's no taking chances so she told me to call security and I called them, and then she told me that I needed to go back to England and sort myself the fuck out.'

Again, I don't know what to do other than probably send flowers to this woman I've never met for saving me.

'Okay,' I say slowly.

'And she asked me why we weren't making a go of things.'

My stomach twists. 'Well, if you took the job in Dublin then maybe you could try—'

'Not me and her,' he interrupts. 'You and me. She asked me why I wasn't making it work with you.'

I stare at him, once again trying to process the vast amount of information being fired at me. 'And what did you say?' I ask, at once desperate to hear the answer and wishing that he'd stop talking.

'I said I was scared that I'd just realised that I want a family and kids and a wife, and all the grown-up stuff that I've been putting off for my entire life, and I said I was scared that I want you because I want those things and you're an instant route to it, and what if I try it out and I don't like it and I break your heart and fuck Rose over. And then Orla said what if I've only realised I want those things because what I really want is you, and because I'd want any life with you no matter what the set-up was, and I realised that was it – the things she said.'

'Orla had a lot of insight,' I say, slightly dazed.

'I'm making it sound like she talked me into it,' he says.

'A bit. Yeah.'

'It wasn't like that,' he says, talking at double speed. 'Literally nothing like that – I'm just telling this stupidly badly because I'm nervous. What I'm actually trying to say is that I have feelings for you and you know that, and you have feelings for me – I'm pretty sure about that – and we have so much fun, and you're just – you're the best. And I want to be with you. I can't see any reason why we shouldn't be together.'

I look at him – at his beautiful, handsome, wonderful face, at his eyes and his beard and his lips, at his coffee-stained T-shirt and his stupidly overpriced Japanese trainers, and I close my eyes. And I say the only sensible thing. The thing that I know I have to say. The right thing.

'I'm so sorry, Dom. But I just can't.'

He looks like a little boy, and my heart is breaking watching him. 'What?' he asks.

'I'm not…' I trail off. 'I'm not a good version of me at the moment. I'm still very, very broken. And the nicest thing I can imagine would be to let you fix me, but I can't. It wouldn't be fair.'

His eyes fill with tears, and my eyes fill with tears, and I hate every single thing about what I'm going to have to do.

'You're sure?' he asks. 'It's really a no?'

I nod. 'It's really a no.'

Stella

One Year Later

'Happy anniversary,' I say, clinking my champagne glass.

'Happy anniversary.' Gavin smiles, clinking back. 'Wait, how is this our anniversary? We got married in October.'

'Not that anniversary,' I say. 'It's the anniversary of filing for divorce.'

He laughs. 'You've got such a memory. One of the things I always hated about you.'

'And you remember basically nothing, one of the many reasons that you drove me mad,' I return.

The restaurant is filled with couples, having a romantic lunch before a bit of shopping or a gallery visit, getting a quick bite before going to the theatre, enjoying all the reasons that anyone goes to this kind of restaurant, celebrations and indulgences and joy. I imagine that Gavin and I are the only pair here, on a Thursday afternoon, sharing a bottle of champagne and drinking to no longer being together. But then, perhaps I'm being judgemental. Maybe we aren't the only ones with a juicy backstory. If I've learned anything in the last couple of years, it's that people are often dramatically more complicated than they seem.

'How are you?' he asks, like he's really asking.

'Better,' I say. 'Not perfect. But a lot better.'

It's a good question, and I've given him an honest answer, because I really am doing better, though only through sheer bloody-mindedness and willpower.

After the Richard incident, I decided that things needed to change. Obviously, dating wasn't working for me. I was picking terrible men and putting myself in dangerous situations, and if Rose grew up noticing any of that then I'd have failed spectacularly. So no men. An entire year of no men. No apps, no flirting, no dates, no nothing. I bought a better vibrator and a bolster pillow for the bed, and that was it. For a few weeks, I would get itchy fingers, wanting a quick fix, a hit of attention and conversation, the adrenaline shot of great, flirty messages. But instead, I'd start painting or sanding or filling, or doing something else to the house, and by the time I'd made the entire place look half decent (with some paid help from qualified professionals), the cravings had passed. I was clean. In remission.

And it turned out to be a fairly practical use of my time, because three months ago I put our house on the market. Gavin had offered to give me another year – he said his mum liked having him around and he was travelling for gigs so often that there wasn't much point paying rent on his own place. But it was time. That house had seen so many of the lowest days of my life, and it was far, far too big. We got an offer over the asking price within a week of putting it on the market. I found a place down the road for me and Rose – a tiny two-bed cottage with wisteria growing on the front and a pale green front door. It was in need of some work, but owned by a lovely older woman who cooed over Rose and told me to rip out everything

I didn't like without compunction. Gavin even let me keep the profit from the big house, presumably because he still felt guilty for walking out, and I didn't fight him on it. Instead, I ordered a butter-yellow stove for my new kitchen. We move next month and I'm excited about it. The first home I've ever owned on my own.

'How's Louella?' Gavin asks.

'Pregnant!' I say. 'She met this guy in Korea, a Canadian, and they spent six months internationally shagging, then she found out she was knocked up, so he moved to the UK because he's some tech tycoon who can work from anywhere, and now they're having a baby.'

'Wow,' says Gavin, looking dazed. 'That's very your sister.'

'I know,' I agree.

'Give her my best,' he says, looking down at his plate. 'Or does she still hate me?'

'Oh, if she ever sees you, she'll kill you on the spot.' I smile. 'So I won't be passing on the message, but I appreciate it.'

There's a familiar sensation, a reoccurring prickle of sadness in my chest that he knows Louella so well, inside out, that they were friends for so long, but that his shame at leaving and her judgement of him walking away is such that they'll never speak to each other again. There are so many things like that. Friends of his I'd see once a year at a wedding and get drunk with, people he worked with who I'd bump into at the end of a night out and share a cigarette with. I took Rose to the park the other day and saw a man on a unicycle, and still reached to message Gav because of some long, tangled in-joke about unicycles that started in about 2010 and has since lost all sense of meaning. I'll never be able to explain it to anyone, and I don't say it to him because we're not like that and I don't anticipate us ever being like that again, so all those jokes and stories and memories are functionally just lost. Stories about eating spaghetti hoops in our damp flat when we first moved in together, the first shag we had the morning after our wedding, the triumph he had when he finally managed to plant something on our old balcony that actually grew, and the Greek salad I made out of the vegetables when they eventually ripened. None of it exists any more because there's no one to say it to, and eventually, all these moments in time, floating out there, they'll die with me because I've handed them on to no one. And there must be so many others, so many memories that I don't know that I've forgotten, that Gavin has in his mind, that he doesn't remind me of, and so those are lost too.

'What about work?' Gavin asks, puncturing my thoughts. 'How's it going?'

'Great,' I say, in genuine honesty. Because it is. 'I went freelance,' I tell him.

'Wow,' he replies. 'You finally took the plunge.'

It wasn't a plunge that I wanted to take. Nine months ago, after having given the combination of single parenting and working full time in the office a really good try, I came to the conclusion that if I kept doing it for much longer I would have a nervous breakdown. So I handed in my notice, and did the scariest thing I'd done since before I had Rose, and went freelance. And it turned out that the scary thing was also the best thing.

These days I drop her off at the childminder, then I walk back and get a cup of coffee, and work from my kitchen table. I write trend reports for the same magazine where I used to work – in fact, I do as much writing for them as I ever did, just a whole lot less admin. And I do other things too. Colour consultations for men who've just got divorced and don't know how to sort their houses out. Sourcing art for picky couples who don't want anything mass-produced. Writing guides to IKEA make-over hacks. And I love it, all of it, especially the parts where I'm helping other people make their homes feel more like homes. I pick when I work and how I work, and most of the time I work a couple of hours in the evening so I can opt to pick Rose up early and hang out with her in the afternoon. It turns out that parenting for fewer hours a day makes me much better at it – like I've got a certain number of Amazing Mum points and I can spend them all in a couple of hours now, rather than rationing them over a whole day and coming out as a moody cow.

'Why did you want to do this?' I ask, as we finish our food. 'Have lunch?'

'I thought it would be nice to catch up,' he says, stumbling over his words. 'And I wanted to say something, and I wanted to ask you something.'

'Okay,' I say tentatively. 'You're not going to suggest getting back together, are you?'

'God, no!' he says, almost insultingly quickly. Then he backtracks. 'I mean, you're great, but I think I pretty comprehensively killed our marriage.'

'Yes,' I agree. 'I think you did.'

'So that kind of leads me on to what I wanted to say,' he goes on, deliberately staring at a fixed point just left of my face so that he doesn't have to meet my eye. 'I think I should explain why I left.'

I'd assumed that the story would remain the same, that he wanted to do stand-up. Which, to my absolute horror, he is actually doing. Not on television or radio or anywhere that makes money, obviously. But he's doing gigs up and down the country and, on the occasions that I've given in and googled him, he's got pretty good reviews. He's not going to be headlining *Live at the Apollo* any time soon, but he is doing the thing he wanted to do. As well as part-time consultancy work during the week to pay the bills (and, to my relief, child support).

'You wanted to do comedy,' I say. 'I get that.'

He nods. 'It is that, but it was other stuff too. I've, uh. Well. I've been having therapy.' He says it like he's admitting to a war crime.

'That's good,' I say. 'I have too.'

'And my therapist said, or I said and they helped me realise.' He takes a deep breath. 'I never really felt like there was enough space for me in our marriage. You were so good at things. You just did it all, like, even when the baby was born, you'd watched all these videos and read all these books, and you just got on with it, and when I did something stupid you'd roll your eyes and act like I was incompetent, and it made me feel shit. But it wasn't just that, it went back ages, like when we first met and you were so much younger, you didn't know how to do anything either, and then suddenly it was like overnight you didn't like us eating in bed or going on package holidays, you wanted things to be different and "better", and you were, like, in charge of making everything happen and it didn't leave me with anything to do. I felt...' He trails off. 'Small. When I was standing next to you.'

He takes a deep breath, and then a long sip of his drink.

There are a lot of things I could say to this. I could point out that he had the same access to the same resources that I did, that he could have learned about taking care of a baby. I had the exact number of hours of parenting experience as he did on the day that Rose was born, but I made being a parent my sole focus and he just watched from the sidelines. Even if he was scared of the baby, he could have learned to cook, he could have learned to paint, any of it. Or I could point out that when we met, I was twenty-three and he was twenty-eight, and that it was perfectly normal for me to 'grow up' and want a less studenty way of life, that probably he should have done the same thing. But there wouldn't be any point. It's clearly cost him a lot to say it, and he's not my person any more. I'd gain nothing by telling him any of that and I'd probably hurt his feelings. And while I don't think it's my fault he felt small, he's someone I used to love. I don't like that he felt that way. So instead of telling him that nothing he says changes the fact that he abandoned me when I needed him the most, I nod.

'I get that,' I say. 'And I never meant to make you feel that way.'

'I know,' he says. 'I just wasn't right for you.'

'Not by the end,' I agree. 'At the beginning, I think we were great. And at some point, I don't know when, we stopped being a good fit. But if we'd realised that then we wouldn't have had Rose. So I'm glad we screwed it up.'

He nods. 'Me too.'

'What did you want to ask?'

Another deep breath. He must have been absolutely terrified on the way here, with the amount of stuff he apparently needed to unload on me. 'I'm seeing someone.'

That hurts. It has no reason to hurt, but it does. 'I met her on the circuit – the comedy circuit.'

'I didn't think it was likely to be the Formula One circuit,' I interrupt.

He doesn't respond to my sarcasm. 'She's a comic, and she's great, and we've been seeing each other for about six months. And I wondered how you'd feel about her meeting Rose?'

Terrible. Horrible. Awful. I hate the idea. But none of that is rational, or fair.

'What's she like?' I ask.

He shows me pictures of her. She's a smiling, busty, blonde woman in her late thirties or early forties. Gavin offers to show me a video of her current set, but the idea of playing sound out loud in a restaurant makes me feel like a criminal. I watch a couple of TikToks of her, with subtitles, and she seems funny. And nice. And normal. And even if she didn't, I have no leg to stand on. Legally, I can't stop him from introducing her to Rose if he does it during his visitation, and if I wanted to I'd be a huge hypocrite because I would have done it with Richard. I shudder very slightly at the memory of Richard who, to my relief, blocked me on every platform, including LinkedIn, and hasn't been in touch once.

'She seems great,' I say, handing Gav's phone back. 'I'm glad you've found someone you like.'

'Thanks,' he says shyly. 'She's the same age as me, so we can talk about kids' TV shows we both watched.'

This is meant to be self-deprecating, and I know he's trying to be nice, so I try not to mind that he's telling me the ways that this woman is a better partner for him than I was. 'You're very welcome to introduce her to Rose,' I say.

'I've got some articles you can read about how to introduce romantic partners without screwing your kids up.'

'Thank you,' he says earnestly.

We order hot drinks, because we might as well, and he asks me an inevitable question. 'What about you? Are you dating anyone?'

I shake my head. 'Absolutely not.'

'What about that bloke I met?'

'Dominic,' I say, forcing my face into a fixed position of neutrality. 'He was actually just a friend.'

Gavin raises one eyebrow. 'Right.'

There's a lull in the conversation while Gavin stirs a sugar cube into his coffee and I think we should probably get the bill, because it's been a very nice hour and I'm glad we did this, but there's a reason that we're exes and the chances of this turning into an argument are never zero.

'Can I say something?' he asks, when he's finished clinking his spoon against the china of his cup.

'Sure.'

'I know it might sound strange coming from me, but I...' He takes a moment to consider what he's going to say. 'I don't want you to be alone.'

It takes a lot of self-control to not point out that he could have prevented that from happening by not leaving me.

'I think you should think about dating,' he says. 'You deserve to find someone who makes you happy.'

I half laugh. 'I did quite a lot of dating last year and it was a disaster. I picked terrible people, I got into some shitty situations, and it's not going to work, so there's really no point in trying. This isn't my time to be happy, this is my time to focus on Rose, and work, and getting my life together. Then I can think about meeting someone.'

'Why do you have to have your life together before you can meet someone?' asks Gavin, bemused. 'When I met Hannah I was living at my mum's—'

'You still live at your mum's—'

'And I wasn't legally divorced and I was trying a whole new career—'

'I know, but that's different—'

'Why is it different?' he asks. 'The right person can help you get your life together.'

I'm exasperated. 'That's not how it works.'

'Says who?'

Everyone. Literally everyone says this. 'I don't know.' I sigh. 'The experts, the relationship influencers, every magazine I read when I was a teenager, everyone knows that you're supposed to get your life together and then meet someone. That's just… it's just a fact.'

Gavin considers me for a moment, looking at me like he's doing a really hard maths problem. 'But if you get your life perfectly sorted before you let yourself meet anyone, how is there going to be any space in your life when you do eventually meet them?'

I think about it for a minute. Then for another minute. And I really, truly, genuinely don't have an answer to his question.

Dominic

I kiss Orla on the cheek as the taxi driver revs the engine of his Honda, very obviously clear that he wants to get to the airport right now.

'How are you feeling?' she asks, smiling up at me.

'Dreadful,' I say. 'You must have given me poisoned whiskey.'

'That'll be it,' she agrees. 'And poisoned Guinness. And poisoned malbec. And poisoned apple Sourz.'

I whimper. 'I'd forgotten about the apple Sourz. This is the roughest stag I've ever been on.'

'It's a sten,' she corrects me. 'For the hundredth time. Now get on the plane and I'll see you for the wedding.'

She slams the door behind me and I wince at the impact, then wave weakly out the window. 'Is there a really smooth, non-bendy route to the airport?' I ask the driver.

'No,' he says.

Orla's 'sten', a word that I'm never going to use in good conscience, was a two-day event at a house a few miles outside of Dublin. She figured that she'd only known her soon-to-be-husband for nine months, so none of their friends had met each other and this was the best time to get us all in one place, building some bonds so that there's good craic (another word that I can't use out loud without sounding stupid) at the wedding.

I was surprised to be invited, if I'm totally honest. But her new bloke didn't seem at all worried that Orla and I had shagged on and off for some years, and had invited a couple of his own exes on the trip. Maybe this is how grown-ups deal with their past flames? Anyway, I'd originally said no because it was too far and I felt like it was a pity invite, but Orla rang me and bullied me into booking a plane ticket. It's a strange, lovely thing, the friendship that we've fallen into. After everything went wrong last year, and I didn't get offered the job in Dublin because I left before the interview (a fair call on their side), she decided that we were going to be sorting-our-shit-out buddies. So she came up with a list – a boyfriend, a better job and some new friendships – and I tried to do the same, and we checked in every week to see how we were doing.

In the first few months, Orla met Jason, who teaches English at a posh school in town, went on a date with him, fell spectacularly in love with him and quit her travelling-all-the-time job (that did not promote her to partner) in favour of a local one so that she could spend more time with him. He popped the question after they'd been together six months and I – and it turns out also her other friends, as I found out at the 'sten' party – was sceptical until I saw them together and then it made so much sense that no one had a word to say on the matter. Whichever way you cut it, she's smashed her list of life improvements out of the park. I, on the other hand, am still working on mine.

'Are you flying back to London now?' asks the driver.

'Yes.' I nod.

'Home to the wife and kids?'

'No,' I say. I shake my head and then regret it. 'No wife, no kids.'

'What's wrong with you, then?' He laughs.

It's a good question. In fact, it's a question that I've spent some of the past year trying to figure out. And how have I been doing that? Therapy. The thing that I swore I would never do, because it's self-indulgent and unnecessary and pointless, the thing that I thought was basically a Ponzi scheme for having too many feelings. Turns out, I was wrong.

It took a bit of shopping around. The first guy I saw seemed to have a kind of men's rights activism streak to him, and kept telling me how the women I'd picked weren't worthy of me. I explained that they were all not only worthy of me but dramatically better people than I am, and that was kind of the problem, and we ended up in a weird row. So then I found Martin, a tiny man in his sixties, who wears little round glasses and helped me realise – without telling me anything – that I'm still a bit traumatised from the failure of my marriage. The joke marriage, the marriage that I use as a punchline on first dates, the silly youthful mistake that I totally don't care about. Turns out, I weirdly did care about it. And even though I was a complete shit during that marriage, I was still hurt by the stuff my ex-wife did that wasn't great, which is how I found myself sitting on a sofa in a flat in Wimbledon, sobbing over the fact that my ex cheated on me over a decade ago, and then sobbing some more about the fact that I failed at being married, at the idea that my parents were disappointed, and the reality that I've missed out on being a young dad and then, of course, the big fat juggernaut at the end of it all, Stella.

I waited several sessions until I broached Stella because I felt a bit like the scared horse in one of those films I secretly like where a sad girl meets a sad horse, and they heal each other. I was scared that he'd say something I didn't want to hear about Stella and it would break all the good stuff that I've started feeling about him. But he didn't. I raised it, very lightly, as a new strand of something I wanted to talk about. And then I very slowly unpicked it, meeting her and liking her, and being afraid that I was going to ruin it, and then the weird waltz we did around each other where we didn't date or sleep together, but we couldn't stop spending time together. And then the bit where she got together with that arsehole, and the way I was horrified at my relief when he turned out to be evil, even though that probably traumatised her. And then, finally, the moment where I told her I was ready and I knew what I wanted, and she turned me down. Point blank. I just stood in her kitchen trying not to cry and then I picked up my stupid wheelie suitcase, which really didn't add any dignity to the horror of the situation, and walked to the end of the road and then waited for a bus, which didn't come, before eventually calling an Uber. When I got home I'd spent so long holding the tears in that I couldn't even cry.

'I'm a commitment-phobe,' I reply to the taxi driver, having given my answer far too much thought.

'Oh, right,' he says. He doesn't ask any more questions for the rest of the journey.

The flight home is easy and my flat is exactly as I left it, because no one else lives here and no one else visits and that's a depressing thought. I put all my clothes straight into the washing machine, unpack all my other stuff and then I turn my TV on and load a game of FIFA, hating myself for having an endless, empty evening to play video games.

There is a fix for this, obviously. Martin has pointed out that I'm probably ready to start going on dates again and that we're not going to know whether my commitment-phobia has improved until I actually try to commit to someone. Several times I've tried to download the apps and force myself to write witty responses to stupid questions, but I feel too old for it all, too world-weary. I don't want to tell the world what my death row meal is, or two truths and a lie. I don't want to go to Clapham for a first date with a management consultant named Jess or Tess or Beth who broke up with her long-term boyfriend because he didn't want to move in together. I don't want any of it. And I'm astounded by the bravery of everyone who manages to keep doing it, all those women who had feelings for me, who I couldn't love back because I was broken and refusing to sort out the brokenness; how did they get back on with it? Presumably they just swiped until they met someone who wasn't emotionally unavailable and started again. Which is what I should do. I know that.

The doorbell goes. I must have ordered something from Amazon and then forgotten about it. Most likely someone on the 'sten' mentioned some life-changing product and I drunkenly ordered it in a desire to prove that I was listening and really in earnest when I said it sounded great. I shove my feet into a pair of trainers, treading the backs down like they're a pair of clogs.

'I'm coming!' I shout down the intercom. 'Please don't take it next door, they steal stuff.' Then I clatter down the stairs, throw open the door and standing on my doorstep isn't a tired-looking delivery driver about to take a picture of me holding my parcel, but a woman. A woman I haven't seen for almost exactly a year.

Stella.

'Hi,' I say.

'Hi,' she replies.

The sky outside is moody. It was warm when I got back from the airport, but it's cooled since then.

'I just got back from Dublin.'

'I know,' she says. 'I used Louella's Instagram. That sounds like stalking. I mean, I went over to Louella's to talk to her – she's having a baby by the way – and I mentioned you, and she showed me your Instagram story, and so I knew you had just got back, so, yeah... Instagram.'

'You deleted yours,' I say. It's not a question. I know she deleted it because I initially thought she'd blocked me and was massively relieved when I realised she hadn't.

'Yeah,' she says. 'I was trying to sort my life out, and watching loads of videos and seeing loads of pictures of people from school who were mean to me now having these great lives wasn't really helping.'

'Fair,' I agree. 'Would you like a drink?' I ask, trying to sound normal. So far, we've mostly talked to each other like our sentences are being put through Google Translate five or six times until they barely make sense any more.

'Yes,' she says. 'Water. Please.'

'Water. Good.' I go to get her a glass. 'How are you? How have you been?'

She smiles, but she also looks sort of tearful, which is really confusing. 'I'm good,' she says. 'Better, at least. I went freelance. Sold my house. Rose turned two.'

I know quite a lot of these things because I've googled her at least once a week since I last saw her and I got a property alert for her house when it went on the market, then looked at the pictures of all the work she'd done to the house and desperately wanted to message her and tell her what a fucking amazing job she'd done.

'That's great,' I say weakly.

'So, Dublin,' she says, similarly strained. 'Are you… living there? Or just visiting?'

'Visiting,' I say. 'I went to see Orla.'

Her face falls.

'No!' I say, too quickly, too panicked. 'She's getting married. To someone else. Jason, she's marrying a guy called Jason. He's nice. He's an English teacher. He likes *Of Mice and Men*, which is a red flag but nobody's perfect.'

She laughs. 'Wow. That's great. Good for Orla.'

'Good for Orla,' I echo.

I hand her a glass of water and then we sit on the sofa, both bolt upright, facing forward, not touching. The screensaver is on the TV, showing pictures of various natural-beauty sights in the world. 'I think that's probably Iceland,' she says eventually.

'Yes,' I agree. 'Or Norway.'

We wait until the picture changes.

'I think that's Cornwall,' I suggest.

'Or it could be Scotland.'

Neither of us says anything while we wait for the picture to change again and time moves more slowly than I ever imagined it could. I rack my brains for something to say because this is going about as badly as it possibly could. Then I shift slightly and knock the controller, which wakes the TV up and reveals that I was playing a football video game against a teenager somewhere in central America.

'Can I say something?' she asks.

'Please,' I reply. 'Please say something.'

She turns on the sofa so that she's facing me.

'I had lunch with Gavin earlier, and he told me—'

'Gavin? Don't we hate Gavin?' I interrupt.

She laughs. 'I mean, yes and no, compared to some of the men I've met in the last eighteen months, he's actually okay.'

'Fair.' I laugh.

'Anyway,' she goes on. 'I thought I had to get my life in perfect shape before I let myself have someone, and I thought I was meeting the wrong people because the universe was punishing me for dating when I should be happy at home with my baby, and I… I had all these rules and these plans, and I had such a strict idea about how it had to work. And it was all pointless because it all went wrong anyway, and I'm sorry. I'm sorry that I didn't deal with it better last year, I'm sorry I didn't tell you where my head was at, or that I was too ashamed of what had happened with Richard to contemplate letting anyone else touch me again for a long time. I owed you that. You were a really, really good friend to me and I didn't return that because I was selfish and self-involved, and I think, sometimes, when bad things happen to you, it's easy to become selfish and self-involved, but I shouldn't. And I'm sorry.'

She takes a deep breath.

'I'm sorry too,' I say. 'I'm sorry that I didn't realise that the morning after you'd been assaulted by your boyfriend wasn't the moment to tell you that I was falling in love with you. And I'm sorry that I was so hurt by being rejected that I just fucked off home and never made contact with you. And I'm sorry that I missed an entire year of you doing amazing things without me there to see them.'

'That's a lot of sorries. From both of us,' she says. 'And I'm sure we'll have cause for a few more. In the future. If you're maybe, potentially, up for that.'

'I might be open to it.' I grin. I lean down and for the first time since that night in her kitchen, I kiss her. I wind my hands around her torso, feeling the warmth of her, running my hands under her top and she giggles at my fingers on her skin, kissing me back hungrily.

'Wait,' I say, pausing for a moment. 'It's Monday. Not Thursday.'

'It's Monday,' she agrees, looking bemused.

'Where's Rose?'

She smiles. 'I accidentally poured my heart out over lunch, and Gavin read me the riot act about not putting my life on hold and then he offered to take Rose this evening instead. So that I could come and see you.'

I smile. 'I always liked that guy.'

She rolls her eyes, laughing at me. 'No, you didn't.'

'No, I didn't,' I agree. 'But I'm coming around to him.' She kisses me this time, her lips full and delicious.

'Hey,' I say, breaking away for a moment. 'Seeing as you've got a free evening, do you fancy going on a third date?'

Acknowledgements

Stella is Starting Over is a love letter to being a single parent, inspired by my life after I split with my first husband and decided to swipe away the pain on various dating apps.

I can't tell you how strongly I feel that we need more stories like this one, love stories for people with complicated lives, and I owe a debt of gratitude to all the people who made this specific story possible.

First to thank for the existence of this book is Darcy Nicholson, who commissioned the book and let me have the freedom I needed to make it a proper ode to single-parent dating, without wanting to sanitize the knotty, complicated business of falling in love when society wants you to be at home singing 'The Wheels on The Bus'. Her second-in-command, Maisie McCormick, who makes everything happen, and Darcy's maternity cover, Caroline Hogg, who handled me so kindly and gently as the latter stages of the novel coincided with the early stages of my having a newborn. I don't think I've ever thanked a copyeditor before, which is probably very rude of me. But Judith Long did such a beautiful job on it, and was so enthusiastic and celebratory about the book, and I'm enormously grateful to her for that.

As ever, my agent Eve White and the rest of the team at the Eve White agency – Ludo, Steven and Emmanuel, are invaluable. Similarly my agent Charlotte Knight, always a guiding light, stewarded the book so elegantly into development for the screen, and the team at Mainstreet Pictures, especially Lucy Tomalin, have been just wonderful in helping me grow the story into what will (hopefully) be a very special show.

On a personal level I must thank the following people. My family: Lucy, Matt, Ellie, George, Tim, and Charlotte. My best friend and writing partner Nick. The gals, Steph, Felicity, Hannah, Liv and Emily. Also my team of childcare providers / babysitters, who made it possible for me to go and have my own little life outside of home: Faye, Angie, Visara and Maria.

The biggest thank you, predictably, has to go to my daughters Margot and Eliza, and to my husband, Mark, who isn't Dom but is, in lots of ways, Dom. Falling in love with Mark has been the most magical second act. Sometimes I look at him, wearing Eliza in a sling or reading Margot a story and I can't believe he's the smirking hot boy I used to smoke cigarettes with outside dreadful pubs in Clapham. Falling in love with Mark was magic, but becoming a co-parent, home owner and proper adult with him makes the heady early days pale by comparison.

Rather self-aggrandisingly, I'm also going to thank myself, or rather, my 2023 self. I'm very proud of that version of me, the very broken, very tired, very frightened one, who decided to choose fun instead of misery, because I owe the wonderful things about my current life to her.

Lastly, and not really an acknowledgement but rather a cri du coeur: I would compel any woman who finds herself in the same position as I was to go on as many dates as possible. Not to find a husband or a partner, not to replace what you've lost, but because it's fun. And you deserve to have fun. While it is utterly terrifying, there is nothing quite like the balm of drinking white wine and talking about yourself to a complete stranger who is occasionally dropping their gaze down to your cleavage. Your marriage ending is not really the end of anything. It's the start. I promise.